MRS. HUDSON
GOES TO
IRELAND

Susan Knight

Paperback ISBN 978-1-78705-627-5
ePub ISBN 978-1-78705-628-2
PDF ISBN 978-1-78705-629-9

Published by MX Publishing
335 Princess Park Manor,
Royal Drive, London,
N11 3GX
www.mxpublishing.com

Cover design by Brian Belanger

To Phyl Herbert, for her constant support and encouragement

Chapter One

If I could have foreseen what was awaiting me across the Irish Sea, I am not sure I should ever have agreed to set out. However, hindsight, as they say, is a wonderful thing, and Kitty Melrose was in such a state I felt it would be unchristian of me not to support her as much as I was able.

I had no particular duties in Baker Street at that time, the events I am about to narrate having taken place during the sad period when we all believed that Mr. H had fallen to his death at the Reichenbach Falls. To tell the truth, I was finding myself somewhat at a loose end and was rather down in spirits, so that when my neighbour, Mrs. Melrose, flew in the door in great distress, I am afraid I rather welcomed the distraction. Her problems proving so much greater than my own – hers having a solid foundation while mine were simply comprised of a combination of enforced idleness and sorrow – that I soon reproved myself for indulging in self-pity.

I should perhaps start by telling my readers a little about my neighbour. Kitty Melrose, a widow woman of my own age – that is to say fast approaching the half-century – was born Kathleen O'Kelly in Ireland in County Wexford. A neat little woman with the pinkish, freckled complexion and curls still burnished with red typical of her race. Her grey-green eyes peer rather, due to short-sightedness and a touch of vanity that makes her reluctant to wear the eyeglasses that would fix the problem. Despite her marriage to an Englishman and despite having spent long years in London raising her family, she has retained her soft Irish brogue. In addition, she is of the Roman Catholic faith and, in past times, liked often to inform me that if I did not renounce my Protestantism, I was bound straight to hell when I died. To which I would reply, quite sharply that I was willing to take the risk, since I did not consider God to be

1

so small-minded if one's motives were pure, and that, moreover, I should never dream of consigning her to the same fate, despite the many superstitions of her faith. After all, did Jesus Christ himself not say, "In my father's house there are many mansions?" Kitty Melrose is perfectly entitled to believe whatever she pleases, and take up residence in her Romish mansion, but I hope and pray, as I have told her, that she would grant the same tolerance to me in my Church of England one. I am glad to say that, as we became closer friends, our disputes on the subject became less frequent. However, even lately I have sometimes caught her looking at me with sad eyes, as if envisaging my horrible destiny on the Day of Judgement.

On this occasion, however, religion was not on her mind, except insofar as it concerned the holy state of matrimony. Once she had done sobbing and once Clara, my faithful maidservant, had brought up a tray of hot tea and some crisp cinnamon biscuits that I had cooked up that morning, Kitty thrust a letter at me, adding that it would explain all.

Clearly she had a somewhat exaggerated view of my powers of deduction. Even though I pride myself on having learnt much from my distinguished tenant – lessons that have stood me in good stead on a number of occasions, as I have recounted elsewhere – this time, failing to make sense of the ill-scribbled note, I was entirely at sea and told her so.

"It is from my god-daughter, Lily," she explained. "She is to be married."

"Surely a cause for rejoicing," I remarked.

"I fear not." Kitty nibbled a corner of her biscuit. "I suspect that she is being forced against her will."

"In this day and age!" I exclaimed. "Surely we have passed from the dark ages by now. And yet…" I considered what little I knew of Ireland, considered by many an uncivilised place beyond the Pale, its denizens, as depicted by Mr. Punch, tending to the ape-like.

2

"Lily's mother, Nora, was my dearest friend," Kitty continued. "We grew up on neighbouring farms and attended the same school. She was married very young to a man who turned out... well, I never knew the details for, by then, I was living here about to be married to dear Edward," (her late husband), "but William Cullen turned out a rough sort of person, and the three sons she bore him were patterned after their father. Only Lily, the youngest, inherited the gentle and yielding nature of my friend."

Here Kitty collapsed into tears again. "I fear her sweetness will be the undoing of the poor girl as it was of her mother."

"What happened to Nora?" I asked.

"I cannot say for certain. Only that her husband, when he had drink taken, was liable to raise his fists against her. He was not ashamed in front of me, and I witnessed as much on the few occasions I stayed with the family, once for Lily's christening, then again for her First Communion and for her Confirmation at the age of twelve." She shook her head.

"How horrible for her and for you," I said. Violence against women by those who are supposed to cherish them is truly shocking but, I am sorry to say, all too common even here in England, even among so-called respectable people, where it is often a hidden crime.

"Yes," she went on. "It was horrid indeed. And I have to say I was never made welcome by the menfolk in that family. Not threatened as such, but I felt most uncomfortable in their presence, and only remained on for Nora's sake. On that last occasion, indeed, I could tell that she was sickly, and shortly after my return home, I received a terse note from William to say that she had passed away. Not a telegram, mind, but a letter which took several days to arrive. It seems she was already buried. In Ireland, Martha, the funeral takes place very soon after death, just one or two days later. Even so, I thought it brutal of him to so say in so many words no need to come over, as I otherwise might have hastened to do." She was deeply moved and I reached out and took her hand "Since then," she said, "as I understand from reading between the lines of Lily's rare letters to me, and from those of my sister-in-law, Annie – she is wedded, do you see, to my brother Peter – that the poor girl has become a general dogsbody for the men in the household, as was her mother before her. And now this…" She took up the letter again, which I had lain on the table.

"I am afraid," I said, "that you will have to read it to me, since I cannot decipher Lily's script." Clearly any schooling the girl had received had not included the fine art of calligraphy.

Kitty held the letter quite a distance from her face – as usual she was come without her eye-glasses.

"*Dearest Godmother,*" she read, "*I trust you and your family are well, as we are here. It will no doubt surprise you as much as myself to learn that I am to be married in two short weeks. It would greatly comfort me if you could attend in the place of my dear mamma…*"

"You know, Martha," Kitty said, breaking off her reading. "I begged William to permit Lily to come to live with me after Nora died. I felt it was not a healthy atmosphere for a young girl to be alone with men who cared little for her. He did not even bother to reply."

"Not if you put it to him that way."

"I did not, of course not. I told him that as one who only has sons, I would dearly love a daughter, and should intend that Lily, as the offspring of my beloved friend, would fill that space in my heart."

As someone who only has daughters, I well understood the sentiment, even though my two lovely girls mean everything to me. Still, I should have liked to have borne a boy. At least I have my little grandsons. They are so loving, even though I see them infrequently, their mother, Judy, living in far off Edinburgh.

Eleanor, who lives nearer, in the county of Kent, has yet to bear me a grandchild, but I live in hope.

"So will you go to the wedding?" I asked.

"I have to. I have to stop it, I think."

I stared at her.

"Stop it! Goodness gracious, Kitty! Whatever do you mean?"

"Just listen."

She resumed her reading.

"My husband to be is Francis Kinsella. You may remember the Kinsellas who have land that adjoins ours... I remember that tribe only too well, Martha, and for no good reason. As for Francis, he is an absolute horror."

"In what way?" I asked.

"A nasty cruel boy, a bully who takes pleasure in inflicting pain on innocent creatures. Cockfighting, hare-coursing, bull-baiting, you name it. Francie will be at the centre of all."

"Surely that is all against the laws of the land. Do the police not intervene?"

Kitty gave me a pitying look. "The police, is it, Martha? Not at all. Don't those boyos enjoy the sport as much as anyone else, down the country anyway. Or at the very least, they turn a blind eye." She sighed. "Anyway, that's not all regarding the bould Francie Kinsella." She hesitated.

"What is it?"

"They say... No, I cannot utter the words." A flush spread over her countenance.

"Come, Kitty," I said. "You must tell."

"It is too horrible, Martha." She lowered her voice to a whisper. "I have heard it rumoured that he is the spawn of his sister with his father."

My shock must have shown on my face.

"Now do you begin to understand?" Kitty asked.

5

"Not really. Why ever should this man be forced on Lily? How can her father agree to such a match?"

"Greed, plain and simple. Listen on: *My father will not have to provide a dowry for me. Quite the contrary for he will receive a fine parcel of land once the knot is tied.* A knot, Martha? A noose more like. He is selling his daughter to a monster who already has blood on his hands."

"What are you saying? That this Francis is a murderer on top of everything else?"

"Well, as to that," Kitty conceded, "I have never heard his name associated with the death of any man, woman or child. But if to torture and kill God's creatures makes a murderer, then yes indeed. When he was a lad, my brother told me, Francie and his gang would set fire to cats, for the fun of seeing them run off screeching. I doubt that he has changed."

"This is indeed dreadful news," I said. "No wonder you are distraught. Poor little Lily."

"I intend to travel to Ireland tomorrow, and to bring Lily back here, and…" She paused then and looked directly into my eyes, "I want you to come with me."

"What!"

"I cannot manage it by myself, Martha, and you have been in such situations before and know what to do."

I had to protest. "I have never ever been in such a situation, Kitty, I can assure you of that."

"What I mean is, you have faced dangers and withstood them."

She was no doubt referring back to certain adventures I had recounted to her, the case of the Smiling Man, for instance, or that of the Demon Within. These, however, bore little resemblance to the enterprise she was now suggesting.

"I know it is a lot to ask but I am desperate. I will pay all your expenses…"

"That," I said, coolly enough, "would not be an issue." I am not a wealthy woman, but I can certainly pay my own way. "But tomorrow?" I added. "It is too soon."

"There is no time to be lost, Martha. It is now little over a week until the wedding day, and it will take two full days to travel to Wexford." She lifted a locket from her breast and opened it to show me the face of a child. "This is Lily. She is just fifteen."

A pretty girl, with long dark hair, but a mournful face. I even thought I detected fear in her eyes, but perhaps that was simply the effect of hearing of her impending fate.

"Really, Kitty, I do not see how it would be possible for me, at such short notice…"

"What is there to keep you at home now that he," she lifted her eyes to the ceiling, indicating the upstairs rooms of Mr. H, "is no more?

Despite the somewhat heartless nature of this remark, I confess that Kitty's tale intrigued me greatly. In recent times, moreover, I had developed a fondness for travel, and Wexford, being, as I understood it, on the eastern coast of Ireland, was not so very far after all from the mainland of Great Britain. I felt myself tempted.

"How would a person get there?" I asked.

The mail train to Holyhead was crowded and stifling. Impossible to open a window because the smoke from the engine would fly in and the atmosphere become far worse. Kitty was not inclined to converse, no doubt being deep in thoughts of poor Lily, so I tried to distract myself with a volume of the latest Marie Corelli and, when that failed, to stare out of the window at the spring countryside we were racing past under an ominously louring sky.

It had indeed been a hard task to get packed up in time for the early morning departure. My good black bombazine serves for most purposes, though somewhat heavy for the spring season, but it was in need of a good airing and brushing. Luckily my maid Clara is a wonder in that department. My travelling dress was simpler, a grey woollen fabric. Moreover, I had the good fortune to have just acquired a lighter gown in brown muslin, which fitted neatly into my trunk. I pride myself on keeping my linen in good order, so sufficient chemises and the like were laundered clean and ready.

I left instructions for Clara regarding the management of the household – and most particularly to keep an eye on young Phoebe, our flibbertigibbet scullery maid, who is a cross I feel I have to bear for the sake of her poor mother and countless siblings.

When Clara asked how long I expected to be away, I could not answer her exactly.

"No more than a few days," I told her optimistically. How little I knew then.

Kitty and I had taken a cab to Euston station in good time for the train. My friend had booked us two first class seats, for which I was grateful even though the comfort, as I have already indicated, was far from complete. The journey was long – more than ten hours – and made more tedious by the aforementioned gloomy silence of my friend. I have found that chit-chat, however idle, can pass the time most effectively, but any attempts I made in that direction were met with monosyllabic replies. It was not encouraging.

If only the landscape had been worth a look, but the midlands of England, at least along the railway line, proved dreary, and only became interesting when we reached north Wales. By that time, however, darkness had set in, so that I could only imagine the entrancing prospect of mountains, castles and fashionable watering places along the way.

I have to say that more than once I asked myself whatever was I doing there when I could have been sat contentedly at home in Baker Street. However, for poor Kitty's sake, I tried to convince myself that we were embarked upon an adventure. Indeed, such it turned to be, though hardly a pleasant one.

It was thrilling, of course, to cross Mr. Stephenson's iron bridge to the island of Anglesey. Even Kitty perked up then. "We shall soon be at Holyhead," she said. The destination for boats to Ireland.

Rather than proceed straight on the night ferry, we were to stay in an hotel near the port, having agreed it would be too fatiguing to keep travelling. In addition, to arrive at the port of Kingstown in the early hours of the morning would, as Kitty explained, be most inconvenient, since from there we had to travel on to the county of Wexford, and would be forced to wait some hours in the station for the first morning train.

The hotel was simple and not luxurious, but clean enough. I sank gratefully into my bed and was soon fast asleep.

The next morning, a dull and windy one, we took ourselves to the ferry. For Kitty it was no novelty, since she had travelled this way quite a number of times over the years, and in addition, as it turned out, was a bad sailor. For me, however, whose entire experience of boats consisted of a few turns on the Serpentine with my dear late husband, Henry, as well as a trip one time to the Isle of Wight, it was most delightful, not to say exciting. The wind churned up the sea mightily as our vessel plunged through the great grey waves, rocking from side to side, so that it was necessary to hold on tight to avoid being flung across the deck. Luckily, my hat was secured to my head with a strong pin. Poor Kitty stayed below, most unwell, and could not be persuaded that the fresh air would make her feel better.

After little more than three hours, the hilly coast of Ireland came into view and we soon safely docked. I was pleasantly surprised, having understood Ireland to be a savage place, to find Kingstown as agreeable as any port on the southern coast of England, with charming formal gardens and stately buildings. I should have liked, indeed, a stroll around to view more of it, but we had to press on. A cab took us to the railway station where, without too much of a delay, we were able to board a train to the Wexford town of Enniscorthy. The line followed the coast for much of the way, providing a pleasing vista of my friend's native country. By now, I was feeling more sanguine about the trip, and even Kitty cheered up and pointed out landmarks on the way: the thrilling stretch of rail around Killiney Bay and Bray head, the train emerging from tunnels to a stretch of sheer mountain on one side and cliffs plunging to the sea on the other. It was only after we were safely past that Kitty informed me of the terrible accident of 1867, when the train crashed through the barrier incurring loss of life and many injuries.

"But they have buttressed it since and now it is perfectly safe," she said. The which I was most relieved to hear since we should have to return that way again in due course.

We then found ourselves in a flatter part of the county, the mountains, including the striking Sugarloaf, further off in the distance. When the train halted in the coastal town of Wicklow, Kitty told me of its famous jail where many of the rebels of 1798 had been held. I nodded wisely, although my knowledge of Irish history is, I am afraid, sorely lacking. I had never heard either of the famous jail nor of the rebels, though I noticed that Kitty spoke of them in tones of pride.

Refreshed as we both were after our sleep and bathed as the landscape was in pretty May sunshine, the prospect ahead seemed much improved, and we both, I think, felt more optimistic about the success of our enterprise as the train trundled ever southwards.

Chapter Two

Kitty had sent a telegram ahead telling of the time of our arrival, and we were duly met at Enniscorthy railway station by her brother, Peter, a stout, red-faced man in his middle years, with a friendly manner and curly gingery hair going grey. I could see little resemblance between him and his trim sister, however, except for the hair and the grey-green eyes.

Although I was again somewhat fatigued, our travels, or should I more correctly state 'travails,' were not yet over. It seemed we had some way yet to go to reach the family farm near the small town of Ferns.

My first view of the Wexford countryside was not propitious. Rattling along rough tracks in what was little more than a cart, with no shelter but our hooded coats from the wind and rain (the weather having turned again as I am told it often does in these parts), I found it difficult to display good humour, even though Kitty's brother Peter kept up a lively chat. Unfortunately, his brogue was so much stronger than his sister's that I could comprehend only the occasional word. It was lucky, then, that he directed most of his remarks at her. He was pleased to see her, I could tell that much from his affectionate tone, and she came out of her silent gloom at the sight of him and was soon chattering away.

I had thought Ireland would be a country like Scotland, with picturesque prospects of mountains, valleys and lakes, but this place was hardly different from the home counties of England, its rolling fields stretching far away. One mountain was faintly discernible on the horizon, and this Kitty named proudly as Mount Leinster, Leinster apparently being the name of the province in which we found ourselves. What differed greatly from home were the wretched hovels of the rural poor which we passed along the way, quite literally mud huts with ragged and rotting thatched roofs, and all around barefoot children in rags, gaunt women with babes at their breasts, bent old folk sitting on rough benches, watching us go by with blank eyes.

Peter turned to me, and this time I understood him quite clearly.

"Your English landlords care little for their tenants, Mrs. Hudson."

Although, as Kitty had informed me in advance, Peter himself was one of the growing band of Irish Catholics able to own their farms, her brother was also active in the Land League, an organisation which seemingly wished to get rid altogether of the English landlords and their excessive rents, stop forcible evictions, and enable tenant farmers to own the land they worked. He was, she had added, for Irish Home Rule as well, and warned that it would be wise to avoid disputes with him on the subject. But, she had insisted, although I myself was English, I might expect no prejudice on his part against me personally, the which, I confess, I was most relieved to hear. In fact, while I had an open mind on the subject of Home Rule, I completely agreed with his views regarding the landowning question, finding them only just and Christian. Nonetheless, I could not condone the violent methods to which certain supporters of the League had resorted in the past. On this occasion, rather than stir the pot, I took my friend's advice and simply nodded as we proceeded on our bumpy way.

I was trusting that our destination would provide better accommodations than I had seen heretofore and so it proved. The farmhouse was a fine stone building, slate roofed and freshly whitewashed, with outhouses of a similar sturdy nature. My spirits at last started to lift. The yard was wet and mucky, however, and I was worried for my skirts. Suddenly I felt myself lifted bodily from the cart by Peter and carried to the threshold of the dwelling. I was too astonished to react, and Peter had already returned to fetch his sister in a similar fashion. Then he went back for our trunks. Meanwhile, a plump woman with a welcoming face and clad in a plain but clean brown dress and white apron, had heard the noise of our arrival and opened the door, several little ones hanging on her skirts.

"Come you in," she said. "Kitty, *mo ghrá*, I am so very, very happy to see you," (embracing her). "And you, too..." she turned to me with a smile.

"This is Mrs. Hudson, Annie," Kitty explained. "My very dear friend."

"Call me Martha, please," I said.

We were led into a cosy room with a big open fireplace in which logs glowed and sizzled. Two sleek sheepdogs were stretched out in front of it and came to sniff us, until Annie ordered them off, and they returned, quite docile, to their nice warm place.

Meanwhile I sank down gratefully in the proffered chair, while the three little children stood and stared at me as if they had never seen the like before. But I love young ones and had soon drawn them next to me, asking them questions to which I got no response. I suppose they found my accent as strange as I had found their father's. Annie meanwhile had hastened to the range to prepare a dish of tea, as she called it, Kitty accompanying her.

I looked around me. The white plastered walls were covered in religious objects, a crucifix, prints of various biblical scenes including the Madonna and Child and what looked to be the Good Samaritan. My eye was particularly caught by a framed image of a bearded Jesus Christ on the mantle, his two hands, marked by the stigmata, pointing at his shining heart which in turn was pierced by a lance and cruelly embedded in a crown of thorns. A candle burnt in front of this fearsome image, which I later learnt was called the "Sacred Heart" and much venerated. Despite this horror, the effect of the room was cheerful. Brightly patterned curtains hung by the windows, a rag rug partly covered the floor, the furniture was fashioned crudely enough of wood – no fancy Chippendale or Hepplewhite here – but was strong and serviceable. The seat of my chair, woven of straw, I found most comfortable, and all in all Annie's housekeeping skills met with my full approval.

Peter soon entered from the yard with our trunks, and set them down. I was pleased to see how he kicked off his boots, not to soil the clean floor, a thoughtful habit. The children rushed over to him shouting "Dada," and he swung each of them up in the air, to their great delight.

"You have a lovely family," I said.

"Ah, ma'am I do, that's the plain truth, and this isn't the half of it. There's five more childer at school."

Did I understand him right? I still had problems with his accent, though I could tell he was making an effort. Speaking out and not mumbling.

"Five more, did you say?"

"I did, to be sure." He laughed merrily.

I tried not to look too surprised. Even back home, large families are common. Indeed, our dear Queen has borne nine children. Yet Annie looked barely old enough to have reared so many.

"Here's Pegeen, Mickaleen and Sarie," Peter said, patting each on the head in turn.

"And I am Martha," I said.

Little Pegeen asked me something I could not understand. Her father smiled and answered. Then looked at me.

"She asked if you be her auntie," he said. "I told her, no that would be the other lady."

"But she can call me Auntie Martha if she wants," I said. "I should like that."

He told as much to the little ones who smiled broadly and tried out the name.

"I'll take your box above, so I will," he said, or something like it, and headed off, the children scampering after him.

The two women then came forward with the tea and a plate of freshly cooked drop scones. Their expressions were serious. I imagined they had been discussing Lily, since they continued the conversation while they set the ware on the table.

"'Tis from the frying pan direct into the fire she'll be going," Annie said. Her voice was softer and clearer than her husband's, and I had no difficulty at all understanding her. "The poor craytur."

"You do not think my plan will succeed then?" Kitty asked.

"To take her away, is it? I think it would be a difficult and dangerous thing to attempt, and I would strongly advise against it."

"But I cannot leave her to her fate. It is too horrible to imagine."

I feared the conversation had distracted from the tea, of which I was in dire need, so I damned etiquette and took the initiative, reaching to pour the pot.

"Oh," said Annie. "I am forgetting myself. After that long journey, you must have a right thirst on you, Martha." She performed the necessary duties.

The tea was strong and hot and the milk that was added was creamy and fresh.

"From our own cows," as our hostess informed us.

After several sips, I began to feel restored.

"We will go and call upon the girl," Kitty resumed, after setting down her drink. "I need to talk to her straight."

"Not today," Annie replied. "Leave it 'til the morrow, do. You will be refreshed and strengthened by a good sleep. As you will need to be, Kitty, for William has become even more difficult than ever and keeps Lily away from company."

15

"You mean he has her locked up," Kitty exclaimed.

"No, no… well, not exactly. But she is watched. It is impossible to get the girleen alone."

Peter and his brood returned then, and we talked of other things, it not being appropriate to discuss poor Lily's fate in front of the children.

I was happy a little later to go to my room to rest. Mine was a large room with a view over a well-stocked kitchen garden at the back of the house, while Kitty meanwhile was to sleep in a little box room, where there was just enough space for a low truckle bed. I felt bad at such preferential treatment, but neither my friend nor my hosts would have it otherwise. Moreover, I feared I had taken over the little girls' room for the quantity of dollies heaped on a cupboard in the corner. I said as much to Annie, who just smiled and said the girls would be happy in the boys' room.

"But where will the boys go?" Surely they would not all bed down together.

"The boys will sleep in the barn," Annie replied.

"The barn!" I exclaimed. "Oh dear. I am causing you a great inconvenience."

"Not at all, Martha. It will be an adventure for them, surely. They slept there before when my aunts came to visit. And the nights are warmer now."

With me thus reassured, she went out. I laid myself down thankfully on the big bed that almost filled the room, imagining how the girls would all cuddle up cosily together there, the way indeed I had slept with my own two sisters when very young. How strange to find myself there, all the same, when two days before I had no notion of travel. If people had told me then that I would soon be bedding down in a farm in Ireland, in the County of Wexford, no less, I should have laughed in their faces.

Musing thus, I found myself staring at an object above the door facing me. It was a cross but unlike any I had seen before, being woven of rushes. Since another, more traditional crucifix hung over the bed, I wondered what it could signify, and determined to ask Kitty later, and then forgot all about it.

I did not think that I slept, but when I next opened my eyes, I could faintly recall a dream in which, clean and sweep as I might, I could not get rid of the dirt that piled up around me. Shaking my head to disperse the unpleasant sensation this engendered, I looked out the window and saw that the rain had stopped and a watery sun was low in the sky. I brushed myself down and descended the stairs. Everyone, excepting Peter, was in the kitchen, Annie and Kitty Melrose bustling about feeding supper to an army of noisy children. Conversation stopped as I entered, and eight pairs of young eyes fixed upon me. Then Pegeen skipped up to me and took my hand,

"Auntie Marta," she said. "Auntie Marta."

There was a chorus then of "Auntie Marta, Auntie Marta" which made all us grown-ups laugh merrily. (I had noticed already that the Irish in general have a difficulty with the 'th' sound.)

Kitty and I then took ourselves back to the parlour to sit quietly and leave Annie to the feeding of her brood.

"So tomorrow first thing we will go to visit Lily," said Kitty, "and we shall see how the land lies and how we can best accomplish our mission."

Good gracious, I thought. It sounds like a military operation.

I reckoned, after my doze in the afternoon, that I should have trouble sleeping that night. Following a light repast, however, after which the household made to go to bed – they having of course to arise at dawn or near enough – I fell asleep almost immediately, the which I ascribed to the fresh country air, so different from the thick and heavy atmosphere of Baker Street. And this time I did not dream, or, if I did, there was no memory of it in the morning.

Chapter Three

"Get away with ye!" the man was shouting. "Away off of my land."

"Not until I see Lily, William," Kitty asserted, placing her foot in the doorway so that the door could not be closed. This was a new Kitty. I had never seen her so determined before.

"Lily's resting," the man replied.

Now I have to admit I had been expecting William Cullen, the declared despot of the household, to be a big brute of a man, and so was astonished when this under-sized, shrivelled, ill-favoured person answered to the name.

"I am her godmother, William, and I am sure she would like to see me."

"Some other time, Kathleen. She's resting, I tell ye. She has bad head on her."

"All the more reason I should attend to her, then."

"Best leave her be." There was no shifting him, and I feared he would crush Kitty's foot in the door sooner than let her past. "You'll see her soon enough, Kathleen, on her wedding day."

His small bloodshot eyes turned past us and the grin that suddenly spread over his face revealed a sparse number of long yellow teeth.

"There you be, lads," he said.

I turned to see two equally diminutive figures and one great oaf ambling across the yard towards us.

"Good morning, boys," Kitty said. "We have come to call on your sister."

"She's resting," said the smallest one with a leer.

"She needs her rest," said the other, "for what's ahead of her, like." They all roared with laughter. Then they pushed past Kitty and myself, entering the house and slamming the door behind them.

"Well," said Kitty, looking at me.

"What now?" I asked. "If they will not let you even speak to her."

"Tomorrow is Sunday. They must take her to church. I will make sure to speak to her then."

"Or at least to slip her a note," I said.

"Yes, indeed. That is a good idea, Martha. I will pen something at once and have it ready, in case I am thwarted again."

Even though Kitty had somewhat prepared me, I was still most taken aback at the uncouth and disrespectful behaviour of the Cullen menfolk. In such surroundings, was it even possible for young Lily to remain untainted? I did not express this notion to my friend, however, for she remained convinced of the girl's purity and innocence.

We walked away, most disheartened by this first set-back to our enterprise, Kitty at the gate turning to regard the house in case Lily should signal to us from a window. Nothing of the sort, however. All was closed and blank.

"I cannot believe," Kitty said, "that he would actually forbid me from seeing my own goddaughter? There is badness at work here, Martha. Worse than I had thought."

It was indeed hard to be cheerful but, to try to divert my friend, I asked inconsequential questions regarding the land we were passing through, which seemed to me more prosperous than any I had observed before. Gleaming brown and white cows chomped on the rich grass and followed us with their eyes; a donkey hopefully approached the stone wall in case we might have some treat to give it. Kitty showed no interest in any of this, nor did she respond when I remarked on the beauty of the hedgerows, burgeoning now with bright yellow gorse flowers and filled with twittering birds and dancing butterflies.

Only when we came to a stile near a stream did any animation return to her.

"Will we cross here for a moment?" she said.

"Is it a shorter way back?"

"No, I want to show you something."

It was a good thing, I thought, that no one was around to see us clamber in ungainly and unladylike fashion over the stile and into a field. A little path ran alongside the stream for a way. We followed it under willows until we came to a pool set around with flat stones. What caught my eye in particular was the curious tree beside it.

"This is the holy well of St Brigid," said Kitty. "I had forgotten it until just now, as we passed. Oh, St Brigid will surely answer my prayers."

I regarded my friend with astonishment. What new superstition was this? She laughed at my expression.

"Dear Martha," she said. "I cannot expect you to understand, but please indulge me."

"I will if you explain to me what this is all about. This tree for instance. What do these rags signify?"

I indicated the hawthorn that stood over the well. It was white and fresh as a young bride with May blossom, but its branches were queerly festooned with strips of cotton fabric, some newly tied on, some dirty and rotten with age.

"They are clooties," Kitty said. "An offering to the saint, if you like."

She pulled out a handkerchief and, to my astonishment, proceeded to rip a thin strip out of it. Then she bent down and soaked the strip in the water of the well. I stepped back because I could see that she was praying. After a few moments, she rose up and tied the bit of cloth to the branch of the hawthorn.

"St Brigid will hear me," she said. "She will understand Lily's plight and help the child."

"Who is this St Brigid? I confess I have never heard of her."

"She is a very strong and powerful Irish saint," Kitty replied. "You will have seen her cross hanging in your room over the door."

"The cross made of rushes?"

"That's the one. The girls made it to protect the house from fire."

"Well," I replied, somewhat nonplussed at this leap into fantasy, "it is certainly a very pretty thing."

Kitty shook her head, but said not another word on the subject. I am sure she found my lack of knowledge and faith another indication that I was surely damned. We walked back along the path by the stream, clambered over the stile and headed home at last, and, whatever reservations I might have about the previous proceedings, they at least had the effect of making Kitty much more cheerful.

That afternoon, as she had explained to me, Kitty planned to take the opportunity to call on friends. She had suggested, rather half-heartedly, that I accompany her, adding, "Although, Martha, we will be gossiping about old times and people you don't know, and I fear you will be very bored."

I replied that I would be content to stay in for the rest of the day and help Annie mind the children, which seemed to be the hoped-for answer.

As it turned out, however, the children, this Saturday, were all out with their father helping, or perhaps hindering, on the farm, and there was nothing for me to do in that respect. Now I am not at all used to idleness, and it troubled me, for Annie would not permit me to assist with any of the chores. I had finished reading my Marie Corelli novel, and now wished aloud that I had thought to bring some embroidery with me.

21

"Well," Annie conceded at length, "if it's sewing you want, I have a pile of linen to be mended. I never seem to find the time. But only," she added with diffidence, "if you wish it, Martha."

"That would be perfect," I replied. I sat myself quietly out of the way in the parlour and sorted through the linen basket. Most of the contents, I found, were sorely in need of the attention of a needle and thread.

After a while, Annie came to see how I was getting on and pronounced herself more than happy with what I had achieved.

"I could not have done it near so good, Martha," she said with a smile. Indeed, I must confess that I pride myself on the neatness of my stitching. "But," she continued with a worried expression on her broad face, "tomorrow being Sunday, I have been thinking about church."

As I was not of her faith, Annie felt it would not be appropriate or even possible for me to accompany the family to the local chapel. The nearest Church of Ireland, as she called it, was at some distance, too far to walk.

I tried to reassure her that, under the circumstances, my Maker would surely not object to me staying home and worshipping Him in private, but Annie was having none of it.

"Peter will drive you," she said, and I recalled with dismay the bone-shaker in which we had arrived. Indeed, I still felt the bruises.

"Then Peter will miss mass, because he will have to wait for me," I objected.

She pondered the matter for a moment.

"I have it," she exclaimed. "I will send Veronica on the bicycle to ask the Timminses."

Veronica was the oldest girl, a pretty young thing of thirteen, with a mass of curly ginger hair like her father's, and a charmingly freckled nose. The Timminses, apparently, were a Protestant couple who lived not too far off.

"I am sure they will be willing to fetch you in their carriage."

There was no arguing the point. Veronica went and Veronica returned. The Timminses, it seemed, were more than agreeable, so it was with them that I would go. I only hoped their carriage would prove more comfortable than Peter's.

The rest of the day passed, I must say, rather drearily for me, although I had a most pleasant chat with young Veronica, who showed herself bright and intelligent. I was already tuning into their way of speaking, and I suppose the same was true of her, for we had little difficulty understanding each other. (Perhaps here I should remark that I have taken the liberty of translating the colourful local accent into the Queen's English, so that it might more readily be understood by my readers, and also because the task of rendering it as spoken is far beyond my meagre capabilities).

I asked the girl about her school work, and was most impressed when she showed me her copy book, written in a clear round hand. To those people in London who have often expressed the opinion that the Irish are nothing but a bunch of unwashed savages, incapable of self-government, I should like to show them this simple young girl's work, which to my eye was superior to much that I had seen at home. Certainly no effort of my maid, Phoebe, would be up to anything like the same standard.

In the course of our conversation, Veronica informed me with some excitement that a match was soon to be made for her Aunt Sal, her mother's sister.

"A match?" I asked. "Do you mean that others will find her a husband?"

"Yes, indeed."

"She does not mind? She does not want to choose for herself?"

The girl looked at me wonderingly then, as if such a possibility had never occurred to her.

"But they will choose well, like they did for Mamma. They know best, you know. And anyway, Aunt Sal is already nearly an old woman."

"What age is she, then?"

"Well, over thirty anyway. Maybe forty, I don't know."

In that case, I thought, I must be ancient in the girl's eyes. A veritable fossil, indeed.

"I hope they will choose Luke Collety," she went on. "Aunt Sal is great with him, and we all like him, too. It would be nice to have him as an uncle."

"So who makes the match?" I asked.

"The matchmaker, of course. Mikey Dan."

How foolish of me not to know that!

"I do not like him so much though," Veronica said. "He smells of whisky and tobacco, and he's not very clean."

At that moment, my companion was called away by her mother to attend to the little ones, and I was left to my mending and to the conclusion that, after all, the Irish really are far behind the English in so many ways. Matchmaking, indeed! A practice that has, as far as I know, died out long since with us. Imagine if my parents had had the choosing of a husband for me. Would they ever have settled on dear Henry? On the other hand, I could see nothing but affection between Annie and Peter, and had Veronica not just informed me that was an arranged match as well? Perhaps I was lucky: when all is said and done, there are many so-called love matches that end in trouble.

Chapter Four

In Roman households they do not eat breakfast before Sunday morning mass – another custom most strange to me. Why ever would God mind his worshippers arriving at His house with comfortably full stomachs, instead of having them rumble irreverently throughout the service? Yet Catholics, as I understand it, like to punish themselves in many different ways, and there was to be no stretching of the rules on my behalf. So before I left for church, I was disappointed not to able to enjoy the delicious porridge that Annie had prepared the previous day. She had given it the quaint name of stirabout, making it with nutty oats and that same creamy milk from their cows. I could only hope to partake again on my return.

The Timminses proved to be an elderly couple, most respectable in appearance. The delight the lady expressed at meeting me, was quite excessive, and certainly more than my poor person warranted. My own delight consisted in the discovery that their carriage was covered and upholstered, so that the journey to church was comfortable enough, although they could have no control over the rough terrain and the potholes. They even had a driver, Barney, who, apparently, as Mrs. Timmins told me in hushed tones, was an absolute "Treasure," his worth consisting apparently in his being prepared unreservedly to take on any number of tasks relating to the Timmins' household.

The Treasure in question proved to be a young man with an empty countenance, crowned with a thatch of untidy straw-coloured hair. He was accoutred in some sort of a bottle green livery, which fitted rather bizarrely on his lumpy frame.

"I do not know what we should do without him," Mrs. Timmins whispered. She was a tiny person, with white hair puffing out under her bonnet and the sharp, bright eyes of a bird. "He is utterly devoted, bless him, and does everything for us. We are not able for much anymore, do you see." And she smiled a little sadly. "The Colonel has a bad leg."

That individual was a rigidly upright gentleman with a sanguineous complexion, sporting a bristling grey moustache. The few remaining strands of steely hair on his scalp had been combed into strictly regimented lines. He had served, as he hastened to inform me, in the Crimean War, the gammy leg being the result of an old wound, which troubled him more now as the years passed. I was reminded of Dr. Watson, though I could never remember, in his case, if the wound he had incurred in the Afghan campaign was in his leg or in his shoulder.

The Colonel shook his head.

"It was a bad business," he said. "Very bad."

I was not sure if he meant the wound or the war, until he added, "Hell on earth, Mrs. Hudson, if you can imagine that. Hell on earth."

I replied that I could not imagine any such thing, and was afraid I knew nothing more about that particular war other than Tennyson's poem "The Charge of the Light Brigade." I asked if Colonel Timmins had been part of that doomed band, but he laughed a bitter laugh and shook his head.

"I am no cavalryman, madam," he said. "I served my country in the infantry."

"The Colonel served his country well, Mrs. Hudson," Mrs. Timmins added. "He was a hero. He has medals, don't you know."

I duly expressed my admiration.

"The Battle of Inkerman was a bad business," the Colonel said. "Very bad. I was with the Durham regiment, don't you know, and we were nearly wiped out... The siege of Sebastopol was even worse."

"In trenches, Mrs. Hudson," his wife added. "Pits in the ground. It must have been horrible."

"I'll never forget one terrible storm," he continued. "I'm not a superstitious man, far from it, but that November 13th was unlucky for us. The storm blew down our tents, scattered our supplies and sank the transport ships in Balaclava harbour. By God, we were in a bad way then, but we hung on by the skin of our teeth. British spirit, Mrs. Hudson. British spirit. It can't be beaten."

He gazed at me with penetrating pale blue eyes.

"No, indeed," I said.

"Later, you know, we got the new Enfield rifles, and it was easier to pick the Russkies off with those."

"Goodness." I suppose shooting people is what you do in war, but still I did not quite like the relish with which the Colonel expressed himself.

They explained how, after the Colonel's discharge from the army, the couple had come to Ireland, twenty or more years earlier.

"I have family connections here, do you see," said Mrs. Timmins.

"Not that we have much to do with those cousins of yours, thank goodness." The Colonel spoke with a sharp edge to his tone.

"No, we don't," she replied, and smiled at me again. "Well, sometimes we pay them a courtesy visit, you know."

The Colonel snorted. It seemed Mrs. Timmins' relations were no favourites of his.

"I still keep busy," the Colonel went on. "Idleness would not suit me, Mrs. Hudson. Not at all." He looked at me accusingly, as if suspecting me of that same vice. "I serve as Resident Magistrate and am Master of the Hunt during the season, which is sadly over until October. Otherwise you might have been pleased to join us."

27

I nodded politely, although I have never hunted, not yet mounted a horse, and will be perfectly pleased never to do so in the future.

"We also keep bees," the Colonel added.

"Bees. Ah, how interesting that must be."

"It is, indeed. The beehive, don't you know, is quite a microcosm of society. We can learn a lot from bees."

"They are ruled by a Queen, I believe," I said, adding somewhat archly, "even though there is no King."

"Just so," said the Colonel frowning.

"Just like England at the moment," Mrs. Timmins trilled.

I nodded, thinking it was not the same at all.

"Oh, Mortimer," Mrs. Timmins continued. "We must give Mrs. Hudson a pot of our honey."

"Indeed we must."

I thanked them, adding that I was most partial to that confection and thought it must taste delicious here, in view of all the lovely flowers that graced the hedgerows.

"Oh yes, we encourage lilac, lavender and honeysuckle in our garden," she replied," and there are cornflowers in the fields."

"You have forgotten the snapdragons, Augusta," added the Colonel. "Bees are very partial to snapdragons, Mrs. Hudson, don't you know."

I replied that it was news to me and most fascinating to learn, the which seemed to satisfy him. In this fashion we chatted amicably enough along the way, despite his somewhat abrupt manner.

At a certain point we passed a farm I took to be derelict, by the broken-down nature of the house and the evident neglect in the yard, where implements stood rusting. Had the occupants been evicted? I asked.

"Not at all" Colonel Timmins replied gruffly, "that's the Kinsella place."

As if on cue, a young man of extraordinary beauty came out of a barn, and regarded us with an inscrutable expression as we passed.

"Francie," said Mrs. Timmins shortly.

"That is Francie!" I exclaimed in surprise. Had Kitty not described him as a horror?

I turned to try to see more of Lily's betrothed, and caught a glimpse of him still staring after us as we turned a corner.

"It's a bad business," Colonel Timmins said, shaking his head. "A bad business."

Was he referring to the state of the farm or the impending marriage? I did not feel that it was my place to question him on the matter, and soon again we were talking of other things.

St. Michael's church was a small neat structure dating, I supposed, from the earlier part of the century. It had an attractive tower surmounted with decorative cornerstones, mullioned windows and an arched wooden door. Inside, the walls were plastered white, and inset with commemorative brass plaques and memorials. The congregation was reduced enough all the same, reflecting, perhaps, the predominance of adherents of the Roman church in this part of the country. The Timminses were well-known among this small community, and, on greeting their friends and acquaintances, made sure out of politeness to introduce me as a visitor to the area.

The rector, a Mr. Webber, slight and pale, with thinning black hair raked back and an unfortunately long red nose, was a man in a hurry. Perhaps Mrs. Webber had a good Sunday dinner awaiting him; he certainly looked in need of feeding up. Whatever the reason, he conducted the service in brisk fashion. We sang "Onward Christian Soldiers" at break-neck speed – Colonel Timmins' assertive baritone booming out beside me. This was similarly followed by "A Mighty Fortress is Our God" and "Stand up, Stand up for Jesus, Ye Soldiers of the Cross." All rather bellicose, I could not help thinking, but possibly the Protestants here felt somewhat under siege. There had, as Peter told us, been some incidents locally, though mostly directed at absentee landlords. Continuing in the same warlike spirit, the reverend's sermon, delivered in a high-pitched reedy voice, exhorted us as Christian soldiers to hurry up and fight the good fight. All in all, before the service ended our loins were well and truly girded up, if you will forgive the crudeness of the expression.

It seemed Mr. Webber was not in such a rush as to dash off after all, but positioned himself at the door of the church as we made our way out, to thank us all for coming. A gentleman I had not noticed before – even though his somewhat curious appearance would surely attract attention anywhere – stood at his shoulder. As Mr. Webber uttered a few bland words to me, this individual stepped forward, a smile broadening his already wide face.

"A new addition to our little company," he exclaimed in voice like a tinkling bell. "What larks! Welcome. Welcome. Welcome, dear lady."

This extraordinary outburst elicited no amazed looks from the crowd, so I supposed they must be well used to the gentleman. He stood no taller than myself, and I am not considered tall. A fleshy man of advanced years with a complexion as soft and pink as a girl's, he was strikingly dressed in a tan velvet jacket, light trousers and an emerald green waistcoat. A pink rosebud decorated his buttonhole. At home in London where many such gentlemen can be seen, I should have called him a dandy. Here, amid the soberly dressed folk, he seemed quite out of place, a curiosity, an orchid in a field of hay, if that is not being too unkind to those of us less flamboyantly dressed.

"Mrs. Timmins, Mrs. Timmins," he urged that lady. "Pray introduce me without delay to your most attractive companion."

Attractive! Now that was a compliment I had not heard for many long years.

Mrs. Timmins smiled indulgently and stated that I was Mrs. Hudson.

"Oh!" He clapped his two hands together as if amazed. "*The* Mrs. Hudson. Can it really be? *The* Mrs. Hudson who was housekeeper to the late and much lamented Mr. Sherlock Holmes. A little bird whispered that you were come among us, but I could scarce credit it. I am honoured, madam, honoured." He made as if to take my hand and kiss it.

"Well," I replied with some asperity, while dodging his attempts at gallantry, "in point of fact I was Mr. Holmes' landlady, not his housekeeper." It is a distinction I often find myself obliged to make. Mine is the house, Mr. H was the lodger (and is again, I can now happily state, he having returned by some miracle from the dead).

"Well, well," the little man repeated, not in the least put out. "His landlady, indeed. Well, well, well. A woman of property. Good, good."

Mrs. Timmins then introduced him to me as Mr. Florence Sweetnam.

"Florrie, please," he said. "Everyone calls me Florrie."

A name that surprised me, I must admit, as I thought it only assigned to the female sex. Nonetheless, it seemed fitting, since Mr. Sweetnam showed himself more than somewhat feminine in his manner.

"Widowed, like myself," he added, shaking his head sadly, "three lovely ladies having preceded me into paradise." Then rather inappropriately, he winked.

"Now how do you know, Mr. Sweetnam, that I am in a state of widowhood?" I asked. My bombazine is black, of course, and yet that hardly signified. Many women of my age choose that to wear that colour.

"Ah," and he tapped a chubby and beringed finger to the side of his nose. "One can have no secrets here, dear lady. Not here. You will soon learn that."

"I doubt I shall stay long enough to learn any such thing," I replied. "I am only over for a wedding."

"Do not say that, I implore you. We shall all be utterly broken-hearted if you abandon us so quickly, will we not, Mrs. Timmins?" Regarding that lady but giving her no time to reply. "After the wedding, indeed!" He bent his head sideways, a cajoling expression on his plump face. "But perhaps, Mrs. Hudson, you will stay on for your own wedding. Who can tell?" With a chuckle and another wink, he skipped off, light enough on his feet all the same for one of his bulk, I looking after him in astonishment, wondering if I should be insulted by his familiarity.

"Florrie, Florrie, Florrie," exclaimed Mrs. Timmins smiling. "He is quite irrepressible, is he not?"

"Has he really buried three wives?" I asked. "I took him for a confirmed bachelor."

"Not at all. He loves the ladies... Of course," she added piously, "he took the bereavements very hard."

Did he indeed? I saw no sign of it.

"He is the kind of man who needs a good woman to look after him, being such a child at heart," and she smiled. "You are already a favourite with him, I can see that."

Make of those two statements what you will.

Colonel Timmins then rejoining us, we soon found the Treasure and the carriage and bumped our way back. Again we passed the Kinsella place, but this time the only creature in the yard was a big black dog, that barked angrily as we went by.

"You know, Martha," Mrs. Timmins was saying, we now being on first name terms, hers, as she had confided, being Augusta. "The Colonel and I have decided you would be so much happier staying with us." She paused.

"Among your own people, don't you know," added the Colonel, with whom I was not on first name terms.

"You would be so much more comfortable, I am sure," Mrs. Timmins continued.

"That is most kind of you, Augusta," I replied, privately thinking that in no way were these my people. "But you know, Mrs. Melrose is my very good friend and companion. I think she would find it most strange, not to say rude, if I were to move out."

"What a pity. We have so many empty rooms, you see, while Peter and Annie's house is so small for all those children, let alone two extra guests."

"That is true." I did not feel inclined to inform them that the boys were sleeping in the barn. "Thank you again. I will ask them what they would like me to do."

"Oh, no, no, no," said the Colonel. "Do not think of it. If you ask, they will press you to stay, even though they would much prefer you to go. It is the way with these people. You must just tell them, Mrs. Hudson. Tell them that you are coming to stay with us."

"The Colonel knows these people well, Martha." Mrs. Timmins smiled prettily. "He is forever helping them out with advice."

Your people. These people. I did not feel at all comfortable with the tone of the conversation. "I shall ask Mrs. Melrose," I said, smiling back. "She will give me good council."

"I am sorry to have to say it," remarked the Colonel, not looking sorry at all, "since these people are related to your friend, but Peter O'Kelly is not to be trusted."

I looked at the Colonel in astonishment.

"He seems a very sound man to me," I replied.

"Appearances can be deceiving," Mrs. Timmins put in.

"He is something of a Fenian, you know."

"A Fenian?"

"A Brotherhood dedicated to overthrowing the status quo in this country. Oh, they claim to have been disbanded, but I know better. O'Kelly and his gang of brothers are against British rule, Mrs. Hudson. As if their poor benighted race can rule for themselves." The Colonel sniffed disparagingly.

I knew, of course, even from the little conversation we'd had on the topic that Peter had strong views, but again did not feel like sharing this with the Timminses. Instead I remarked, "Well, Peter has always been perfectly civil to me."

"That's as maybe. I suppose since you are friends with his sister, you run little risk of having your throat cut."

I said nothing to this extreme remark. The pause lengthened uncomfortably.

"You should at least come to take luncheon with us," Mrs. Timmins persisted at last.

"I am sure they gave you no breakfast," the Colonel added, smirking.

"Thank you again," I replied, "but I am expected. It would be most impolite of me to stay away without telling them."

"Barney can carry them a message."

"Another time," I said. "You are both really too kind. Anyway," I could not help adding, "I doubt they are planning to poison me."

"It is no laughing matter, I can assure you Mrs. Hudson. People have been killed. Lord Frederick Cavendish and Thomas Henry Burke to name but two."

"Yes, yes, the Phoenix Park murders," I said, adding somewhat sharply, "and yet I rather think more of the deaths were on the other side of the divide. In any case, I am sure Peter is not allied to these bloodthirsty organisations."

"*You* are sure!" The Colonel sniffed again, emphasising the first word with disdain. "Let me tell you, Mrs. Hudson," and he actually waved a pointing finger at me, "Wexford is a hotbed. A veritable hotbed. Just think of Father Murphy. Think of Vinegar Hill."

I could not think of them, indeed, for I knew nothing of either of them. However, I was disinclined to ask the Colonel to explain. I did not appreciate that finger in my face, not at all, and kept silent.

Poor Mrs. Timmins did her best to diffuse the poisoning atmosphere. "You must at least stop by for the honey, Martha." Did she never give up? I rather feared once they got me in the house they would lock the door on me, like poor Lily.

"I shall be delighted," I repeated firmly, "to call on you on another occasion."

Seeing that I would not be further moved, the subject was dropped, although I noticed a tightening of the Colonel's expression and a heightening of his already high colour. I imagine he did not like to be gainsaid, especially by a woman.

They left me at the farmhouse gate, Mrs. Timmins giving me instructions to send Veronica over with word to fetch me and my things, if and when I decided to move to their house. The Colonel barely bade me farewell, merely giving me a curt nod.

The O'Kelly family was already back from mass and, I am afraid, awaiting my return before breaking their fast. It was as well then that I not been tempted to join the Timminses for luncheon.

Annie asked me how I had got on with the pair. I glanced at Peter, who, however, had his nose deep in his dish.

"Well enough," I said. "They were very kind to take me."

Did Peter grunt?

Today being Sunday, the stirabout was embellished with cream and a dash of a local beverage I was told called poitín. It proved even more delicious as a result. I told Annie she must give me the receipt. To which she gave me a look I can only describe as ambiguous.

Later, Kitty informed me that poitín was an illegally distilled local spirit.

"But you can always use whiskey," she said.

"I see."

Kitty had urged a walk after breakfast and, it being a bright morning, I readily complied. As I am usually an active woman, I did not wish to spend the rest of another day confined indoors. In any case, there was no more linen for me to mend.

On the way, I told Kitty of the Timmins' invitation.

"I hope you do not wish to avail of it, Martha," she replied. "Annie would be most offended, and I know the children love having two aunties to attend to them."

"I do not wish to at all," I replied. "Augusta Timmins is pleasant enough, I suppose, but I do not care much for the Colonel. He has a bullying, patronising way about him. Although," I added, "I am sorry the boys have to sleep in the barn."

"Get away out of that," she replied. "They love it. I am sure they stay chatting far into the night, something they cannot do in the house. In any case, you know, you have to stay by me for the success of our enterprise."

The path was taking us through a small wood carpeted with bluebells. It was a most pretty sight, especially as the rays of the sun seemed quite to dance through the leaves of the beech, oak and birch trees upon the bell heads of the flowers. Rustlings of woodland creatures could be heard; a red squirrel ran across the path and up a tree, and a thrush perched on a branch over our heads and started to sing. It was all most idyllic, and yet and yet the ominous shadow of Francie Kinsella seemed to lay over all.

"How did you get on with Lily?" I asked. "Were you able to talk with her?"

"Barely. And not alone. The menfolk stayed clustered about her. But I managed to present her with a prayer book into which I had placed a note. I only hope no one will intercept it."

"Did you mention the plan?"

"No, I did not, in case, you know, that it did indeed fall into the wrong hands. I merely wrote that I would love to chat with her and introduce her to you, adding that we would walk this very path every day at a certain time and that she should try to meet with us."

I nodded. I could not have thought of a better plan myself. Occasionally, my often scatter-brained friend showed herself to be quite resourceful.

"I do not know," she went on, "if it will be possible for her to escape the house, and even if she manages to come out, I am sure she will not be alone."

We had now emerged from the wood and faced a slight rise in the path. From the top we could look down a short distance on a farm house.

"That is surely the Cullen place." I recognised it although we had previously approached from a different road.

"Indeed," Kitty replied. "This is the quicker and more secluded way. The land you can see beyond belongs to the Kinsellas. The field they will gift to William."

A miserable enough patch to exchange for a daughter.

"There is Lily now," my friend exclaimed.

A slight girl, her long dark tresses loose about her shoulders, had come out a back door to hang sheets on a washing line strung across the yard. The large oaf of a brother ambled out behind, not offering to help with the heavy laundry. His only task, it seemed, was to keep a watch on her, and he sat himself down on a log, to do just that.

After a moment, she glanced up at us, then at him, but he was occupied in whittling a stick and noticed nothing. She dodged behind a sheet, so that he could no longer see more than her feet.

37

Looking up at us again, she nodded her head and waved, a wan smile on her pretty face.

"She has found the note," Kitty said. "I think she will not come today but maybe she can find the means tomorrow. I hope so, for the wedding is in four days."

"Four!" I said. "I thought more."

"The banns were read and the announcement made. Everyone was surprised." She paused. "Everyone but the bould Francie and the rest of his wretched tribe. He was all grins and smirks. But you know, Martha, it is unlucky to be married on a Thursday. And a Thursday in May, as well."

"Is that bad?"

"Marry in May and you'll rue the day. That's the saying. But what cares Francie for that?"

"I saw him," I said, "as I was passing the farm with the Timminses. I must admit I was most astonished, Kitty. The way you described him I thought he must be some sort of a freak. Yet he looks very well. Very well, indeed."

"Do not be fooled, Martha," she replied. "I think you have read the book by Mr. Wilde about Dorian Gray. Francie, you know, is very like that character."

Oscar Wilde's book had been a sensation a few years before, and we had all rushed to read it, thrilled by the horrid truth that lay hidden in the attic portrait. But surely that was a fiction? No one could be as evil as Dorian Gray in real life.

"I confess I am puzzled," I went on. "Why would his father so desire the match as to sacrifice a field for it?"

"It is indeed a mystery," Kitty said. "Although I know that Francie can be pure savage if he does not get his way, and it seems he has his heart set on poor Lily."

We had now turned back and descended the path into the woods. I was minded to pick a bunch of bluebells to give to Annie.

"She will like that," Kitty said.

I could see my friend was low, contemplating her goddaughter's impending fate, and so, to make her smile, I regaled her with an account of my meeting with Florrie Sweetnam.

"I do not know him," she replied. "We will ask Annie."

That young woman looked askance at the bluebells, by no means as delighted as I thought she would be at the offering.

"You have forgotten, Kitty," she said.

"What?"

"About bluebells."

Kitty looked puzzled.

"How their tinkling bells attract the faeries."

"Oh, Annie," Kitty said. "You don't still believe that old superstition, do you?"

"I suppose not." Annie fetched a pot to put them in, although I do not think she was at all happy about it, which surprised me greatly.

"Do you not like to think of faeries, Annie?" I asked, almost laughing.

"You want to keep well away from them, Martha. They can be very spiteful, you know."

She was quite serious!

Later I saw that the flowers had been left outside the door and later still that they had quite disappeared. For Annie, it seemed, the faery-folk did not just live on in children's stories.

We were on safer ground discussing my recent encounter.

"Florrie, is it?" Annie said. "Oh Lord, yes. Everyone knows Florrie Sweetnam."

"I do not remember him," Kitty said.

"You would if you had ever seen him," I remarked.

"Indeed and you would." Annie started to laugh. "He has been here I suppose fifteen year or more. After you went away, Kitty, he married the Devine girl and moved in to their house. When

39

she died, he stayed on there. You should just see what he has done to the place."

"Ah, yes," Kitty replied. "I know it. Over the hill on the Boolavogue side. I remember Miss Devine as well, but she was hardly a girl even then. A real old maid, in fact."

"Well, Florrie took a shine to her, or at least, to the house. No," Annie stopped herself, "that is unkind of me. He is a harmless old body, who still thinks that he is a young feller."

"He told me he has buried three wives," I said.

"Yes indeed, the poor man. But all of them women of property," Annie said. "More power to him."

Chapter Five

The following day, we again set out on our morning walk, hoping to meet up with Lily, for time before the wedding was running out. The older children being back in school, I suggested bringing the little ones,

"Why?" Kitty asked. "They will delay us."

"But they can also cause a distraction. Surely Lily's chaperone will not act roughly if there are babies present."

"Perhaps," my friend replied doubtfully.

"And it will give Annie much needed respite," I added.

There could be no argument with that, so with three delighted children in tow, along with the two dogs, Bella and Star, we set off once again to the bluebell wood. The children were happy to run round and explore, and the dogs were finding all sorts of interesting scents to absorb them. This suited us very well, for if we ventured into open ground, we might be observed from the farm and all thoughts of Lily joining us would be dashed. And if there were faeries around, attracted by the tinkling of the bluebells, I for one did not see them.

The children had just started a game of hide and go seek among the trees, with Kitty calling out to them not to wander far, when Lily herself rounded a bend in the path, not alone, alas, for the oafish brother was with her.

Close to, she was even lovelier than her image in Kitty's locket, a delicate-looking girl, porcelain-skinned with dark eyes and hair that I could now see had reddish flecks in it

"Goodness," exclaimed Kitty, as if greatly surprised. "Imagine that children. Here's Lily and Oliver."

It was lucky, I thought, that this was the lad we had to deal with rather than one of the others, who, even at a brief encounter I had judged the more canny.

Oliver, for his part, was regarding us with stupefaction.

"Come Lily," he said. "We must go back."

"Oh, not yet, Ollie. It is so nice here and I love to see the children." Clearly a favourite with them, she embraced them one by one. Then she was introduced to me, and smiled warmly. Her brother I suppose I had already met. In any case, he displayed no interest in making my further acquaintance.

"The children have been playing hide and go seek," I said. "Perhaps we could all join in."

"No," said Oliver, looking terrified.

"Just for a few moments, Ollie, please… No one need know." His sister looked at him pleadingly. Surely his heart must melt.

"Oh, Oliver don't be a spoilsport. What harm?" Kitty said.

He hesitated. I jumped in.

"Oliver and I will stay here and count to twenty while you all go and hide." I took his arm, doubting the while that the lad could actually compute that far.

"No," he said, and tried to pull away. "No, no." But the others were already dashing off giggling into the woods.

"One… two…You must close your eyes, Oliver," I said, "three… four. Close them or you quite spoil the game…" He was looking wildly about, but I had him gripped firm, and I am a strong woman. He could have pushed me down, I am sure, but retained at least some native courtesy. "Five…six…" And so on slowly up to twenty. Only then I let him go, and he bounded off in his search, carelessly where he trod and crushing, I am sorry to say, many bluebells in his path.

When everyone finally emerged from among the trees, the children laughing and pushing each other, I noticed that Kitty and

Lily had both been weeping and now hastily wiped their faces. The gormless oaf, thank goodness, saw nothing amiss.

"You will say nothing about it to no one," he hissed at his sister, hoping thereby, I imagine, to save his own neck, rather than protect hers. Then he pulled his charge roughly back along the path towards their farm.

The children scampered after them for a way, calling Lily to play some more, but she just turned and waved before he dragged her off and out of sight. Kitty was too overcome to get control of herself so I assembled the children, then, and Pegeen called to the dogs. I doubt they would have responded to my unfamiliar voice.

"How did you get on?" I asked.

"I shall tell you later," she whispered back.

Home at the farm, Annie asked if they'd had a good time.

"We did, mammy. We played hide and go seek. And guess what? We saw Lily and Ollie."

"Did you indeed?" Annie replied, turning her eyes on us.

"Yes, they were walking in the woods as well," said Kitty. "Such a nice surprise."

I understood she did not wish to involve her sister-in-law further in our plan, and Annie, for her part, said no more about it, whatever her suspicions. Claiming fatigue, Kitty and I then repaired upstairs, allegedly to rest, my friend accompanying me to my room to report on what had transpired.

"I told Lily of our plan," she said. "But she fears it cannot work. She is afraid of her father and brothers and has quite despaired of finding a way out of this marriage."

"Well," I replied. "It is the best we can hope for. I trust she will at least consider it unless she is determined to sacrifice herself for a muddy field."

"But how can it work," Kitty asked, "when they guard her so closely?"

The plan we had fixed on had come to us following a chat over the supper table the previous evening. It seemed it was the custom in these parts for the groom to take dinner with the bride's family on the eve of the wedding. A fat goose would be cooked and quantities of ale and poitín would be drunk.

"Sometimes so much," Peter had remarked, chuckling, "that the groom and the father of the bride have to be carried to church the next day."

That would assuredly be the time for Lily to leave the house and meet up with us. She could pretend to be worn out and go to her bed. Then creep out when the men were otherwise occupied.

The problem would be how to get her away quickly. This Kitty and I now discussed, agreeing that they would surely come in hot pursuit once her absence was noticed.

"Of course, with any luck," I said, "that will not be until the next morning, assuming, as Peter said, the menfolk will be stupid with drink. Might we persuade your brother to come with his cart to drive us all to Enniscorthy? We can then wait there for the next train to Kingstown."

"I should not like to involve Peter in this," said Kitty. "The Cullens and Kinsellas are his neighbours and he will have to continue to live here with them after we have gone."

"You are right," I said. "Of course, Peter and Annie must have no hand in this."

We sat thinking for a few moments and then I clapped my hands.

"The Treasure," I said. "I will ask for the Treasure."

Kitty looked at me open-mouthed.

"What?"

"The Timminses told me that they would send Barney, their driver, to fetch me if I needed him. I will call for him to fetch me on some excuse."

"So late at night?"

"Will it be so very late? Lily can pretend to retire early. I am sure they will not want her to witness their carousing." Then a better thought struck me. "I have it. I will arrange to visit the Timminses that day. They will surely insist I stay and dine with them, and then the Treasure will have to drive me home."

Kitty considered the idea for a moment. "It could work. But what will you tell this Barney Treasure, or whatever his name is, for him to consent to take us all the way to Enniscorthy?"

"He did not strike me as a very bright young man, but I am sure even he understands the attraction of silver coins. We can make it very much worth his while."

I spoke with more confidence than I felt. Between Lily agreeing to flee from the only home she had ever known, to this being accomplished without discovery, and with the uncertain involvement of a young man of whom I knew very little, the outcome was far from sure. Yet Kitty felt she had to try, and we could think of no other way.

The next problem facing us was how to get word of the plan to Lily, and how to find out if she intended to go along with it. It was Kitty this time who had the solution.

"We should send a basket over to the house. Gifts for Lily with a note secreted among them, but also a purse of sovereigns for the men. I will say it is to help with the wedding breakfast. The money will, I hope, distract them. If I know William Cullen, he will build a little tower of the coins and reckon how few of them he needs to spend on food and drink for the guests."

"It is risky," I said. "But I suppose it must be done."

"I wonder if Lily even has a decent wedding dress," Kitty mused. "Her father is that mean; he is quite capable of sending her to church in any old garment."

"Well," I said, "even if she has something fine, let us hope she has no occasion to wear it."

"I have in any case brought some little bits and pieces with me," Kitty continued, "including a fine lace bag for Lily to carry, an embroidered linen handkerchief and some seed pearl rosary beads. I will hide the note in the bag under them."

"How will we know if she has found it and, more importantly, if she is willing to go along with the plan?" I asked. "You said that she is reluctant."

"She is afraid. Yet I think she is even more afraid of this marriage."

For a while more we scratched our heads over the problem, and then I had an idea.

"Tell her to hang some coloured item on the washing line if she wishes to come with us. If the line is left white or empty we will know that she is unwilling to risk flight."

This plan was agreed on at last, and we duly engaged in preparing the basket. Indeed, when Annie heard of it – without knowing its clandestine purpose, of course – she insisted on adding gifts of her own, including a fine linen tablecloth from her own trousseau.

"What use have I for it?" she asked. "The children would destroy it in an instant. Peter too."

One might well ask what use would Francie Kinsella have for it either, but no one remarked on that.

Annie suggested sending the basket over to the Cullens with the oldest boy, Gerald, "I should not like Veronica to go there."

We did not ask why, but could well imagine.

The deed was done, and we could only await the outcome, hardly able to settle to anything. I could not read, and wished once more that I had brought some sewing with me, to distract from troubling thoughts.

The next day, being Tuesday, two days before the wedding, we yet again went walking in the bluebell wood, hastening to the hill top from which we could view the washing line. There was nothing hanging there, and no sign at all of Lily. We walked home dispirited. After all our plans, was she not going to bite?

On the other hand, it proved simplicity itself to get myself invited for dinner with the Timminses for the following day, the wedding eve. Having sent the obliging Veronica over with a request to pay them a visit in the afternoon, I received an effusive invitation directly back with the girl. I could not flatter myself, however, that my company was so very much sought after. More likely it was that any variation to the restricted and humdrum social circle of the local Protestant gentry was to be welcomed. Particularly since, despite the hunt, their honey-making – the which I imagined was anyway delegated to the staff – and the Colonel's less than onerous RM duties, time must hang heavy on their hands.

In the morning, Kitty and I set off yet again on our walk, to the astonishment of Annie. Country people, I often find, have little use for the beauties of nature. To indulge in contemplation of such, takes away from the hard work needing to be done. We explained it, I think satisfactorily enough, however, by stating what a delightful change it was for us city folk from the stifling air of London. And that, for me, was no lie even if I would never wish permanently to exchange my life there for a rural one.

Reaching, with some trepidation, the top of the hill, we greatly rejoiced to see a red petticoat hanging from the line, waving in the breeze like a flag of freedom. Lily wished to flee her fate. We returned in much better form, Annie commenting that truly the fresh Wexford air had brought a bloom to both our cheeks. We sat down to eat a plate each of bacon and cabbage, oozing toothsome juices, which we heartily enjoyed.

The day had turned into another fine afternoon, and rather than risk my bones in Peter's cart – Gerald, the oldest boy, kindly offering to drive me by that conveyance, his father being occupied as ever with farm duties – I expressed a desire to walk the short enough distance, especially if Veronica could be spared to accompany me. I had taken a strong liking to the girl, and it seemed she to me, since she liked whenever possible to sit next me and hold my hand.

The direction we took, she wheeling the bicycle in order more quickly to return, was the opposite one to the bluebell wood. We skirted fields that belonged to the O'Kellys, and passed another and another farm, some miserably poor and some looking to be more prosperous, along winding and undulating country roads, edged with hedgerows of sweet-smelling gorse. In the distance I could see the distinctive outline of Mount Leinster, a light web of cloud around its summit that it seemed a breeze could brush away.

"Really, Veronica," I said. "You are blessed to live in such a lovely spot."

"But I should like to see London," she replied. "It must be a great place." It was a favourite topic with her: the big city seeming like something out of a faery tale to one who had never ventured much farther afield than the small town of Ferns.

"It is," I said. "It is splendid. But, you know, the air is often bad and the streets are always dirty, and there is disease and the people... well, some are very rough."

"Some people here are rough, too."

"That is true. But perhaps in a different way. There are cut-purses and villains of all sorts on the lookout for the likes of you and me. I cannot walk so freely there, you know."

I was making more of it than was strictly true, but I did not want her to think of London as some kind of El Dorado.

"So would you like to live here instead?" she asked, setting clear green eyes upon me.

"Ah well, you know, I have my family and friends over there. And of course my own little house. I should miss all that."

I had my memories too, of dear Henry and of Mr. H, but of those I did not speak to a girl of thirteen years.

As we passed the next field, I noticed in the midst of it a strange little hill, covered in dense bushes and rocks.

"You would think," I said, "that the farmer would wish to clear that away."

"Oh no, Auntie Marta," the girl replied, shocked. "No, he mustn't be doing the likes of that. 'Tis a faery fort and the faeries would get very angry."

I am afraid that I burst out laughing until I realised Veronica was quite serious. I was reminded of her mother's reaction to the bluebells, which I still could not quite take seriously.

"Do you mean to tell me," I said, "that people round these parts still believe in the faeries?"

She nodded, adding ominously, "Some have seen them to their cost."

"Whatever do you mean?"

"There's a hill near here, Knocknacoill, 'tis called. There's a ring of stones on top, from the old times, and that's where the faeries gather. Haven't people seen strange lights up there by night?" She looked at me, all eyes. "If you hear the faery music, they say, you can't stop dancing for ever and ever. No, you wouldn't want to go up there in the dark, Auntie, or the faeries might take you away and you'd never get back."

The remainder of the walk passed most entertainingly with her telling me all manner of tales of the little folk, as she called them, their spitefulness or worse if crossed.

"There was a woman," she said, "left her baby boy in the house while she went to collect sticks. She saw a great pile of them around the rath – that's what we call the fort, you know, in the old language. Anyway, her friend told her not to go there, but she said they were fine sticks, so they were, and she had no fear of the faeries. But then when she went back to her cottage with her bundle of sticks, what did she find in the cradle, only a little wizened old craytur where her lovely bonny baby used to be. The faeries had took him because she took their sticks."

"Now, Veronica..." I started.

"My Grandda Gerald was taken by the faeries too, but he got away."

"Is that so?"

"He was coming back home one night and didn't he see a fine rabbit in the field near the rath. So he went into the field to chase the rabbit. Around and around he went but couldn't catch the rabbit at all. And when he tried to find the gate out of the field he couldn't find that either and ran around the field all the long night until the day came, and then at last he found the gate. But he always said that the rabbit was a faery that cast a spell on him."

"I see. That's an amazing story, right enough."

I could not help but wonder, nonetheless, if the grandfather was coming home from some inn, his head swimming with the drink, and that was the reason he could not find the gate, and there were no faeries in the place at all.

"Two men of this parish saw the banshee on the bridge one dark night," Veronica went on.

"Stop," I said. "Whatever is a banshee?"

"A banshee is a faery spirit. If you hear her wailing, it means someone in the family is going to die."

"So I suppose these two men heard her wailing, did they?"

"They did not. They saw her combing her long hair, dark as the night."

I suspected that Veronica must be telling a story that was so often retold that it had acquired a script of its own.

"They seized her comb and ran off with it as fast as they could, with the banshee running after. They locked themselves in their house, but when they peeped out the window, there she was reaching up for her comb. They were terrified out of their wits and in the morning they went to the parish priest to ask what they should do…"

"Yes, but why did they take the comb in the first place?"

Veronica looked at me with pity for the foolishness of my question. "Divilment, I suppose. Anyhow, the priest said to return to the house, and at night open the window just a little tiny bit, and hold the comb out with the long tongs you use for the fire, or the banshee would have the hand off them along with the comb. And that's what they did."

"Aha," I said.

"But that's not the end of it," said Veronica. "The men had reared five fat pigs to take to market, but when they went to fetch them, the pigs were lying stone dead. The banshee had killed them out of spite."

She shook her head in satisfaction, and scrunched up her freckled nose while her ginger curls danced.

"Dear me. Five dead pigs. That's bad."

"'Tis, and that's not the end of it either, Auntie Marta."

"Good heavens. There's more?"

"Indeed and there is. The next morning again they went to check on their hens and the hens hadn't feather among them. The banshee had taken them for her pillow. The men had to knit little jackets for their hens to keep them warm. They learnt their lesson after that, Auntie, and stayed well away from the banshee."

"I'm sure they did," I said. "Well, I hope I never meet one of those ladies."

Veronica shook her head grimly, "Please God," she said.

We had now come over the brow of a hill.

"There's the Timminses' place now," Veronica said, indicating a large squat grey-stoned manor set squarely on a sward of lawn, a little back from the roadway. "You'll be fine from here, so you will, Auntie. I don't wish to go in. Mrs. Timmins is always laughing at me, and I'm a-feared of the master."

I thanked her for her company, sorry indeed, that I had unwittingly put her in their way twice before.

"Oh, no, Auntie. That is no harm. Mrs. Timmins gives me a farthing sometimes, so I don't really mind her laughing."

A farthing, I thought drily. Generosity has no bounds! I gave the girl a silver sixpence, which she was loath to take. I insisted however.

"I shouldn't have found the place without you, my dear. And you have delighted me with your tales of the faeries."

"There's many more about them, Auntie," she replied and reached up (not so far for she is tall for her age) to give me a kiss on the cheek. Such a sweet and innocent child and not so very much younger than Lily. I admit I was moved, even having to brush a tear from my eye.

It was the Treasure, in the same incongruous bottle-green livery he had worn before, who opened the front door and who showed me into the parlour. I was somewhat taken aback to find there none other than the gallant Florrie Sweetnam, ensconced with the Colonel. Both men stood up on my entry, Florrie beaming and pressing his hand to his heart, as if the sight of me represented the acme of his desires. The Colonel simply gave me a nod without benefit of a smile. Still, he bade me welcome and requested me to be seated.

There was no dearth of chairs to choose from. The room was crammed full of heavy mahogany furniture the which I imagine must have been brought from a larger house in England when they left it, and not really suited to the limited space. I had to walk carefully round each overstuffed armchair to avoid brushing against one of the occasional tables with my skirt, knocking flying the bric-a-brac with which it was laden. A huge cast iron fireplace surmounted by a mirror dominated one wall, although there was no fire lit in it, just chopped logs. The walls themselves were covered with paper of an unattractive greenish hue, resembling to my eye a sort of mould or verdigris, while heavy velvet drapes in a wine-dark shade of red, dusty-looking, hung at the lattice windows. A towering grandfather clock steadily ticked the hours away. The antlered head of some poor massacred deer hung over a case containing a large fish, a pike perhaps, that was itself placed on top of a cabinet containing more fussy ornaments. A portrait of the Colonel as a younger man in full dress uniform dominated another wall, his cold blue eyes fixing the viewer's however much he might try to avoid them. In short, a room that crowded in unpleasantly, not a room in which to feel at ease.

Florrie, however, seemed quite relaxed and unaffected by his surroundings, plying me with questions about what I had been up to, as he put it, winking betimes as if there were something a little dubious about it all. He could not know, of course, what Kitty and I had planned, but at the same time I felt uncomfortable at his probing.

The little man was attired as flamboyantly as before, this time in a jacket of dark blue velvet with a silken waistcoat in a lighter shade of turquoise blue, decorated with exotic orange birds, the whole outfit surmounted by a white cravat fastened by a large emerald pin. A white rosebud in his buttonhole completing his attire, the contrast between himself and the soberly dressed Colonel could not have been more striking. I could not imagine what the two of them might talk of between themselves when not constrained by the presence of others. Perhaps it regarded the golden liquid which Florrie was sipping from a tiny glass, since they continued on this theme.

"I agree, Timmins," he said. "Most superior. Most superior."

The Colonel nodded, clearly pleased at the praise. He hastened to inform me, with some degree of self-importance, that he arranged for the Amontillado to be sent over expressly from Cadiz. I evinced an amazement which seemed to gratify him.

"You see, Mrs. Hudson, I cannot readily obtain the variety of delicately fragrant grape I like from anywhere else. A dozen or so bottles from time to time is after all not so great an indulgence. I'm sure you will agree."

Florrie nodded vigorously and said, raising his glass to me, "You are not averse to partaking of a sip or two of such a superior sherry, I hope, Mrs. Hudson."

"Not at all," I said, more out of politeness. I did not wish to cloud my mind with spirits in view of what lay ahead of me that night. "But only the merest drop, if you please."

The merest drop was all I was given. I imagine the Colonel was anxious to husband his fine wines, and not waste them on those he reckoned unable to appreciate the true delicacy of the grape.

"Here," he said, passing me a glass. "I do not imagine you have been offered the like at the O'Kelly's." He and Florrie laughed heartily.

"I am very well fed there, I can assure you," I replied. "Annie is a most excellent cook."

"If you like crubeens – pig's trotters, don't you know – and stirabout."

I had not been offered the former delicacy, but was on the point of praising the latter. The Colonel did not let me, however, interrupting to explain to his visitor my stubborn refusal to come and stay with them. He made light of it, but I felt that he was still offended. "Unless," he added, fixing me fiercely with those blue eyes under the grey bushes of his eyebrows, "you have changed your mind, madam."

"You are most kind, Colonel," I replied, calmly returning his gaze, "but I think I must stay with my friend."

"Perhaps," said Florrie, swallowing back the rest of his sherry. "Mrs. Hudson prefers the smells of the farmyard to those of your flower garden."

"The which I am longing to see," I said quickly to try to dispel the souring atmosphere. "If that is at all possible. And by the way, this sherry is indeed most agreeable."

The Colonel did not offer me any more of it, but neither did he refill Florrie's empty glass.

It was true that I longed to escape to the garden. Between the Colonel's judgmental demeanour, Florrie's nods and winks, the very room itself, I felt quite stifled. And where was Augusta Timmins? No explanation had been made as to her absence. I hardly thought she would be busy in the kitchen concocting our supper. If the household could afford to import wines from Spain, they must have a cook. It was all rather strange.

"I trust Mrs Timmins is well," I ventured, as we made our way out to the garden.

"Augusta will join us shortly," replied the Colonel, which was, in fact, no reply.

The garden was indeed most attractive in the late afternoon light. Not too formal, its paved paths lined with neatly trimmed box hedges, a herbaceous border full of peonies, freesias, pansies and other late spring flowers, including the famous snapdragons in pink, white and purple that the Colonel had already informed me were much favoured by his bees. A waterlily pond was crossed by a little white bridge to a six-sided wooden summer house nestling under an elm tree.

We had no sooner crossed the bridge for a closer view when, suddenly, the scent of a lilac bush took me back to my childhood. Our garden at home had several bushes of that most aromatic shrub, and the memory quite moved me. I turned to the Colonel.

"It is all utterly enchanting," I said, and the treacherous thought came to me that if indeed I were staying with the Timminses, I could sit out here every day, indulging my senses.

"We like it," said the Colonel. "And so do the bees."

"It is a veritable faeryland," Florrie put in. "Although you know, Mrs Hudson faeries in this country are not the sweet little creatures you find in England. They are often spiteful and wicked."

"So I am coming to understand," I replied.

"The superstitions of these people are most amusing," he went on. "Though you know, I am not inclined to dismiss them altogether."

The Colonel merely snorted.

We walked back round the pond to a walled area containing a well-stocked herb garden. I rubbed a sage leaf between my thumb and forefinger and sniffed its sweet scent. Again I complimented the Colonel on his husbandry. His expression was becoming ever more smug, as if to ask, now my lady, are you not sorry you have refused our invitation to stay here?

At the end of the herb garden stood a high wooden fence with a gate in it.

"That is where the apiary is situated," said the Colonel.

"I should love to see it," I said. "I am most fascinated by bees."

"Are you indeed?" He looked at me as if he very much doubted it.

It was nothing less than the truth, however. Mr, H was used to describe to me how one day he wished to retire to the countryside and keep bees, a dreamy look in his usually sharp eyes. He would give me long disquisitions on these little creatures and their world, which started by boring and ended up enthralling me. I did not convey this information to the Colonel, however, hardly thinking it would be of any interest to him.

He opened the gate for us to glimpse the ranged hives but advised against going too near.

"Angry bees can be very dangerous," he warned, "and I have bred these to be particularly protective of their hives."

"Can you do that?" I asked. "How very interesting."

"Well, of course," he conceded, "I did not personally breed them."

"You had them shipped from Cadiz with the sherry perhaps, Colonel." I ventured a joke. Florrie laughed but the Colonel frowned.

"It is a serious scientific enterprise. The breeding of killer bees ..."

"Killer bees, oh my!" exclaimed Florrie, stepping back. "How frightful."

"Not at all," the Colonel continued. "They are perfectly safe unless they feel themselves to be under attack. Like any of us, indeed." He shut the gate. "I should be delighted to show you more but alas, one must only approach wearing the proper protective clothing."

"I should hate to get stung," Florrie trilled. "At least, not by a bee." He winked in, I am afraid, a rather suggestive manner.

But before anyone could respond to this, there was a welcome interruption.

"Martha," I heard called out. "Oh my dear, I am so sorry not to have welcomed you when you arrived. Most inconsiderately rude of me." It was Augusta Timmins, hurrying up the path behind us. I suspected the delay had been occasioned by her elaborate toiletries on our behalf, for she was all frills and flounces, perhaps a little inappropriate and overly youthful for a woman of her age.

"I see the Colonel has introduced you to our dear little honey-makers. I have a pot all ready to give you. You must not forget to take it with you." She twinkled at me. "Unless of course, you have decided to stay."

Oh dear, I thought. Am I to be harangued on the subject all evening?

"No, Augusta," said the Colonel. "I have already enquired. Mrs. Hudson insists on keeping to her prior arrangements."

"Well, never mind," his wife replied. "We have you now, Martha, and we will make the most of it."

She came up close to me, and her breath, I was somewhat shocked to discover, was rather strongly scented with Amontillado, or maybe with something not quite so delicate and fragrant.

The dinner was trout (caught locally, as the Colonel informed me, in the river Slaney), while the spring lamb was from one of their tenant farmers. A milk pudding that was too hard set and rubbery to my taste rounded off the meal. In fact, I considered that, despite the richer ingredients, the preparing of it was far inferior to Annie's cooking. Of course, I said nothing of this and instead praised the cook.

"Dear Maggie," said Augusta. "The Treasure's mother, don't you know. I have done my best to instruct her in gourmet cooking."

"You have done it admirably, Augusta," said Florrie.

The Colonel said nothing, cutting into his pudding.

These banalities concluded a conversation over the meal that, however, had earlier taken an uncomfortable, not to say unfortunate turn.

To begin with, they had all been shocked to hear that I had actually walked over from the O'Kelly's farm.

"You should have sent for Barney," said Augusta. "That is what he is here for."

"I could have fetched you in my carriage, dear lady," said Florrie.

The Colonel was inclined to blame my hosts.

"To think that they left you to walk and did not provide a conveyance." He shook his head as if to indicate that his sorry suspicions of the inadequacy of the O'Kellys had been all too justly realised.

"Oh, they offered to bring me," I was finally able to retort, "but it being such a lovely evening, I was delighted to indulge myself with a ramble through your most attractive countryside. Young Veronica showed me the way, and, after all," I added, "it is not far, surely not above three miles, and I enjoy the exercise."

"Well," Augusta replied. "If that is the case... Indeed, I suppose it is a novelty for you as a city dweller, while for us to walk three miles is an awful chore."

"Ten steps is more than enough for you, my dear," said the Colonel to his wife, with some sharpness. She laughed, a little nervously, I thought.

"Mrs. Hudson is a phenomenon," Florrie put in. "You know, I suspect she has quite fallen in love with this little corner of Wexford. Maybe," and again one of those tiresome winks, "she can be tempted to stay for ever and ever."

The Colonel meanwhile glowered at the remains of his trout, all bones and meagre flesh, and shook his head a little, as if still convinced my having to walk was the fault of the Irish peasantry.

"Will any of you be attending the wedding tomorrow?" I asked, after a pause.

"What wedding?" said the Colonel. "Oh, you mean the Cullen girl. No, indeed. We will be staying well away from that particular carnival of the animals."

Florrie laughed, but I was deeply shocked at the man's language, etiquette of course forbidding me from showing it, except by frowning.

"I suppose that Francie Kinsella will be round at the Cullens this day, as is their drunken custom," the Colonel went on.

"I believe so," I said.

"His goose is cooked," chortled Florrie.

"I beg your pardon?"

"That's what they say hereabouts, don't you know, Mrs. Hudson. The bride's people give the groom a feed of goose the day before so that he cannot wriggle out of the arrangement. And then, as they say, his goose is well and truly cooked."

They all laughed heartily.

"I do not think it is Francie who wishes out of the arrangement," I could not help but remark.

"No, indeed," Florrie replied, suddenly serious. "Poor little Lily."

For a few moments, we all concentrated on our lamb. The potatoes were watery and the gravy insipid. This was far from gourmet in any understanding of the word, and if I were Augusta Timmins, I would have a few sharp things to say to Maggie the cook.

"On the way here," I said finally, to break the uneasy silence, "I saw the strangest sight. A wooded and rocky mound in a field that was otherwise flat and well-tended. When I asked Veronica why the farmer did not remove it, she told me quite seriously that it is where the faeries live. Despite what you were saying earlier, Mr. Sweetnam, surely only children would believe that."

"Oh no," said Augusta. "It is a faery fort, and the people round here believe in it as much as they believe in the Holy Bible."

"More," replied the Colonel. "These people are drowned in superstition of all sorts. Faeries, indeed. Pah!"

He drained his glass of Burgundy wine, before refilling his glass.

"Yet, you know, Timmins," Florrie put in, "that when the Maxwells removed a faery fort from their land, they had nothing but trouble after, their crops failed, their livestock got sick and Mrs. Maxwell broke her leg in a fall from her horse. They say it reared up suddenly at nothing in particular. Folk say it was a faery barred its way."

"Humbug," roared the Colonel, bringing his fist down so hard on the table that the glasses all shook, and poor Augusta nearly jumped out of her seat. "Poppycock! My God, these people demand Home Rule and yet they are still living in the dark ages."

"Well," Florrie replied sententiously," I am just repeating what I heard."

"The Maxwells failed because of poor husbandry, nothing more," the Colonel asserted, "and I expect Mrs. Maxwell's horse simply wanted to rid itself of its fat burden."

There was a moment of silence.

"I hope," I said, very sorry for having mentioned the faeries in the first place and in order to change the subject to my one reason for visiting the Timminses, "that Barney will be able to take me back later."

"Are you sure, since you enjoy exercise so much, that you would not prefer to walk back in the dark, Mrs. Hudson?" said the Colonel, adding in a sarcastic tone, "I am sure it must be beautiful by moonlight."

"So romantic," sighed Florrie, and he sniffed at his flower.

"Of course, Barney will convey you home," said Augusta. "We should not let you walk."

"Why bother Barney, when I can easily bring Mrs. Hudson back?" Florrie smiled at me. "It would be my pleasure."

Now this was an unexpected hitch.

"Oh," I said. "Thank you, but I am sure it is quite out of your way, Mr. Sweetnam. I should hate to put you to any trouble."

"No trouble at all, dear lady, I assure you. I should be only delighted."

"Well," added Augusta. "That is nicely settled then." She looked so complacent that I was sure that she had planned this all along. Especially when the men withdrew to smoke, and we returned to the parlour.

"He likes you very much," she told me merrily. "Martha, you have made a conquest."

"One I do not wish for, I can assure you," I said. "You know, Augusta, Florrie's attentions make me most uncomfortable. I am an old widow woman and long past any thoughts of romance." Although inevitably my mind slipped back to Jimmy, the Darlin' Boy, who had not so long before turned the head not just of myself, but of Kitty Melrose too.

"Too old! Goodness, Martha, do not say that. You are still a fine-looking woman."

Or at least one of property, I thought. "No, but really, Augusta, I should greatly prefer to be brought home by Barney."

"Fiddlesticks," she replied. "Florrie is a harmless dear man. A little eccentric, as of course you can tell. But his heart is good. Now, dear, please try some of this wonderful Amontillado. The Colonel has it sent from Spain, you know."

"I tasted some already," I said.

"Well, then you know how simply delicious it is," and Augusta filled two large glasses for the two of us. She giggled. "Why should the men have all the fun?"

I had noticed at dinner that she had merely sipped at her wine, even seeming to prefer water, but perhaps that was because the sharp eyes of the Colonel were ever upon her.

"Your very good health, Martha," she said, and clinked her glass against mine.

I set it down after a mere taste. I had to think and fast. Whatever was I to do about Florrie? Perhaps I could involve him. Perhaps, being the man I thought he was, he would find it an adventure to run off with a bride and two women. I sighed and looked at poor Augusta and her secret little habit. Something to get her through it all, perhaps. Marriage, after all, was not always a state to be relished. Imagine – and I looked up at the portrait on the wall, with its domineering expression – imagine being locked in marriage until death do you part with Colonel Timmins!

It was not a moonlit night after all when we set off, although the sky was whitened with the stars that are so often visible in the countryside. I could see the Great Bear, Orion's Belt, even the Seven Sisters, my dear Henry having been an amateur astronomer and having, on evening strolls through the Regent's park, enlightened me as to the various constellations.

Stars just then were hardly uppermost on my mind, however. While Florrie babbled on, I was debating the wisdom of asking him to assist in the night's endeavour. On the other hand, what else could I do if we were to hope for any success?

"Mr. Sweetnam," I said finally, taking a deep breath, "I have a rather strange request to make of you."

Chapter Six

It had been a foolhardy enterprise from the start, of course. Yet to think it could have gone so very disastrously wrong! I blamed myself, although at the time we had not been able to come up with a better plan, and something had to be ventured, since Lily's very future was at risk.

Florrie turned out to be all for it. I had assured him that if he refused to take part, I should quite understand, though without any idea how I should next proceed. However, his little eyes sparkled.

"What an adventure," he said, rubbing his hands together. "What larks."

We drove then to the Cullens' farm, but I made him stop at some distance in case the noise of the carriage wheels or a whinny from his horse caused suspicions in the household. Kitty and I had trusted, all the same, that the menfolk would be well stewed in porter and poitín by then, having started carousing early in the afternoon. With any luck, they would all be asleep in their cups.

I warned Florrie that we might be some time, and then joined Kitty, who was already waiting at the rear of the house, seated in the shadows on the block by the clothes line where I had first observed the girl and her brother. We exchanged not a word but clasped each other in an embrace. I could see that Kitty was greatly moved. The stars still provided a white canopy over the world and, although there was a slight dampness in the air, it was neither too cold nor unpleasant to sit out. I felt, indeed, I could sit there forever, wondering at the enormity of God's universe and hoping that He was looking over us and our endeavour.

From time to time I consulted my pocket watch, straining to see the hands. I think we must have waited about forty minutes before the back door creaked open and the slight figure of Lily emerged, clutching a bundle. She flew over to us and Kitty held her tight. Then, as silently as possible, we started back to where Florrie was waiting for us. It seemed so easy, after all. There was the carriage ahead of us. We were nearly upon it.

"Well, well, well, now, ladies. Goin' off for an evening drive, are ye? Well well."

The voice was high and sharp. Lily trembled and let out a cry.

"Maybe I'll join ye, so. 'Tis a fine night for it."

The speaker emerged from the shadows, a tall shapely figure, the starlight glinting white on his fair locks, his pale face. He approached us and caught the girl by the arm. She gave another cry.

"Ah, Francie. Is it yourself?" said Kitty, her own voice trembling. "We just came to see Lily before she... before you..."

"In the middle of the night. How very curious."

He giggled then, and the sound, I admit, made me shudder.

"You weren't a-goin' to run off on me, girl, were you now?" he said.

"No, no, Francie... I just... Kitty's like a mother to me. I wanted to see her. You must understand..."

"Oh, I understand, girl." His voice was unctuous. "I understand you very well. All those men in your house and no woman. Any young one would want the reassurance of her own sex before the big day."

"Yes, Francie. That's it. That's it."

"But, see now, what I don't understand, Lily girl, is why you packed a sack to bring with you, just to chat to your friends."

She was looking down, but he pulled her hair back so that she was forced to face him.

"Don't you want to marry Francie?" he asked. "Don't you want to be Mrs. Francis Kinsella, girl? Don't you want to wake up and find your little slippers under my warm, cosy bed?"

I could see her trembling and felt it had gone on long enough.

"And if she doesn't," I said, "isn't that her right? She should not be forced."

"Ah, now," he said, looking at me for the first time. "The Englishwoman, is it? Is it your one that's behind it all, then, Lily? A-comin' here with her English ways, her black Protestant ways, A-comin' where she's not wanted. Comin here to tempt you away from the right path, the agreed path. The path that's been signed on. Comin here to tempt you away from your family, your own kind. Mebbe to make a black Protestant of you, too. Ah, Lily, Lily, Lily, whatever was you a-thinkin' of?" His face was almost touching hers. "You're promised to me, Lily. And a promise, don't you know, is a promise."

"Yes, yes." The girl seemed almost transfixed by his gaze. "I'm sorry, Francie, so I am. Only…"

"Only? Only what, girl?"

She took a deep breath. "Could we not just wait a bit? It's all been such a… such a rush. Could we not wait to be married, Francie?"

'Wait, is it? How long would you say, then? To wait, like?'

'Like… till I'm eighteen, maybe.'

He roared with laughter. "Ah Lily, Lily. What a joker you are? Three years, is it? The marriage feast will be well stale by then. No, girl." His tone turned menacing. "You'll be mine tomorrow, so you will. Understand? All mine."

Silence, then. I think we all felt the barely repressed violence in the man. Lily slumped.

"All right, so, Francie. I'll come back in with ye now."

"Indeed and come back in you will. And I'll give you a pinch or two for the bould girl that you are." He giggled again. "Wasn't it a right blessin' now I let the others do the drinkin'... See, I'm not much of a drinkin' man, Lily, you should be glad of that. I won't be beatin' you in a drunken rage, like yer da does." He laughed louder. "Oh dear me, no, indeed. I'll beat you cold sober, so I will. But only when you deserve it, girlie. Only if you try and run away some more."

I shuddered at his words and his tone. Surely Florrie could hear it all, too? Was he not going to come to our aid? With his help, perhaps we could still pull the girl from the brute and drive off. Francie must have seen me glancing in the direction of the carriage, for he continued, "So who's the eejit was a-goin' to bring you away?" Francie peered over. "Not little Florrie Sweetnam. Not the flower of the valley himself." He chuckled and then called, "Come out, Florrie, where I can see ye. Come out, man."

But Florrie, like John Falstaff before him, evidently felt that discretion was the better part of valour, for he whipped his horse and was away.

Francie laughed merrily at that.

"Well, ladies, there goes your ride now. You have a long walk ahead of ye, I'm that sorry to say. Unless I wake the lads and tell them what's been a-happenin', so they can drive you home. Will I do that? Will I?"

"Ah, no," begged Lily. "No, Francie. Don't tell, dadda. Please don't tell."

"Who could resist that sweet appeal?" he replied. "Anyhow and all, last thing I want is my blushin' bride black and blue tomorrow from the beatin' the bould William will be sure to give her if I tell. No, Lily, mebbe you and me... mebbe we'll stay out under the stars a while. What do you think of that? 'Tis right romantic, so it is. Under the stars and all." He laughed some more, while Lily squirmed, and tried to speak. "Hush, now, girleen," he continued. "Now I've an idea. Why don't we go and visit my field, for the last time, like, before I give it over in exchange it for my darling' girl? Wouldn't you like to visit the field, Lily? With Francie. Come, girl. Let's go visit the field." His free hand glided round her waist.

"You are not married yet, Francie Kinsella," said Kitty sharply. "Show some respect."

"Respect is it?" he snapped back. "Ye're a fine one to talk of respect, Kathleen O'Kelly. I could have you before the magistrates for attempted abduction. What about that? And mebbe I will yet." He threw back his head and laughed. "But tonight, yes indeed, I will respect my little bride-to-be and send her a-packin' back to her maidenly bed. And with the greatest respect, I'll sit outside the door all night, to make sure she don't attempt another ramble in the dark." He licked his full lips under the stars. "Tomorrow night, well, well that will be another matter, eh Lily, eh, eh. I can wait until tomorrow night. Oh yes. I've waited a long time. I can wait a tad longer, so I can." Laughing the while, he dragged her back to the house and shut the door behind them.

Kitty and I looked at each other in dismay. Disaster. Our plan in ruins. And indeed a long walk ahead of us in the dark.

"Do you think he will really set the magistrates on us?" she asked, as we set off. "What a terrible scandal it would be."

"Not at all. Lily would surely say that she was being forced into a marriage against her will. We were merely helping her escape that fate."

"I do not think that would carry any weight in this country, Martha. Women here you know are very much the property of their fathers and husbands. Still and all, you being such great friends with Colonel Timmins, and him being the Resident Magistrate, the ruling would be up to him. So I suppose Francie would think twice about it."

Not that I was such a great favourite with the Colonel, but I refrained from mentioning that fact right then. Instead I said, "I confess I am most surprised at Francie."

"How is that?"

"Despite all, he seems an educated man."

"He is. We Irish are not so barbaric as not to educate our people, you know, Martha."

"I did not mean that. I see good education in Peter and Annie and their children. Yet Francie seems different."

She laughed bitterly. "Ah, that he is."

"I mean intellectually. He speaks well, even if what he says is vicious."

"He was always one for the books, was Francie. Some say that's what turned him... strange, you know. Too much book-reading."

It was my turn to laugh. "Blame the books! Ah no, Kitty. That won't do."

"It is not what I think, Martha. It is what they say."

"You do not learn cruelty from books... But look there!"

Away ahead of us now, in the gloom, a mass of black loomed like some huge crouching beast.

"What is it?" Kitty sounded fearful.

No faery fort, nor yet a banshee combing her hair on a rock "I think our carriage awaits."

Indeed, Florrie had only driven a little way along the path to stay for us. We were most pleased to see him, even if he had not shewn any great gallantry back at the Cullens' farm.

"No Lily, then?" he said observing the two of us. "You could not get her away."

"If you had helped us, perhaps we could have," I replied tartly.

"Oh no. No, indeed. I was never there, don't you know. Pull me up before the magistrates and I'll deny it. Florrie Sweetnam, esquire, wasn't there at all, at all."

"So you think he will indeed call the law on us," said Kitty.

"Who knows what a quare fellow like Francie Kinsella will or won't do? Oh Martha, Martha, I should never have agreed to your silly game if I'd have known Francie was still around the place. He's not a man to make an enemy of."

Martha, now. Not Mrs. Hudson or dear lady.

"I am sorry," I said, genuinely contrite. "But I was at my wit's end, Florrie. We had to have a carriage for Lily, I was intending to pay Barney well."

"I forgive you," said Florrie jovially, whipping the horse on its way. "But you will owe me, Martha, and I don't mean in silver coin. You will owe me dearly, my lady. Yes, indeed."

Kitty threw me a swift glance. I said nothing. I knew that I was wrong in so many ways.

How could we attend the wedding, after that? How could we not? Annie indeed fussed at my intended presence – it would apparently be a mortal sin for a Roman Catholic to attend a Protestant church – but I told her that there were no mortal sins as such in my Church, and that if I had no qualms about going to the wedding then neither should she.

"Who knows," I said, "but I might be convinced to turn."

She regarded me then to see if I jested but I kept my face solemn.

"That would be wonderful," she said.

It would be a miracle, I thought.

"I will pray for it, Martha," she went on, clasping me in her arms, and I felt bad at my duplicity.

"In any case, I will not of course take communion," I said. Their faith, as Kitty had informed me, teaches that the blessed bread

70

is substantially transformed into the flesh of Christ and the wine his blood, a barbaric superstition that makes me shudder.

It was unlike any wedding I have ever attended. When my daughter Judy married Dr. John McFee, a strict Scottish Presbyterian, in Edinburgh where they now live, the service was just that, a service before God, with a simple wedding breakfast to follow for the immediate family. As for Eleanor, my other daughter, her nuptials to Clive Hazelgrove were an altogether more jolly affair, with a feast and dancing to follow the ceremony, and yet, even though it took place among the hop fields of Kent, there was nothing to compare it with the unbridled revelry that we attended in the county of Wexford on that Thursday in May.

Dressed in our Sunday best finery – my black bombazine having to serve as usual but with the addition of a fine shawl I wear for special occasions, and I sporting a once plain hat which the girls had insisted on decorating for me with coloured ribbons – Kitty, Annie and I sat ourselves in the bone-shaker to travel the short journey to their local Roman Catholic chapel, the Church of the Annunciation. Peter meanwhile walked thither with his eight excited children in tow. Only Veronica, I believe, guessed that the event would be anything but a joyful celebration.

The small building was already packed to overflowing and noisy, quite unlike my experiences in the local Church of Ireland with its rows of empty pews and its sedate congregation. Indeed, we had some difficulty in finding enough seats to accommodate us all. I was surprised at the turn-out, but Annie whispered that most people were attending out of curiosity, to see how the wayward Francie would conduct himself in this holy place.

"I am afraid some are hoping for a scandal," she said.

The bridegroom in question was already waiting in front of the altar, or to put it more accurately, was lounging on that holy table in what looked to be a deliberately sacrilegious way. As outwardly attractive as ever, he was accompanied by a couple of disreputable looking fellows, comporting themselves more like ruffians outside a tavern than young men about to take part in a sacred ceremony, grinning and muttering and even sparring a little. Francie, at the same time, was keeping a sharp eye on all those entering, and, catching sight of Kitty and myself, gave a mocking salute and whispered something to his two companions, who stared back at us with smirks on their faces.

The priest, meanwhile, had emerged from the sacristy, Father Joe, as Annie told me, surprising me rather with the familiarity of the nickname. Now, I know that Roman Catholic men of the cloth are not permitted to get married, but surely that can be no excuse for the dismal sight the man presented, a decidedly grubby white surplice over a raggedy black cassock. No, there was nothing reverend about this particular gentleman. He was, moreover, excessively stout, with an apoplectic complexion under a head of astonishingly white and abundant hair that seemed to be standing on end, perhaps in shock at what he was about to do. Still, he at least murmured something to Francie and the others – perhaps chiding them for their lack of respect – for they moved back and stood up straighter, though still with insolent grins on their faces.

An unseen organist soon struck up a solemn, if ill-played tune, and the congregation at last fell silent. We turned our heads to see Lily faltering up the aisle, clinging to her father's arm, he nodding to right and left and smiling broadly, perhaps in imagined contemplation of his new field. Following behind, as maid of honour, walked an awkward, ill-favoured girl, aged maybe thirty or so, her yellowish face wary, her skinny body tensed as if to block any last minute attempt at flight by the bride-to-be.

"Briege," whispered Annie. "Francie's sister."

I studied with interest this strange little person, recalling only too well the scandalous rumours regarding Francie's parentage. Surely it was not possible that she was both sister and mother to the bridegroom. To my eye, she lacked any physical graces whatsoever, and it seemed more like to be a cruel joke at the girl's expense. Indeed, Briege Kinsella hardly appeared old enough to be mother to Francie, unless she had been little more than a child when she bore him. However, what did I know of the ways of this alien world, with its repressive religion and primitive beliefs? In any case, under the circumstances in which we found ourselves, that was neither here nor there. As our Lord says in the good book, he that is without sin among you, let him cast the first stone.

Meanwhile, Lily herself, her sweet face tear-stained – although she was evidently trying her best to smile – looked lovely, but oh so fragile, in her simple blue dress, her auburn hair no longer hanging loose but coiled up in a plait around her head and crowned with a garland of daisies. One hand clutched a bunch of calla lilies which, despite the accord with her name, seemed more suited to a funeral.

The girls gasped so see her so pretty, while Kitty exclaimed softly and with emotion, "Oh, I do believe that was same dress her poor mother, Nora, wore to her own wedding."

If so, it must have been carefully preserved in some trunk to maintain its condition, for it looked well, the cornflower colour of it not faded at all. How affecting it was to think of the mother and daughter planning ahead to a day which should have been full of joy but which was proving to be so very different.

The service was in Latin, so I imagine that I was no more in the dark than anyone else as to what exactly was being said, even though the congregation seemed well able to mutter their responses in that ancient tongue. We knelt, we stood, we sat, we knelt again, I following the others in their movements, although I refrained from making the sign of the cross over my breast and refrained too from partaking of the host, the only person in the whole church to stay in my seat and not join the queue to the altar, excepting of course the younger children who had not yet made their first communion. I was most grateful to little Pegeen for holding tight to my hand during the lengthy ritual.

When all were back in their seats, the priest, assisted by a boy hardly as high as the table itself, made a great show of putting away the bread and the chalice, not before he had drained it dry of the altar wine.

It was over at last, and Lily and Francie were one. Kitty and Annie wiped away discreet tears, while I was moved to pity for the poor girl we had tried and failed to save. Already, even in church, Francie's hands were over her, immodestly touching her breast as he grabbed her to him in a kiss that was anything but chaste. On her release, she looked utterly terrified, while Francie's two friends, along with Lily's own father and brothers, laughed and clapped.

Outside the church, Lily was lifted by her husband onto an old nag, and, in this way, headed a motley procession along the country lane that led to the Cullen farm, Francie strutting by her side. The sun smiled on the scene, where I reckoned black, weeping clouds might have been more appropriate. Kitty and I said not a word to each other the whole way, although we could not help but be beguiled by the innocent gaiety of the children skipping along beside us. Only Veronica looked solemn. Again, I suppose, being just two years younger than the bride, she was more aware of the true nature of the event.

Arriving at length at the farmyard, we found trestle tables had been laid out, piled with bread and cake and pies and sausages of all sorts, as well as bottles of porter, and squash for the women and children. It seemed that after all, William Cullen had not stinted on the comestibles. When I expressed this thought to Annie, she just laughed.

"Not at all," she said. "The guests have brought most of it. Peter even killed a pig so I could make black and white pudding."

"Didn't we help you, mam?" said Sarie.

"You did indeed, good girls. Sure, I could not have managed it without ye."

"And I helped me da," young Gerald put in. "Lord, didn't that poor pig squeal something awful when we strung him up." He laughed merrily. "You shoulda seen it," he said to Kitty and me. "That ould pig, all blood and guts."

Though a little shocked, I reflected that it was not my place to judge. Country folk to be sure look upon such practices differently from squeamish city dwellers, and indeed, was I myself not raised in a small village, well away from the city of London. That however, was neither yesterday nor the day before, and country ways, I am afraid, have been well rubbed off me by now.

It was then that, with some dismay, I saw the bridegroom was heading our way, and hoped that he was not about to make a scene. Perhaps he would reveal to everyone what we had been up to the previous night, and send Kitty and myself packing, with a flea in our ears.

No such thing. He had come to crow, rubbing his hands gleefully, and warmly welcoming Peter and Annie and the children. Then he turned to us two.

"And ladies, ladies," he chuckled. "So good of you to turn up to see with your own eyes the matrimonial knot fast tied. I am humbled, indeed and I am. I never ever expected such an honour. For you two London ladies to come here today, to see me darlin Lily and me, tied together in holy wedlock till death us do part. Well, words fail me, so they do."

Hardly, I thought.

"Congratulations, Francie," Kitty replied. "I wish you every happiness."

"Thank you for your very kind words, Mrs. Melrose. Very kind indeed, and kindly meant, I truly hope. And," turning to me, with that horrid smile, "you too, missus. Though I haven't yet heard you say anythin of the sort."

He'd wring blood out of a stone if he could.

"Of course," I said. "May Lily and yourself live in joyful harmony, all the days of your life."

"Thank ye, for that, missus," he replied. "That a good blessin to hold in my heart." He laid his hand across his breast, at the spot where that organ generally resides. "Of course, you might have added may we be blessed with many childer, childer as lovely as these. Such little sweethearts," gazing at Peter and Annie's brood with an apparent fondness belied by his menacing chuckle. "I hope so, indeed and I do. In fact, you know, I'll be startin work on that particular enterprise this very night, so I will."

With a leer and a wink, he moved off.

"Well!" said Kitty.

"What in heaven's name was all that about?" asked Peter.

Kitty just shook her head.

A lucky distraction just then was caused by a fiddler who started up playing a lively jig to welcome the guests and we soon got seats for all of us at one of the tables. Looking around, I found I recognised no one apart from the members of the Cullen family, William the father and large, gormless Ollie with the two undersized brothers I had learnt were called Tighe and Seb. Unsurprisingly, perhaps, none of the locals from the Protestant church had put in an appearance. I suppose I was half thinking that Florrie might turn up, although after his unfortunate encounter with Francie the previous night, this must be most unlikely.

At what passed for a top table sat Lily surrounded by the Kinsella clan. She looked very small and unhappy, especially since Francie, eyes bright and wild, kept jubilantly proposing toasts – his claim to sobriety the previous evening clearly forgotten, Moreover, at each toast he urged his new bride to drink up, something she was clearly reluctant to do, so that he had almost to force the cup upon her. I felt Kitty beside me stiffen, but there was no way that we could intervene and say, Enough!

76

When all were sated, the fiddler set to again, now joined by a scruffy little fellow, playing a strange type of a bagpipe that he did not blow on but rather squeezed with his elbow. The effect in the open air was not as unpleasant as I find the Scottish bagpipes to be, although I imagine it would not prove so tolerable in the confines of a small room. Francie leapt to his feet at the first notes, and, to general applause, dragged Lily out to dance. The drink had surely fired him up and increased his sense of triumph, and he twirled and spun the girl like she was a rag doll. Soon, many more were up, dancing wildly. Peter even led Annie out, and the children joined in too, laughing and pulling at each other. Someone fired shots from a gun which terrified me at first until Kitty reassured me that it was not at all unusual at country weddings. I smiled then to think how different the staid event that was Judy's nuptials, where we all sat stiff as ramrods on our hard chairs, sipping cups of weak tea. But, unlike poor Lily, Judy is blissfully happy with her kindly Dr, John, and I could not have wished a different outcome for her, at least.

As we watched the dancers, I saw how Lily, almost fainting with fatigue, at last prevailed on Francie to let her sit back down, whereupon he seized the hand of his sister and leapt and hopped around the yard with her instead. It was a strange and cruel pairing, for while the bride and groom, in beauty at least, were equals, his undersized sister, for all her attempts to follow his nimble steps, stumbled and several times almost fell, and I suddenly realised that she was lame.

"The poor girl!" I exclaimed.

"Briege, is it?" said Annie now back and breathless beside us, with a becoming flush on her cheeks. "Ah, she's well enough able for him, Martha. Believe you me."

Still, watching the clumsy woman frowning with effort, while her brother grinned and taunted, I could not help but wonder if this was truly the case. I again recalled the rumours regarding

Francie's maternity, but, looking from plain sister to potato-faced father, just then roaring with laughter that exposed black stumps of teeth, and sharing a bottle of poitín with the parish priest, it seemed to me utterly unlikely that they could have made such a one as Francie.

As if reading my thoughts, Kitty remarked, "Usually the faery folk take a beautiful baby and leave in its place an ugly changeling. It seems that this time, for fun, they did the opposite."

"Kitty!" exclaimed Annie, shocked, nodding a warning head towards the children.

"They cannot hear me," Kitty said. "And you must admit, Annie, that Francie has enough spite in him to be spawn of the little people."

I looked at my friend. Was she serious? After the recent episode at the holy well, I could well suppose that the eminently respectable Mrs. Kathleen Melrose of Baker Street, widow of a banker – that most materialistic of professions – still, in her heart of hearts, believed in the faeries she had heard about as a girl. Before I could inquire further, however, we were joined by a jolly stout young woman in the company of a gawky fellow with sandy hair and eyes the colour of hazel nuts.

"It's Sal and Luke," said Annie welcoming them to our table.

This then was the 'old' aunt of thirty, mentioned by Veronica, for whom a match was to be made.

"Ah sure no, we won't be sitting down with ye," Sal said. "We're only arrived now and are dying for a dance, aren't we, Luke?"

"If we must," he replied, his grin splitting his face amicably.

"We just came to say good day to ye."

"Mammy let you out then?" Annie asked.

"Ah, wasn't she asleep and snoring to beat the band. Mags from down the boreen is keeping an eye out. Sure and Mammy'll be grand for the couple of hours." On that note, Sal and her beau rushed off among the dancers.

"Please God," said Annie, "it'll be them two tying the knot next."

"And a more joyous occasion it will be," Kitty added.

"Indeed."

Kitty and I watched the couple, laughing together comfortably as a close couple should, along with the rest of the merry throng, until both of us wearied of the spectacle. We discussed then how soon we might leave, dependent as we were on Peter to drive us back, unless, that is, we took the short cut through the bluebell wood. I think both of us were keen to get away, not least because of Francie's unpredictable moods. The man in his cups might yet turn upon us. Yet Peter, who worked so hard every day, was clearly enjoying hobnobbing with friends, while Annie too had found other young mothers to chat to. The children, meanwhile, rosy-cheeked with excitement, ran around whooping, snatching snacks from the still laden tables and showing no signs of flagging. Only Lily sat, a still point amid the clamour. We had thought of joining her but reckoned it would only incur the wrath and suspicions of her husband, so we decided for her sake to leave her be.

Finally we decided to take a chance on the woods – already the sun was sinking into purple clouds, so we should have to make haste, not to find ourselves caught in the dark. As we rose from our seats, it was at that moment that terrifying new spectres burst into the yard. Five figures dressed in conical masks woven of straw, with more straw stuffed into their shirts, and skirts of the same weave round their waists, appeared like visions from a nightmare. There was uproar as they leapt into the crowd and joined the dance, wresting women from their partners and spinning them round. In response, the jigs and reels got faster and faster. It was primitive and wild and reminded me of a medieval painting I had once seen.

"Straw Boys," Kitty explained, placidly enough. "They bring good luck to the newly-weds."

"Good luck?" I said. "They look like demons to me."

"Later they will make a bonfire of their costumes."

"Why?"

"All part of the fun."

An explanation with which I must be satisfied.

Just then, one of the Straw Boys spotted Lily, sitting all by herself, and with a howl of delight rushed over to her, lifting her bodily and making as if to run off with her. She let out a scream, whereupon Francie, drinking with his friends, must have looked around to see what was happening, for he precipitated himself on to the pair, knocking them to the ground. With a queer screeching cry, he started beating the poor mummer and must have inflicted severe harm upon him, had Peter and others not dragged him off at last. The Straw Boy then picked himself up with an oath, and shaking his fist at Francie, strode off out of the yard and away, followed by his companions.

The crowd fell silent.

"Not good," Kitty said, shaking her head. "Not good at all."

"What do you mean?"

"Bad luck will surely follow."

As if, I thought drily, that was not already apparent.

Francie was trembling all over, frothing at the mouth and continuing to emit those inhuman sounds his sister now kneeling beside him, stroking his forehead and whispering soothing words. Annie meanwhile had rushed to comfort Lily, who was still prostrate. She lifted her gently and sat her back at the table. The girl was shaking and Annie put her arm around her.

"Keep playing, boys," shouted William Cullen. "Keep dancing, all of ye." But the joy had gone out of it, and despite his entreaties, many people were already creeping away.

Peter rejoined us then and said that he would fetch the pony and trap so that we could ride home, but we demurred and stated that, since there was still some light, we would walk. I could tell that he was relieved to hear it, since he clearly wished to get the bewildered children from the place as soon as possible.

Away from the noise and crush of the wedding party, the evening proved balmy and aromatic with the scent of flowers. It was nonetheless eerie in the woods, inky with shadows and echoing with strange calls – an owl, perhaps – and we had some difficulty making out the path. The children, now suddenly exhausted, huddled along beside us, the little ones jumping in fright at rustling noises in the undergrowth.

"'Tis the faeries for sure," said Pegeen, and clutched my hand.

"Not at all," I told her. "It's just some baby animals settling down in their beds for the night, as you, my dear, will be doing very, very soon."

Chapter Seven

Very early the next morning, I was awakened by a terrible uproar from downstairs. For a second or two, after the lateness and upheavals of the previous night, I could not quite remember where I was. Then Kitty, still in the shift that was her sleeping attire, burst into my room.

"Oh, Martha," she cried. "The most terrible thing. The most terrible, terrible thing… Oh Lord, bless us and save us…" and she threw herself down on the bed and embraced me, sobbing uncontrollably.

"What is it, Kitty? What has happened?"

It was a few moments before she could compose herself. Finally, she lifted her head and gasped out the awful intelligence. "Hasn't poor Lily only gone and murdered Francie."

I could not speak, but gazed at her in disbelief. Little Lily a murderer! And of a man twice her size and strength. It could hardly be.

I held my friend for some moments more, and then entreated her to explain all, as calmly as she could. It seemed that the Kinsella father and daughter had been awakened by a scream from the room of the newly-weds, and, on rushing to investigate, found Lily, all a-tremble, a knife in her hand and Francie on the floor, stabbed to death.

"If only we had got her away the other night." Kitty resumed her sobbing. "The poor girl… What horrors drove her to do it, I can only imagine."

"When did this happen, do you know?"

"Not long since, I think. A short while only."

"So how have we come to hear of it so soon?"

"From Peter. Seemingly he was about to take the cows to pasture when he saw Mossie on the road, running and waving his arms like a madman. 'She's done it, the witch,' he was screaming. 'She's done for Francie.' Or something of that nature. It took Peter some time to get sense out of the man…"

"How truly horrible. But is it sure she was the one killed him?"

"They say she had the knife in her hand. That she was all bloodied over… That's all I know, I don't know anything more, Martha." Kitty was breaking down again.

"Take a few deep breaths," I advised her and clasped her hand. "It will calm you."

She did as I said and once she had gathered her wits, I asked what else Peter had to report.

"He told how he went back with Mossie and indeed found the wretched Francie stabbed and lifeless. The sister was screaming and wailing and tearing her hair, a terrible carry-on altogether, and when Peter looked for Lily, Mossie said he had locked her in the outhouse and could Peter stay and mind Briege while he went for the Sergeant. But Peter said it would be better if he got Annie to go over. Another woman, don't you know. And Mossie agreed… Oh, Martha, what's to be done at all?"

I tried for a moment to order my thoughts. Finally, I said, "We must go in Annie's place. I need to talk to Lily before the Sergeant arrives." I arose from my bed forthwith, and, despite Kitty's presence, started to dress myself as quickly as possible.

"We cannot do that, can we?" she asked.

"Who will stop us? But make haste Kitty. There is no time to be lost."

Downstairs, I explained to Annie that, if she agreed, we considered it preferable for her to stay and mind the children, while Kitty and I went over to the Kinsellas' place, a suggestion to which she was clearly not averse. Peter offering to drive us, I for once was grateful for haste's sake to ride in the bone-shaker. On the way I asked him to describe exactly what he had seen when he entered the bedroom, and he did his best, but, sadly, did not prove very observant. Mr. H would surely have been most frustrated with his answers.

"What did I see? Well, wasn't Francie on the floor, all covered in blood and not a breath left in him."

"Did you touch him, Peter, to make sure he was gone?"

"Sure and I did not, Martha. 'Twas clear to all that the lad was dead, God rest him," He made the sign of the cross. "'Twas the priest Mossie should be calling on, before the Sergeant."

"I just wondered," I said, "if he was cold."

Peter glanced at me as if of the opinion that is was I who was cold even to ask such a thing.

"What difference does it make? The lad is dead, I tell you."

"It could make a deal of difference. To Lily."

However, there was no further enlightenment on that subject to be had.

Mossie Kinsella was awaiting us at the ramshackle cottage, not wishing, as he told us, to leave his daughter alone with the body, she was in such a state. He paced the uneven earth floor of the kitchen, a dark and dirty place, a place where one could well imagine evil might breed. It was evident that, after the break-up at Cullen's, some members of the wedding party must have come back to the house to continue the celebrations, for relics of the night's carousing were visible in the form of empty bottles of porter, stale heels of bread scattered across a greasy wooden table beside scraps of black pudding and a hacked ham, the sickly sweet stench of strong drink over all.

Despite his understandable shock and emotion, Mossie made it abundantly clear that he was not best pleased to see Kitty and myself attending instead of Annie, and even, looking at me, barked, "What's your one a-doing of here?"

Peter explained that Annie could not leave the children, even though that was not strictly true – the older ones, especially Veronica, were well able to mind the babies. Moreover, he continued, since he, Peter was here with us, Annie had to make sure of the well-being of the cows and get young Gerald to get them to pasture in his stead. All of which seemed to satisfy Mossie well enough, even though he still regarded me with dark suspicion.

"Where's Briege?" asked Kitty, even though the woman's shrill wails could be heard from the back yard. "I'll go and mind her."

"She won't come in," said Mossie, "not while Francie lies still in his blood... Oh, the witch, the witch. It'd be well for her to burn for this night's deed, so it would."

"If it was truly Lily who killed Francie," I said. I knew this would rile the man, as indeed it did.

"If... if..." He advanced on me in a threatening manner, and I was glad that Peter was present. "I'll give you 'if', missus. Who else do you think did it and me finding the girl with the knife in her hand and my boy's black blood on her shift? Who else did it? Ha, ha!" He shook a fist in my face. "Or mebbe he did it to himself. Do you think that? He kilt himself, did he?" He laughed a horrible guffaw that ended with him coughing and spitting on the floor, an unsavoury sight to say the very least of it.

"Maybe she killed him and maybe she didn't," I said. "That's for the law to decide, Mr. Kinsella." I spoke calmly, to try to appease him. After all, the man had just lost his only son, and you had to pity him that.

"I am going to the barracks for the Sergeant," he said. "You keep a sharp eye on her, Peter," pointing at me. "No high and mighty Sassenach should think she can come here and meddle in what don't concern her."

"He is very upset," Peter said to me in apology, after Mossie had slammed out the door.

"No," I replied. "He was right to be angry. All the same, this Sassenach has every intention of meddling. Please, show me the body."

"What?"

"Please, Peter. Lily's very life may depend on the next hour."

He was reluctant, but led me through to a back bedroom. Now, I have seen dead bodies before, of course I have, including that of my dear Henry. However, I have never seen one that had resulted from a violent attack, and had to brace myself at the horrid sight.

Francie lay on his back, no longer beautiful, a grinning rictus stretching his lips, his pale blue eyes wide and staring as at the ceiling, for no one had thought to close them. Blood pooled around him, although I could see no wounds or stains on his white nightshirt. It was likely then, that he must have been stabbed from behind with the long-bladed knife that lay beside him, and that the wounds were in his back, though we must not move him to find out. I asked Peter, who, after a moment's thought, concurred with my theory.

At least he was able to confirm that the body was lying exactly as he had first seen it.

My next procedures, I think, rather horrified my companion, but either the conviction that I knew what I was doing (I did not, not completely) or enough of the deferential mentality towards my background remained, for him not to try to prevent me. I touched Francie's forehead to find that he was neither warm nor cold but unnaturally cool. When I tried to close his eyes, I could not and his arm, when I attempted to lift it, was also stiff with rigor mortis. I then dipped the very tip of my finger in blood which was blackened and viscous.

"This man," I said, "has been dead for many hours." I explained my conclusions, and Peter nodded agreement. "Please make a note of that," I added, "in case you are called upon to give evidence." He nodded again, though with a marked reluctance. The thought of standing up in court clearly did not appeal to him.

I then examined the weapon without touching it. It seemed to be an ordinary kitchen knife, but in that case whatever was it doing in the bedroom in advance of the crime. If Lily had brought it with her, it would seem to indicate that she had premeditated the murder, which was surely most unlikely. If she were guilty, given her feebleness and his strength, it must have been a crime of the instant, inspired by some terror. Perhaps indeed Francie had brought the knife with him as a cruel joke or worse to terrify the girl, and that somehow she had turned it on him in self-defence.

"Now," I told Peter, "I have to speak to Lily."

"Oh, no." He was horrified. "No, no, no."

"It is imperative that I do so," I said, rising from the floor and trying to appear more in command than I felt myself to be. "You stay here with Francie. You need not know what I will be about."

He looked hard at me for an instant, then said, "I'll stay and say a few prayers over the poor craytur."

I had already informed Kitty of my intention to interview the girl so that she, if necessary, should distract the sister. When I went out into the yard, the two of them were huddled together, Kitty with her arm around Briege, whose wails had abated to dull moans but whose eyes still flowed with tears. The black dog I had seen before lay at the girl's feet, but now rose with a threatening growl as I approached. Briege muttering to it, it lay back down again, although I cannot say I much cared for the wolfish expression in its eyes. In general let it be said that I like dogs. Didn't the O'Kellys have those two lovely creatures, Bella and Star. However, in this case I made an exception. It was a mangy, dirty beast and smelt bad.

Kitty nodded to me, and then, with a slight jerk of her head, indicated the outhouse where Lily was imprisoned.

"Will we go in and make a nice dish of sweet tea, Briegeen?" she said. "It would do you good."

The woman shook her head. Her hair was streaked grey and greasy and her plain face, so pasty the last time I had seen her, was puffed up and red from the crying. "No, Kathleen, I cannot go into the house. No way. Never again."

"Peter is in saying prayers for your brother," I told her. "And you must keep up your strength, you know, at least for the sake of your father. To comfort him."

She looked at me then with an unreadable expression in her eyes. I shuddered to think what comforts exactly the father might require of her.

On this occasion, however, my words and those whispered to the woman by Kitty must have had the required effect, for she finally let herself be led back into the kitchen, followed, I was relieved to see, by the dog, whereupon I made haste to the outhouse and unlocked the door.

Inside, huddled in the gloom and evidently terrified, was the slight form of the young bride, gazing at the widow as she now was.

"Lily," I whispered in reassuring tones, "it is Martha Hudson come to talk to you."

"Come to take me away?" she asked hopefully. "Oh, please take me home."

"I cannot do that, Lily," I replied. "The Sergeant will be arriving soon to talk to you, but I want to hear everything from you first. Do you understand me? I want to help you, so for that I need you to tell me all you can recall about last night and this morning."

"I want to go home," she repeated, her voice shaking. "Please, Mrs. Hudson."

It would be a hard-hearted person, indeed, not to be moved by her entreaties. "I know you do, my dear," I replied. "And I want you to go home as well." How bad could it have been here, if all the girl now wanted was to return to the Cullens' place? "But please answer my questions."

She drew a deep breath, collecting herself. "I will if I can," she said at last, in a calmer tone. "You see, Mrs Hudson, I don't remember very much. Not at all."

"Just start by telling me, did you kill Francie? Did you kill your husband?"

"Indeed and I did not." She was almost angry now, a good sign, I thought. The girl had some spirit after all.

"Then someone else did," I replied. "And we must try and find out who it could be. Again, I ask you, tell me what happened last night, as much as you can remember."

She frowned with the effort of thinking. "After the feast at ours," she said, "Francie brought a few fellers back with him here and they kept on drinking. Francie made me stay up with them for a while, although... I did not care for it, Mrs. Hudson. Not for the way those fellers spoke to me and looked at me." She shivered. "Then Briege said, 'Let her to bed, Francie, the poor girleen, for the love of God.' Something like that. So then he let me and Briege go to bed, calling he'd be up soon enough. He laughed." She shivered at the memory. "Briege was very kind and asked if I needed anything. To be somewhere else, I thought, dreading what was ahead of me. But I said no and she left me."

"Were you able to sleep?"

"I thought I wouldn't, and for a while indeed I lay trembling, waiting for Francie to come to bed. But then after all I fell asleep. I must have."

"I see."

"Well, you know, Francie made me drink some poitín. I am not used to it, and my head was spinning a fair bit, so I suppose it was that made me sleepy."

"Yes, probably so."

"And Briege brought me draught of tea of camomile, to calm me, she said. You know Mrs. Hudson, she is a wise woman and knows the cures."

"The cures?"

"Oh yes, Briege Kinsella is better thought of around here even than Dr. Ross when people get sick or when women are labouring to give birth. Yes, indeed, Mrs. Hudson. Briege is well known for her remedies."

Maybe for her sleeping draughts, too, I thought.

"So," Lily continued, "between the poitín and the other, I did not hear Francie come to bed. Indeed, I think he must not have, because... because..." She blushed and looked down.

"Because," I said gently, "he did not touch you."

"Oh Mrs. Hudson, I suppose I would have known, would I not?" The innocence of her!

"Yes, indeed. There would have been signs, even if you did not wake up."

"Well..." I could hear that she was relieved. "'Twas the morning light woke me. I was alone in the bed. I looked around and then I saw... Oh, Mrs. Hudson, I could not believe what I saw. Poor Francie on the floor beside me, a knife in his back and so very much blood."

"This is very important, Lily. Are you saying he was beside the bed lying on his front, with a knife in his back?"

"Yes..." She paused. Then added. "Oh, Lord, I have a confession to make."

After all?

"You see," she went on, "at first I thought it was one of his tricks. He loves to play tricks, Mrs. Hudson. He always has. Spiteful tricks. So I thought he had set the scene to half terrify me out of my wits, and then to jump up and laugh at me. That's what I thought, so I did."

"Indeed," I said drily. "That would be a nice trick, to be sure."

"I got out of the bed, pulled out the knife and turned him over. That when I saw... that's when I screamed. Then Mossie and Briege came rushing in and the next thing Mossie had dragged me out here and locked me up. I suppose it looked like I had done it, but they didn't give me a moment to explain."

She broke then and clutched my arm and wept.

I pressed her to me, but continued, "When you touched him, Lily, was he cold, was he stiff? Try to remember."

She scrunched up her face in a frown.

"I... I think so. Not so very cold, you know. But he must have been stiff for it was easy enough to turn him."

"Very good. Very good, Lily."

I heard a noise in the yard then. Mossie was returned with the Sergeant. I pressed the girl's hand again, told her to be brave and, for now, not to tell anyone that she had spoken to me. Then, having waited until the men entered the cottage, I quietly exited the outhouse and locked the door behind me again.

I joined Kitty and Briege in the kitchen. They were still huddled together, although the woman had stopped her wailing now and merely gave a rasping shudder from time to time. Meanwhile the men were all in the bedroom. We could hear the hum of their voices, but not what was being said. Finally they came out.

"A sorry business, Mossie," the Sergeant was saying, shaking his head. "A sorry business! Who would have thought the girl had that much wickedness in her." He was in the dark green uniform of the Royal Irish Constabulary, a smallish neat man of about forty, with rosy cheeks, and a face that suggested its regular expression was a smile, though perhaps not an amiable one. "Well," he went on, in slow ponderous tones. "Where's that young Lily then. I suppose I'll have to be taking her in." He shook his head again.

I decided to speak up. "That might be rather premature, Sergeant."

He looked at me and narrowed his eyes.

"Pre-mature, is it indeed? And who be you, then?" he asked.

"This is Mrs. Hudson, Sergeant Hackett," said Peter, "visiting from England for the... the wedding,"

"From Eng-e-land is it. An En-gel-lish woman. Well, well." The Sergeant's face creased into a smile, but the smile indeed lacked any warmth.

"Mrs. Hudson was the landlady of Sherlock Holmes," Peter explained with something of a boastful tone.

"Indeed... Sherlock Holmes, is it? Well, well, well. Who'd have thought it..?" The Sergeant's smile, combined with his sharp little teeth, was reminding me more and more of the crocodiles in London's zoological gardens. "Sherlock Holmes, is it...? And who be he, now, when he's at home?"

"Why, the great detective, of course," Peter replied in surprise.

"Ah, that Sherlock Holmes. The great detective, is it...? Of course it is." He paused for a moment, then shook his head. "No, can't say I'm acquainted with the gentleman." He stared at me, still smiling. Or sneering, more like.

"Whether you know of my late tenant or not, Sergeant, is hardly relevant," I said, with some acerbity, at the same time suspecting that he feigned ignorance of my famous tenant in order to increase his own importance. "Surely there should be a more thorough investigation of the circumstances of the case before jumping to conclusions. That's all. That's my opinion. The body..."

"Oh, that's your opinion, is it, Mrs. Holmes, or whoever you are? You are of the opinion you're some kind of a de-tec-tive yourself, are you now?"

"Mrs. Hudson has solved a number of cases in the past," said Kitty, trying to be helpful.

The Sergeant turned to her. "Kathleen O'Kelly is it, who went away off from her own place and married a Sassenach. Well, thank you, Kathleen, for enlightening me regarding Mrs. Holmes's achievements. Though, in this case, I am of the opinion, me, that we can manage quite well enough without her valuable assistance. Thanks very much, ladies, and goodbye to ye."

"Meddling women," said Mossie, glaring at me, "thinking they can come over here all high and mighty, hoity-toity like… You can't get away with that any more, missus. Times are a-changing here, and the sooner you realise that the better for you. We Irish are a-rising up and taking back what should always have been ours…" He stepped forward and tightened his fists as before, as if to strike me. No doubt sensing its master's anger, the black dog then rose from its position in front of the range, and made as if to launch itself upon me, which it might well have done if Briege had not again restrained it with a "Down, Conan."

"Now, now, Mossie. Enough of that," the Sergeant said, as if he was not the one who had provoked the outburst. "So where's that young Lily now, then?"

"Safely locked up in the outhouse, Michael. Where she can't murder the rest of us."

"The body was cool, the blood congealed when Lily found him. When they found Lily," I cried out. "She just woke up and found him like that."

Sergeant Hackett rounded on me again. "What's that? She just woke up and found him like that, did she? So let's get this clear. Are you trying to tell me a new bride falls asleep on her wedding night, instead of a-waiting all agog for her man?" he laughed nastily.

"That's a new one on me, missus. Ha! You must have forgotten how it was, 'twas that long ago." I gaped at his effrontery. Then he narrowed his eyes. "Anyways, how do you know all that for sure, missus? You bin poking around have you, old woman, while Mossie here was away out of the place?" He glanced at Peter who lowered his head but said not a word. "Well, now, you can just poke off and leave those that knows about these things to perform their official duties. I'll say it again, madam. Good day to ye."

Mossie coughed and spat on the floor just missing my foot, and then the two of them strode off to confront poor Lily, the dog Conan following behind.

"It is not right," I said. "I am sure she did not do it."

"Who then?" said Briege, rising up with sudden energy. "Who then? Was it me da? Was it me? Is that what you think?"

"No, of course not, my dear." Though I wondered.

"She had the knife in her hand. She was all over blood."

"Yes, but what if she had just found him like that? Would it not be natural to take the knife, to see if he was really dead? It was then she screamed, wasn't it?" Briege said nothing and looked sullen. "Could someone else not have crept in when you were all asleep? What about the men who stayed behind drinking, when you had gone to bed?"

"Why would they kill him? Why? They were his friends. No, the only person who'd want him dead is the young bride who didn't wish to be there in his bed, sold off by her da, hating Francie. Oh, she hated him all right, I know she did."

"Enough to kill him? To stab him? No, it cannot be."

Briege looked at me with blazing eyes.

"She killed him all right. She must have for it was not our knife. She must have brought it with her."

"Not your knife?" This was news indeed. I tried to remember what it looked like. Just a long-bladed knife you might find anywhere. "Anyone could have brought a knife," I continued, thinking, *if it is true what you say.*

"It was her knife. She brought it. She must have planned it from the start." She subsided into sobs in Kitty's arms. "Poor Francie. Me poor, poor brother."

Peter led me away.

"Better leave be for now, Martha. There will be time."

"Will there?"

His kind and reassuring face smiled down at me. "I made a note, like you said. They are more like to listen to me, you know." He paused. "Forgive me for saying this, but mebbe you can only make things worse for Lily."

I supposed he was right. The word of a man always still takes precedence over that of a woman even in England, even in London. I sighed and nodded.

"By the bye," he said, "I must apologise for the way the Sergeant spoke to you."

"It was not your fault, Peter."

"No, but it wasn't right. It was no way to speak to a lady."

"I admit," I said, "that I was taken aback. Shocked, even. I hope he does not speak to his wife in like manner."

"He has no wife," Peter replied.

"Ah," I said.

The same Sergeant and Mossie soon came back in – without the dog, I was glad to see – and, since both remained convinced of the girl's guilt, discussed how best to transfer Lily to the barracks. The policeman had arrived by bicycle, which quite obviously was completely unsuited to the job at hand, and so Lily had been locked up again in the outhouse until an appropriate conveyance could be sent for. Peter offered his cart but was turned down. Apparently, it was not secure enough for Sergeant Hackett's satisfaction, or perhaps he suspected Peter, through his connection to me, of not being entirely trustworthy. Meanwhile, with another glare in my direction, Mossie went off, a bottle of porter in his hand and a foul-smelling pipe in his mouth, to settle himself down in front of the outhouse door, the dog at his feet, to prevent anyone else from having further communication with the girl before she was taken away.

There was also the question of the corpse, which would have to be removed in all haste and taken to the morgue in Wexford town for further examination.

"To establish cause of death," Sergeant Hackett said, sneering at me, "in case there's any doubt but that Francie was stabbed."

I bit my tongue and said nothing.

As we all headed out to watch the Sergeant leave, an excessively fat person in a long black robe came cycling up to the cottage, puffing and blowing and looking entirely discombobulated. I soon recognised the parish priest, Father Joseph. It seemed he had been sent for from the barracks, after Mossie had requested his urgent presence.

"I understand young Francie's dead already, is he, God help him?" the new arrival said to no one in particular, as he dismounted, wiping the sweat off his brow with a large, rather dirty cloth. "Well, I will do what I can."

After a few low words exchanged with Mossie, he entered the cottage, followed by the rest of us.

"A tragic business. I am sorry for your trouble, Briege."

"Thank you, father."

"Bless you, child."

He looked from Kitty to myself in a short-sighted blank sort of a way, clearly not recognising us as parishioners, but nodding acknowledgement.

Then he let himself be led by Peter into the bedroom, Peter murmuring that he had already said prayers over the body.

"Very good, very good."

They were away a while. None of us spoke and the priest's voice could be heard chanting some sort of a requiem. It felt very solemn, the reality of the death at last coming home to us all, and I found myself silently praying too, both for Lily's safety and for Francie's soul. No matter how vicious a person may be, one would never wish the fires and eternal torments of hell upon them.

At last, Father Joseph and Peter emerged, the priest hanging on to the other's arm and looking, despite his erstwhile ruddy complexion, almost grey with shock. I imagine that, although he had ministered to many dying and dead, none would have been in the butchered condition in which he found Francie.

"A glass of whiskey for Father Joe, perhaps, Briege, if you have any such," Peter said.

She jumped up at that, and fetched a tumbler of poitín for the priest from among the mess on the kitchen table. He swallowed it in a single gulp, shivering at the effect.

"I am sorry my dear, that I could not anoint him," he told her. "Francie is dead these many long hours, I fear. The soul long gone from his body."

I looked at Peter, who nodded. More unimpeachable evidence perhaps, for later.

"I am sure you did what you could, Father, and dada and I are very grateful." She refilled his glass, which this time he sipped at more slowly. Then she reached up to a jug over the fireplace and shook out some coins, which she pressed into the priest's hand.

"Ah, you're very good, so you are," he said, after checking to see how much he had been given. "I suppose the funeral will have to be delayed a while."

Briege said nothing to that, hanging her head, so Peter informed the priest that there had to be a coroner's inquest.

"As I thought, in such cases. Very hard on you, Briege, my dear. I'll pray for you."

"Thank you, Father."

Then Peter introduced the priest to his sister, and to myself.

"Ah, Kathleen, of course. I would not have known you, my dear. How are you, how are you?"

"Well, father, thank God."

"And the family?"

She told him of her sons – both far off now in Canada, but doing well for themselves, thank God – and of the passing of her husband. The priest shook his head in sympathy.

"You must be lonely, my daughter," he said, adding a trifle sanctimoniously. "The good Lord giveth and the good Lord taketh away, you know. So this," he turned to me, "is your friend. God bless you too, my daughter."

"Thank you," I said, and after a pause, "Father."

I think he could tell that I was not used to the address – I was not his daughter and the only fathers I readily acknowledge are my own dear late papa and He who is Father to all mankind – but the priest just nodded and smiled, his dewlap quivering.

"Well now, Briege," he continued, turning to her, "I think I'll just have one more top up for the journey back, if you don't begrudge it, now."

"Oh no, Father, of course not. Why don't you take the bottle?" she said, and then opened the cupboard door. "Why not take a full one, indeed. We have plenty to spare."

"Well now, that is most Christian of you, my dear, but no, not at all. I could not possibly agree to it." He gave us all a wry glance. "Heaven forbid you might suspect that I am in the habit of imbibing freely in a general sort of a way. Not at all, not at all… It is just that, under the shocking circumstances today…" He waved his hand in a vague gesture towards the bedroom. Then paused and looked at the proffered bottle. "Ah well, I shall take it so, in the spirit in which it is given. I will be sure to ration it out so that it lasts a good long time."

Thereupon, giving us a final blessing he left us, perhaps with a slight stagger, or maybe a waddle was Father Joseph's usual mode of walking.

"It'll be all drunk up before this night is out, the old soak," said Briege, when he was out of earshot. "God forgive me for saying it, but he is. He made a right holy show of himself at the wedding night after you had gone, I can tell you... Still and all, if it works for him..." She poured herself a shot and swallowed it back, showing that she too was well used to the fiery liquid.

We agreed – Peter, Kitty and I – to stay until Lily was taken away. At least she would have some sympathetic faces around her. Indeed, I whispered to Peter that it might be a good idea to keep an eye on Mossie in case, fired up by the drink, he decided on some rough justice of his own. Peter concurred and went out to keep company with the bereaved father.

It was a tedious enough wait. Any queries Kitty directed at Briege were met with monosyllables or silence, and, while my friend clearly felt that she had to stay with the girl, I could tell that I was no favourite with that person, so I went outside. Glad indeed was I to get out of that oppressive kitchen. I took care, however, to go the front of the farm, well away from Mossie, Peter and the dog, though the breeze carried to my ears occasional murmurs of a conversation between the two men.

What a balmy day it was. A silky breeze caressing the skin. Mount Leinster visible far off, bathed in sunshine, its distant slopes a light blue, the deeper blue of the heavens above it, and occasional fluffy balls of cloud floating by. What a contrast between such tranquillity and the violence within the cottage. Yet I know that nature is often cruel and heartless, "red in tooth and claw," as my dear Tennyson has it. Or perhaps it was simply my mood, coloured by the recent events, that saw the landscape tainted with blood. I am most usually a contented and happy person, after all, and even on that dark day found comfort in the lines from the same poem:

Oh yet we trust that somehow good
Will be the final goal of ill.

While I was thus musing and idly staring about myself, my eyes fixed on a pair of elder trees just outside the gates of the farm. Surely some unnatural movement flickered there. I looked more closely and, to my horror, suddenly found that I was being spied on by several beings whose figures I could barely make out in among the flowering branches. Large and grotesque, these were no human forms, and I am afraid that my reason left me momentarily: with all the talk of faeries, I quite took the things to be supernatural. I must have cried out, then, and quite loudly too, for Peter soon joined me and asked what was the matter.

With a shaking finger I pointed to the trees. He peered up.

"By god," he exclaimed. "It's them straw boys."

"Surely those are not men up there?" I asked. "The branches would not be able to bear their weight."

"No, no, not the men themselves. It's just their costumes, Martha." He shook his head. "Bad cess to them. They have hung their gear from the trees, leaving them to rot, do you see, because of the way they were treated at the wedding. To bring bad luck on the family."

"They have succeeded only too well, then," I remarked, having regained my composure. Now that I knew what they were, I could make out the woven straw of the headdresses, crude and malevolent effigies casting their ancient curse.

"They gave you a fright, did they?" Peter said, grinning.

"Quite a turn," I admitted. "And yet, Peter, you know what this means?"

"What?"

"That there were others around the farm last night, creeping about in the dark. Perhaps they even crept inside. The same men would have borne quite a grudge against Francie for his treatment of them, would they not?"

However, when Peter conveyed this information to the newly returned Sergeant Hackett, bringing him to view the dummies, he was not impressed.

"Another fancy of yours, I suppose," he replied, looking at me. "It won't do, no, it won't do, Peter. Not unless you can bring me a straw boy holding a knife and with blood on his hands. That might be something to look into." He smiled that crocodile smile again. "Now, that's not to say," he continued, "that I hold with what those lads did. 'Tis a cruel joke, right enough but 'twas mischief, that's all. Nothing at all to do with murder."

He walked off.

"Do you know who those lads were in the costumes?" I asked Peter in low tones as we followed the Sergeant round to the back yard.

"I have a notion. I'll ask a few people. But you know, Martha, I can't see it was them did the deed. It would be a violent revenge surely for a small enough matter. And why ever would they leave clues behind them, to show they were here?"

That was true. I suppose I was grabbing at straws, no pun intended.

A sorry sight it was, a while later, to witness poor Lily bundled into the Black Maria and hauled off. At least Briege had permitted Kitty to put clean clothes and other little personal items into a bag for her. Sergeant Hackett, of course, had to dump it out to check it contained nothing irregular, before roughly stuffing all back in again.

We tried to give Lily reassuring smiles and nods, but in truth the outlook seemed bleak indeed.

"Where will they take her?" I asked.

"First back to the barracks," Peter said, "to be held there until the results of the investigation into the death has taken place.

Then, if she is sent for trial, she will go to the Bridewell in Wexford town to wait for the summer assizes." He shook his head. "I should not like any son or daughter of mine to be sent to such a place, though I believe they are better than they used to be, if that is any consolation."

Soon after Lily had left with the Sergeant and the two constables he had brought with him to subdue that notorious criminal, Peter, Kitty and I set off back to the farm.

"I can hardly bear it," my friend said. "Whatever are we going to do, Martha?"

"I think I should consult Colonel Timmins, as you suggested before," I replied, trying to sound confident.

"Oh, yes," she replied. "He will sort it out, for sure."

"Colonel Timmins, is it?" said Peter, with no great respect in his voice. "I doubt he will look kindly upon Lily. He is no friend to the Irish unless they bow and scrape before him, and Willie Cullen has never done that." He whipped his horse with rather more force than necessary, seeing that the beast well knew the road and needed no encouragement to take us back.

"You are both convinced then that Lily is innocent," he remarked after a while.

"Do you not?" I asked him surprised. "After the evidence of the blood and the rigor?"

"She could have done the deed earlier and waited to raise the alarm."

"That would be most strange, surely."

"I am not claiming she is guilty," he continued, "But aren't you ladies letting yourselves be influenced by your love for the girl? Just look at the circumstances. As Briege said, who else had a motive? Although to be honest, I am not saying that Francie didn't have enemies. A man like that... However, who else could have got into the house and not be seen? Lily may not have killed Francie. Just that it looks that way. It will look that way to a judge and jury.

And it will certainly look that way to Colonel Timmins," adding with a bitter twist, "however great a friend of yours he is, Martha."

I knew that he was right, except about my being such a friend of the Colonel's.

"Well, in that case," I replied. "Kitty and I will have to find out for ourselves who did really murder Francie."

Peter sighed and gave the horse another lash. The cart jerked forward and I anticipated more bruises.

Chapter Eight

The next day being Saturday, after a night spent tossing and turning and worrying how to proceed in in a country that was proving so alien to me, I decided at last on a plan, more to avoid being frustrated by inactivity, than with any hope of a positive outcome. In the morning after breakfast, therefore, I set out by myself to walk to the Timmins' place. Such physical exercise in the fine but somewhat chilly weather was most welcome, and I was in a much more sanguine state of mind by the time I arrived at the blocky house. I would lay out the case for Lily's innocence coolly and rationally. The Colonel must surely hear me out.

I knocked on the front door only to learn from a pert housemaid that the Timminses had gone out. No, she told me, they were not expected to return any time soon, and made to shut the door in my face. Before she could do so, I pressed for further details. The Colonel and Mrs. Timmins, she said begrudgingly, had gone for the day to visit a cousin of Augusta's who lived near the seaside town of Arklow. Disappointed that my trip was in vain, I yet begged a glass of water, which the girl brought me with a bad grace, leaving me on the doorstep the while without even inviting me into the house, as if I were some passing tramp. I should be most aggrieved if either of my servants – Clara or young Phoebe – treated a visitor in such a way. Yet I knew that would never be the case, since I have managed to train even Phoebe in the basics of good behaviour and hospitality.

Following the draught of water, for which I thanked the hussy in an exaggerated manner – although I am sure my irony was wasted upon her – I had then to walk all the way back with nothing to show for my outing. At least I might expect again to accompany the Timminses to church on the morrow, the which provided some small consolation.

I saw barely a soul on my path, although one encounter merits a mention, particularly in view of subsequent events. On the way to the Timmins' house, I had passed a tumbledown cabin, surrounded by a tiny walled-in patch of ground over which a couple of scrawny chickens were scratching. Now, on my return, an old crone was sitting outside, chopping muddy roots, turnips I think, into a bucket. She addressed some words to me in what I think must have been the Irish language, for I understood not a single word. Her poverty and wretched demeanour moved me, however, and I took a coin from my reticule to give her, hoping she would not be offended. Quite the opposite. She grabbed my hand in her claw and held it with a strength I could not have guessed in one so apparently feeble.

A torrent of words which I took to be thanks poured from her. Attracted by the sound, a girl of about eleven looked out over the half door of the cabin, and, seeing me, came full out and bobbed a little curtsey. She was a pretty thing, although filthy and in rags and, of course, I had to give something to her as well.

"God's blessings upon you, ma'am," she said in heavily accented English. Such effusive thanks for so little.

"Is this your grandmother?" I asked.

"Tis, surely. Mammo… Mammo Kinsella." The girl laid an affectionate hand on the old woman's shoulder. "And I'm Nell."

"Kinsella," I said. "Are you kin to poor Francie, then?"

The girl translated my question to the old woman, who spat on the ground, and muttered.

105

"Cousins," Nell explained, "but 'tis divil a bit of good it has done us, Mammo says. Poor Francie, indeed. There's nothing poor about them. Them's tight as a duck's arse." She giggled. "Excuse me but that's what she said, ma'am."

"Have you not heard the news, then?" I asked.

"News?"

"About Francie."

"That he got wed and didn't ask us along. Yes, we heard."

"Not that." I wondered for a moment if I should break the news of his death to family members, but concluded it would soon be common enough knowledge. In any case, I doubted these two would be heartbroken to hear of his passing.

"Dead!" exclaimed the girl. "Murdered, you say. Lord bless us." She made the sign of the cross.

Turning then to the old woman, she exchanged more words with her, quite heated ones. Finally, Nell turned back to me.

"Mammo says 'twas his wickedness did for him. Indeed and all, she knew 'twould happen, for didn't she hear the banshee a-howling in the night."

The banshee again, that signals death.

More incomprehensible words.

"So who did it?" Nell asked.

"They say it was his new wife. But…"

The girl babbled to Mammo before I could finish. The old woman shook a gnarled finger at me.

"You say 'twas his new wife kilt him," Nell told me, "but Mammo knows better."

At long last someone who believed in the girl's innocence.

"No, I don't think so either," I replied. "But who then does Mammo think did it?"

"Why sure, 'twas the faeries, because he disrespected them."

Hardly a claim that would stand up in court, I feared.

"Well," I said, taking my leave of them, "I must be on my way. Good day to you, good people."

"Would your ladyship like to step in first and take a cuppeen of fresh milk for the road?" Nell asked.

I thanked her but said that I had but recently satisfied my thirst, reflecting at the same time how much more truly generous were these poor people than the servants of the gentry. The widow's mite, I thought, and all the more valuable for that. Without raising possibly false hopes in the girl, I vowed to myself that I would try to do something to improve their miserable lot. But the banshee, indeed...

The weather has a way of changing quickly in Ireland – four seasons in one day, as has been said before by others – and by the time I reached the farm, a huge black cloud had started emptying little darts of rain onto the surrounding countryside, and more particularly upon me. Luckily, I made it into the kitchen before the full downpour unleashed itself.

Having hung my coat up to dry and quite despairing of the mud on the hem of my skirts, I sat down with Annie and Kitty for a welcome cup of tea and told the others of my fruitless quest, not omitting to complain of the rudeness of the maid. I then added how I had met with Mammo and Nell.

"They are poor souls," Annie said. "You know, the grandmother took the girl in when her parents died of the fever. They barely scrape a living."

"Mammo is most bitter against Francie and his family," I said. "She certainly does not mourn his death." I did not mention the banshee, not wishing to pander further to the superstition.

"Yes, they are distantly related, I believe," Annie said. "Though you know Mossie is not a rich man, either. Look at the state of his farm!" She shook her head. "No, Mossie would be hard pressed to help anyone out, and I believe there is a regular army of poor relations. They are a feckless enough lot." Spoken with the somewhat smug tone of one who was anything but feckless.

I remarked then that I should like to do something for the poor pair, to ease their lot. Annie replied a little sharply that if I wished to help every needy Irish peasant I passed along the road, my purse would soon be empty. I must have looked downcast, because she continued, laughing, "Oh, Martha, I see how you have a soft spot for poor girls, Lily, Nell… who else I wonder? Well, I have to go into Ferns someday soon for some messages. You are welcome to come with me if you like, to make up a basket for them."

I liked that idea, especially since I needed to find a post office to send a telegram to Clara, and inform her that my return would be delayed. By now, I knew that Annie was not intending a similar activity, having learnt that "messages" for her meant "provisions."

The rest of the day I spent with the smaller children at my feet, recounting traditional stories – Cinderella, Jack and the Beanstalk and Little Red Riding Hood among them, the latter provoking wide eyed horror at the mention of the Big Bad Wolf, which soon turned to rejoicing at the little girl's narrow escape and the slaying of the Wolf.

"Just like Lily and Francie," said Pegeen.

"How so?" I asked warily.

She chuckled. "For wasn't Francie big and bad, Auntie, and wasn't Lily the clever girl to kill him dead?"

"Oh no," I replied, rather regretting my choice of a tale to tell. "No one deserves to be killed, Pegeen. And anyway, we don't think Lily killed him, do we?"

Pegeen shook her head, but without conviction.

"Was it the woodcutter did it, then?" Sarie asked.

"Maybe it was. Maybe it was."

To change the subject, as quickly as possible, I asked them to tell me more of their own quaint Irish tales. Like Veronica, they all believed firmly in the little people, informing me with serious expressions that a tiny man guards a pot of faery gold at the bottom of the rainbow, and that whoever finds it will become rich, but that this leprechaun, as he is called, will try to stop you from getting it because he is very bold.

"Bold?" I asked. "You mean brave?"

"Not at all, Auntie. He is very, very naughty."

Which apparently is their understanding of the word, and at last explains why Annie, when chiding one or the other of them is like to fling out that epithet, something that had puzzled me greatly.

Despite this diversion, I found the day dragged horribly. Kitty meanwhile showed herself content enough, although I saw that while I, the guest, was doomed to idleness, my friend was at least permitted to do some light chores. It was in vain that I declared that I too would be happy to help out.

"Don't be thinking of it, Martha. You take it easy," Annie said.

I sighed and asked the children to tell their numbers.

Later, in case I had thought she was less than concerned with poor Lily's fate, Kitty assured me that keeping busy had been a way of distracting herself.

"You were lucky then," I answered.

The following morning, being Sunday, the Treasure duly drove up to the farm to collect me for church. The Timminses were already settled in the carriage and Augusta could hardly contain her excitement regarding the murder.

While I did not approve of the gloating and unseemly way in which – discovering I had actually been present at the scene – she requested sensational details, it did at least give me the opportunity to speak on the subject to the Colonel, and lay out my very sound reasons for thinking Lily innocent.

The Colonel, eyebrows and moustache bristling, was, however, not inclined to hear me out, and interrupted in his customary peremptory manner..

"Mrs. Hudson," said he. "I understand that you may have been able to assist the English police in one or two little ways, whether through luck or judgement I of course cannot say." The expression on his face reflected the certainty that it had to be luck, because I was clearly lacking the other quality. "However, you cannot come here, you know, and expect to explain the case, as Sergeant Hackett has informed me you have been trying to do, to our Royal Irish Constabulary, or, indeed, to our judiciary (presumably meaning himself).

"We are, I assure you, well able to investigate the case without help from misguided amateurs, and I should advise you very strongly, madam, to keep out of it." With which riposte, and with a smug curl to his lips, he sat back in the carriage.

There was a long pause. I must say, I was not inclined, after that, to argue with the man, but found it telling, all the same, that the Sergeant had wasted no time in informing the Colonel of my interest in the case, presumably to head me off. That the Colonel needed little heading off, however, I could not doubt. I can recognise a closed mind when I see it, and the Colonel's was tightly padlocked against anything I might say. Augusta, on the other hand, was clearly embarrassed at her husband's abrupt, not to say downright rude manner and tried to soften its effect.

"Well, you know, Martha," she twittered, "the Colonel has much more experience with these things than either you or I. And it is such a very sordid matter, I am sure it is better for a lady like yourself not to get involved."

I had to speak up. "As for me being a lady – if indeed I can make claim to that elevated station in life – I have to say, Augusta, that in the present case, it is neither here nor there. I wish only, like any righteous citizen of these islands, that justice be served, and I am sure, in that at least, the Colonel must agree with me," giving a swift glance at that personage, who however was resolutely turned away to the window, apparently engrossed in the landscape, "and that he will wish to make certain that the right person has been found guilty of the crime."

The Colonel twitched, but did not otherwise respond.

"Of course, that is what we all wish for," Augusta went on. "Although as I have heard it said, Lily was discovered standing over poor Francie with the knife in her hand, and dripping with blood." She gave a delicious shiver. "Surely that must be proof enough."

Word indeed travelled fast in this part of the country.

"Yes, that is true enough," I replied, "yet when she was discovered like that, the body was cooling. I verified myself that rigor mortis had already set in."

"Oh, I don't know anything about such things," she said, with another shudder. "Rigor what?"

"The stiffening of the corpse after death," the Colonel snapped.

"Oh goodness." Augusta paled. "Oh dear, dear, dear." Perhaps she was suddenly reminded of her own mortality.

"That only occurs several hours after death," I added.

Augusta fanned herself rapidly.

"Even if you are correct, Mrs. Hudson," the Colonel said, "it really has no bearing on the circumstances. Lily was present at the scene, she had motive and opportunity. Ergo, she did it, whether earlier or later." He relented then a little. "I know your friend, Mrs. Melrose, is very close to the girl. You may convey to her that at least Lily is not likely to hang. Everyone knows what Francie Kinsella was like."

Cold comfort indeed.

By now we had arrived at the church. I was bubbling over with a fury and frustration I found hard to conceal, although I suppose I should not have been surprised after all at the Colonel's reaction. A man like him would not welcome instruction from a woman. I could only hope that my words might prompt him to take a more open-minded view of Lily's involvement, although I doubted this very much.

My mind racing in all directions, I am afraid I hardly paid attention to the service until the sermon, when Mr. Webber made reference to the very tragic events of the past few days, urging us all to pray for Francie's soul, and to pray for Lily, that she might repent her evil deed and find some forgiveness in the eyes of God. Evidently the local community and even the Church had already judged the poor girl and found her guilty.

When myself and the Timminses first entered the church, I had noted the presence of Florrie – who could ignore that cherry red jacket? Indeed, he had given me a little wave and a wink. After the service, therefore, I was not surprised to find him waiting for us outside.

"Good morning, Mrs. Hudson," said he, reverting, after his previous familiarity, to my formal title. "What a turn-up. Dear me. Who would have thought it?"

"Yes, indeed," I replied. "It is a very sad business altogether."

He pulled at my arm, so that we were at a distance from the crowd.

"To think," he was now whispering, "that if we had succeeded in our little escapade, Francie might still be in the land of the living."

"I trust, Mr. Sweetnam," I said, also in lowered tones, "that you have not mentioned our little escapade, as you call it, to anyone else."

"No, indeed. It is our secret." Of course, he winked, and would, I think, have nudged me too, if I had not moved quickly out of the way.

At that moment, Augusta approached. "Barney has arrived with the carriage, Martha. We can return whenever you are ready." Adding pointedly, "Mortimer is waiting."

"Oh no, please," Florrie said. "I have just persuaded Mrs. Hudson that it would be an honour for this poor widower to accompany her home in my barouche."

This was news to me. I glanced at the round pink face that was maintaining its characteristic amiable and innocent expression. Then I looked beyond Augusta to the Colonel, who was twitching with impatience and bad temper. If I found myself between the devil and the deep sea, I at least knew which one I preferred.

"Mr. Sweetnam is most kind," I said. "Moreover, it would save you the inconvenience of a detour, Augusta."

She smiled knowingly. At least, she thought she knew what was going on, and I was not about to disabuse her on this occasion. If she considered that Florrie's attentions meant a particularly personal interest in myself, then well and good. For now.

"I hope you will call on us again soon, Martha. Both of you, indeed," she said. "And never mind the Colonel. His bark, you know, is far worse than his bite."

"Whatever does she mean?" Florrie asked, as Augusta moved off. "Did the Colonel bark at you then?"

"Somewhat," I said. "He thinks I wish to meddle in the murder."

"So do you?"

"Yes," I said, "I do."

"What larks!" And off we went to his barouche.

It seemed to me that we were driving a very roundabout route back to the farm, although, the day being fine, it was most pleasant to view the countryside in all its late spring glory from the comfort of the barouche. The hedgerows were burgeoning with holly, hazel and blackthorn; sunbursts of gorse flowers exuded an exotic scent of coconut, while the branches of the May trees were set around with delicate white clouds of blossom. Beneath, anemones, dog violets and cowslips clustered along the road's edge, a treat for the senses. I quite forgot our troubles for a while, lost in the enjoyment of the ride.

How amazed was I, nevertheless, when we at last drove up to the most extraordinary house I have ever seen in my life, a white castle all turrets and battlements.

"What is this?" I asked.

"My apologies, dear lady," Florrie replied, smiling sweetly. "I just could not resist the desire to show you my humble abode."

"It is hardly humble," I said. "And you should have asked my permission, Mr. Sweetnam. It is not seemly to carry me off like this."

"Oh, do say you will come in for a look around, Mrs. Hudson. It is so seldom I meet anyone here with the discerning taste I detect in you."

"I am afraid it is quite impossible," I replied, somewhat flattered nonetheless. "Please take me back to the O'Kellys immediately."

"No. Not until you have come in for a moment. I told you that you owed me. This you can do for me at least."

"Mr. Sweetnam, you have abducted me."

He quivered with glee, like a strawberry blancmange just set upon the table.

"Not at all, not at all. You will be quite safe, I assure you. My housekeeper, Mrs. O'Meara, is a model of respectability, and she will, I am sure, have some toothsome refreshments prepared for us."

Having missed breakfast again due to the O'Kellys' religious scruples, I was in truth rather hungry. I had already instructed Annie not to await my return for breakfast, since I had been hoping to accompany the Timminses back to their house to try to work on the Colonel, a plan which had been so completely dashed. There was thus no great hurry to return, and the mention of Florrie's housekeeper indeed reassured me regarding the propriety of the visit. I must confess, too, that I was curious to see the inside of this most curious of dwellings.

"Well," I conceded, "for a few moments then."

"Splendid, splendid. You will not regret it, dear lady, I am certain of that."

Meanwhile, a young man was approaching us from a mews building situated to one side of the house. Tall and dark, he was most attractive, with something of Jimmy, the Darlin' Boy, of fond if treacherous memory. I hoped this youth was less of a rogue.

"Ah, here is Thomas," said Florrie, hopping down from the vehicle. "We shall be needing the barouche again in a while," he told him, "so keep it ready, if you please."

The young man nodded and smiled a dazzling smile. At that same moment a huge hairy beast came galloping towards us. I stepped back in shock, but Florrie merely laughed.

"Down, Bran," he said, as the creature in its exuberance tried to jump upon me.

"What is it?" I asked, for I had never seen the like before.

"An Irish wolf-hound," Florrie replied. "Good for hunting wolves, you know."

I must have looked aghast, for he laughed all the more.

"Don't you worry, Mrs. Hudson. There are no wolves left in Ireland. Or at least not of the animal variety." He winked. "Bran is an old pet and a good guard dog. Aren't you, boy?" He caressed its ears, on a level with his chest. "Now, go back with Thomas, and don't be frightening the ladies."

The young man whistled and headed back towards the stables, the huge dog trotting obediently beside him.

"A beauty isn't he," Florrie said. "Named for Finn McCool's dog…" I looked askance. "Irish mythology, don't you know. Another interest of mine."

He was full of surprises.

With me still a little shaky from the recent encounter, we proceeded to the front entrance of his extraordinary abode. The portal by itself was quite spectacular, an arched doorway flanked by pillars as if one were about to enter some Italian cathedral – not of course that I have ever done the like, having only see such in illustrations and paintings.

"What do you think so far?" my host asked me.

"I am quite speechless with amazement," I said.

"I fell in love with it the moment I saw it," Florrie went on. "I simply had to have it."

"But was it not the property of your first wife?" I asked, remembering what I had heard from Annie.

"Oh well," and he looked just a little shame-faced, "of course I was madly in love with dear Mary Elizabeth before ever I saw her place of residence." His eyes twinkled at me playfully, and I was not at all sure that I believed him. "In fact," he went on, "I have over the years vastly improved it. To be honest, it was quite ramshackle when I moved in after our marriage. But I saw the possibilities, and luckily had the wherewithal to fulfil my vision."

"So did Mary Elizabeth approve?" I asked as we entered the hallway. "Oh my goodness!"

The sight which had provoked my exclamation was of a vaulted ceiling in decorative white plaster, all curlicues and naked cherubs, surmounting panelled walls painted in a shade of deepest crimson, themselves above a parquet floor of elaborate design. It was spectacular, yes, but not at all homely.

"Did your wife like your...er... improvements?" I asked again.

"During her lifetime it was, sadly, not as you now see it." His face drooped mournfully. "Alas, dear Mary Elizabeth was taken from me far too soon, even though, you know, she was some considerable degree older than myself. Now my second bride, dear Blanche, was of great assistance to me, particularly in the garden. She was quite a follower of Gertrude Jekyll, don't you know."

I shook my head. "I am afraid I don't..."

"You are not acquainted with the work of dear Gertrude! My goodness me. Then I cannot think you are much of a gardener, Mrs. Hudson."

"No, indeed. I have no garden in Baker Street, just a back yard. But I love flowers, and my delight is to walk in a beautiful garden."

He clapped his hands. "Then you will adore my little patch." It hadn't looked so very little to me, from what I could see of it. "It is, I pride myself, even more striking than the Timmins' garden which, as I recall, you greatly admired." He smiled. "Yes, indeed, dear Blanche worked wonders. None of your formal Italianate gardens for Castle Florence, despite the name." He chuckled at his little joke. "No, Gertrude Jekyll and the English country garden constituted the model for our design."

I was rather afraid he would suggest a walk there and then, before I had appeased my appetite, but no fear of that. Florrie Sweetnam, as I was soon to observe, enjoyed his food far too much to postpone that particular pleasure.

He led me into what I suppose was a parlour, although to call it such was to make it sound quite domestic. It was a large room, rectangular in shape, its walls covered in pale green silk and sporting paintings of aristocratic-looking ladies and gentlemen, who were not, Florrie hastened to assure me, ancestors of his, but rather the work of followers of Mr. Gainsborough and Mr. Reynolds. The high arched windows, reminiscent of a chapel, and looking out over the driveway, were each inset with a small panel of stained glass. But what drew the eye most was an elaborate fireplace of white marble, turreted like a miniature castle. It must, I thought, be the very devil to clean. Upright chairs, that seemed to be chosen for the beauty of their design rather than for comfort, stood around in studied carelessness. I was relieved therefore when Florrie indicated a well-padded chaise longue to me, though not quite so happy when he sat himself down close beside me.

"What a most striking table," I said, regarding a piece of furniture that I could not imagine ever set with tea cups and cake.

"Yes, it is one of my treasures. One of my many treasures, Mrs. Hudson. I do so love to surround myself with beauty. The top is Sicilian jasper, don't you know."

I had never heard of it, but again expressed my admiration.

"I am intrigued," I added, "by the stained glass."

"Ah, yes, indeed," Florrie replied. "I researched the Sweetnam coat of arms, you know, and had a charming man in Wexford make the panels up for me."

"Your family actually has a coat of arms!" I was impressed, and rose to study the motif more closely.

"Oh, we are an ancient clan, you know, going back to Anglo-Saxon times." He joined me at the window. The panel featured a helmet over a shield with a slanting green stripe, the whole surrounded by arabesques of leaves. It was not exactly pretty, and I am not versed in the symbolism of heraldry, so I wondered at the design of what looked to be a series of spades down the stripe. There was an inscription in Latin over the whole.

"*Ex sudore vultus*," I read. "What does it mean?"

Florrie fidgeted somewhat. "I thought the Latin added tone," he said.

"Yes, but what does it mean?"

"Hmm," he paused for a moment. "It means 'By the sweat of the face'." He gave me a challenging look.

I stared at him for a moment. Was this a joke? Yet for once he was serious.

"Ah!" I replied. "Is that because your ancestors spent their time digging." I pointed at the spades.

"They were warriors," he said, ever so slightly affronted, "as you can tell from the helmet. The motto is a war cry."

A strange one, I thought, but followed him, without commenting further, back to the chaise longue.

"The family originated in the county of Cheshire, you know. In England," he continued, all affability again. "I am sad to say I have never visited there. One day, perhaps. Although I am rather partial to their cheese."

"Yes," I replied. "I have visited that county and have indeed tasted the cheese. Both are most pleasing, in their different ways."

Florrie became quite excited. "You were there! Did you by any happy chance happen upon the village of Swettenham."

"No, I am afraid not."

"That is a pity. The first Saxon Lord of Swettenham had his estates confirmed by King William Rufus. The family seat, Swettenham Hall, still stands, you know, and is a fine building. Or so I understand it to be. One day, I intend to write a history of the family." He gave a great sigh, as one quite exhausted in advance at the prospect, and lolled back on the chaise longue. "I have some fascinating ancestors, you know, Mrs. Hudson."

"Really?"

"Oh yes. Lords and all sorts. But there was also Joseph Swetnam, the woman-hater."

"Good gracious!"

"Yes, indeed, Joseph wrote a pamphlet denouncing the fair sex in extreme language. It was very popular at the time. But fear not, dear lady, I do not share my ancestor's sentiments on that

119

particular matter." He winked and edged a little closer to me. "Quite the opposite, in fact."

Thankfully, at that moment a woman entered the room, as out of place as it was possible to be, a plump and homely looking body in her early sixties. She was wheeling a trolley on which, oh joy, a plenteous supply of delicacies were arranged.

"Mrs. O'Meara, you are a wonder," said Florrie. "Just as Mrs. Hudson here was about to faint away with hunger."

She smiled at him in a motherly way and nodded pleasantly at me.

"You are very welcome, ma'am," she said, and set to serving the tea in the most delicate cups I have ever seen, translucent porcelain embellished with a design of roses. I was almost afraid to lift mine up.

Plates overflowed with freshly made scones, crisp almond biscuits and dark slabs of what Florrie informed me was something called barmbrack, plump with raisins.

When I praised it, smeared with thick butter, Mrs. O'Meara informed me that traditionally it was prepared for All Hallows' Eve, but since Mr. Florrie loved it so much she made it all year round.

"However, Mrs. O'Meara leaves out the ring." He smiled archly.

"The ring?"

"Whoever finds the ring in the barmbrack will be married within the year," he explained. "I should have insisted, Mrs. O'Meara, if only I had known that we should have such a delightful visitor, that you would have placed a ring in the brack, despite the unseasonable time of year for it." He chuckled and winked.

Oh dear, dear me, such misplaced gallantry.

The housekeeper simply smiled, bowed a nod and withdrew.

Florrie sighed. "I don't know what I would do without Mrs. O'Meara, here all alone by myself. She is a perfect treasure."

Another one.

"I love my house," he told me. "I love, as I have told you, to surround myself with beauty. But it can be a lonely place as well, Mrs. Hudson. Very lonely."

"Mrs. O'Meara's biscuits are quite delicious," I said quickly. "Would it be very greedy of me to take another?"

"Not at all, dear lady. Then I will show you some more of the house."

It only occurred to me long afterwards that, during the seemingly desultory conversation that followed, both while feasting on the goodies provided, and after, while hosting the Grand Tour of the house, Florrie had quite pumped me for information regarding myself and the actors in the tragic drama that had constituted the murder of Francie. Without dwelling, as Augusta had, on the gorier elements of the case, he had managed to extract from me exactly how it was I came to be present in Wexford, how at the very scene of the crime, and all about Kitty and Peter and Annie, apparently only inspired by a friendly interest. I felt myself naïve, in retrospect to have revealed so much, while only learning from him what he wished me to know.

I oohed and aahed a great deal that morning, although privately of the opinion that I should hate to live in what seemed to me a veritable mausoleum of art and artefacts. It also occurred to me that Florrie Sweetnam must be a very rich man indeed to have assembled, and to continue to maintain, such an establishment, not to mention an elaborate wardrobe. He seemed to have no occupation when I asked about it, becoming vague on the subject.

"Oh, I keep myself busy, I can assure you," he said. "I dabble, you know, in this and that."

"Dabble?"

"Let me show you." He led me into what I considered a conservatory, but which he insisted was to be called an Orangery, a mainly glass structure on the south facing side of the house, full of exotic plants set around couches where one could take one's rest, enjoying the view of the garden even if the weather outside were inclement.

As if reading my thoughts, Florrie remarked, "The outlook is lovely and mild today, Mrs. Hudson, but you should sit here during a storm. It is most deliciously exciting. It inspires my art, you know."

In fact, an easel stood in one corner, holding a, to my uneducated eye, a rather loose depiction of what seemed to be a rough sea.

"You did this?" I asked, managing to add awe to my tone.

"Yes indeed. As you can tell, I am a great lover of Mr. Turner."

I had heard of the artist, of course, although I confess I knew little of his work. In general, I am kept far too busy to be visiting museums and galleries, although I do admire the works of Mr. Constable.

"These," he went on, a little timidly, indicating the wall of the house behind us, "are my darlings, rendered in paint by me."

Three portraits hung there, each depicting a decidedly grim and ill-favoured female, each with eyes that stared out balefully. Of course, it might well be that the lack of skill of the artist was to blame for the unfortunate effect.

"Your wives?" I ventured, trying hard to display enthusiasm.

"Dear Mary Elizabeth, dear Blanche and dear Emma Jane," he said pointing to each with loving pride, "God bless them all."

"What a touching tribute," I said.

"Please to note," – he indicated an empty area of wall next to Emma Jane – "how there is just enough space for one more image?"

Oh dear, oh dear, oh dear.

We returned through the upstairs landing, Florrie wishing to show me the bedrooms, all lavishly accoutred – each having a four poster hung around with drapes, windows of a fancifully Gothic style, and some startling additions, such as a full suit of armour in one, a stuffed monkey in another and in the third, Florrie's own room, a tapestry depicting men with the hairy legs of beasts chasing full-bosomed maidens clad only in wisps of drapery. Scattered everywhere, too, were art works of a decidedly amateur nature, gaudy still lives and wild landscapes presumably by Florrie. For such a professed lover of beauty, he showed, I felt, little discrimination when it came to his own productions.

I could not imagine spending a restful night in any of those bedrooms. It would be like walking into one of those spine-chilling novels by Mrs. Ann Radcliffe or Sheridan Le Fanu, with their accompanying perils. However, again, out of courtesy to my host, I expressed only admiration.

At the end of the corridor was a door which Florrie did not move to open. This surprised me for he had opened every other, including, quite unnecessarily, those of the water closets. When I asked what room this was, he twinkled a little as if suppressing a mystery, and stated that this was the one door which was not open to any but himself.

I had no further interest in the matter, and was about to walk on, but that, it seemed, would not do.

"Like Bluebeard, don't you know," he said, staying back so that I was forced to stop and turn around. "Bluebeard, you know."

"Oh yes, Mr. Sweetnam." I did not appreciate his sense of humour and, despite the demands of etiquette, decided to put him in his place "Am I to understand then that your dead wives are all hanging up in there?"

If I thought he would be shocked or offended, I was quite mistaken.

"He he!" he chortled, jumping up and down and clapping his hands. "Oh, Mrs. Hudson, you are a caution. A regular caution. You know all about Bluebeard then, do you?"

"Not at all. Only that one detail."

"Well, I can reassure you, dear lady, that all my beloved wives received a good Christian burial, and lie side by side in St. Michael's churchyard, where one day," putting on a sad face, "I shall assuredly join them."

"Good," I replied, adding hastily, in case he thought I was prematurely anticipating his departure from this vale of tears. "At least, I am glad to learn they are not in there."

"It is just my little den," he continued, "where I can retreat from the whole world if I so wish it."

"I have a room like that at home," I said, "although I have no need to bar the door. When I am there, sewing or reading, my people know not to disturb me."

Not quite true. Young Phoebe has from time to time barged in without a by your leave on some trivial matter, and, in the happy past, Clara had sometimes to summon me to Mr. H. The great man never did respect my privacy and, I regret to say, has not learnt to do so any more now that he is returned. However, I did not feel the need to inform Florrie of that. Indeed, I was becoming tired both of him and his little ways, his secrets, his hints and winks, tired of his pride in his cold and heartless house. When he asked if I now wished to see the garden, I excused myself, saying that I really needed to get back home.

"Well, now you know where I live, you are welcome at any time, dear lady. Any time at all. As long as I myself am here, of course."

I thanked him, and then he asked if I would mind very much if Thomas drove me back, since he himself felt somewhat fatigued. I was more pleased than disappointed with this arrangement, and readily acquiesced.

"But you know," he told me as I prepared to depart. "I am with you on this business of Lily, Mrs. Hudson. You have quite convinced me of her innocence" – we had spoken of it at some length – "and I shall be happy to offer you any small assistance that lies within my power."

That much I was most gratified to hear and thanked him sincerely. Indeed, I considered it quite likely that I should need the services of someone, even if only to take me about.

The handsome young servant then drove me back, mostly in silence, for, although he looked like a statue of a Greek godling, when I tried conversation I could not understand a single word that he said, so rough and mumbled was his accent.

Chapter Nine

Arriving back at the farm, I was somewhat surprised to find in the kitchen no Kitty, who had seemingly gone out with the children. Instead, a disreputable-looking little man was sitting at the table in serious conversation with Peter. In his squashed hat and jacket of motley patches, this quaint individual quite embodied my image of the leprechaun as described to me by the children, though, if there were a pot of gold at the end of his particular rainbow, he had made no good use of it. Annie beckoned me over and whispered that this was Mikey Dan, the match-maker and, for one terrible moment, I feared that he had come from Florrie on my behalf, but soon realised the talk was all about Annie's sister, Sal.

A pungent combination of stale tobacco smoke and spilled drink emanated from the man's shabby clothing, and I recalled the distaste with which Veronica had described him. Would he in due course, I wondered, be required to arrange a match for her too? It was an unedifying prospect.

Meanwhile Annie was busy setting mugs of tea in front of the men, alongside the bottle of poitín that was already there. A little early in the day for that, I thought to myself, but Mikey Dan readily reached for the bottle and splashed a goodly quantity into his cup as far as the very top. Peter himself only added a drop or two, presumably to be neighbourly.

I was most curious to observe the workings of the strange custom of matchmaking, but was unsure if I would be welcome. I need not have worried for Annie motioned me to a chair by the wall and offered me a cup of tea as well, the which I readily accepted, without of course the addition of strong spirits.

She then sat beside me and whispered an explanation of the proceedings, while the men remained engrossed in discussion. I was rather surprised that Sal herself was not present, but apparently tradition demanded she stay elsewhere in the house while her fate was being decided by the men.

Usually, Annie told me, the negotiations would be between the matchmaker and the father of the prospective bride, but in this case, the father having passed away, Peter, as an older male member connected to the family by marriage, was standing in his place.

All the talk, as far as I could tell, was about cows and money, as if poor Sal were a similar commodity to be bargained over. However, there seemed little disagreement, as if the matter were easily resolved, and I understood that, in this case at least, the negotiations were something of a formality.

"Will we set a time to walk the land, then?" asked Peter.

"We can go now and if it please you, sur," the matchmaker said, swallowing the dregs of his drink. "No time like the present, as the man said, and time is marching on where the same Sarah is concerned." He gave a horrible cackle. "She's no spring chicken, to be sure, and 'tis lucky indeed for her I have been able to arrange such a good match."

"Right," Peter replied shortly, and stood up. "Let us be off, so."

Annie came forward then with a full bottle of whiskey which she presented to the man. He looked at the label.

"By god, that's fine stuff," he said. "Thankee kindly, woman of the house."

He looked at me and nodded, a courtesy I returned, and I could hear, as they went out of the house, the matchmaker asking after me.

Annie shook her head, as if apologising for the uncouthness of the fellow, then called to her sister who seemed to have been lurking right behind the door, for she came in at once. I recognised the young woman whom I had seen at the ill-fated wedding celebration. Stout and red-faced though she was, she had the sweetest smile, and in it I could see the likeness with her prettier older sister.

"Settled?" she asked.

"Settled. Just about."

"Thanks be to God. At long last."

I congratulated her, asking if the young man in question was to her liking, and if it was the good-looking fellow I had seen with her at the wedding..

The sisters laughed.

"Luke, is it?" said Annie. "Sure Sal and Luke have been lovebirds since they were wee-uns."

I must have looked confused because Sal then explained why the marriage could not have been arranged before now. For many years, she'd had the care of her mother, an invalid. This person, it seemed, took exception to any man who came looking to court Sal, and especially to Luke Colletty, whom she claimed was of tinker stock and not near good enough for her daughter.

"Tinkers?" I asked.

"Travelling people, who go from townland to townland mending pots," Sal said. "But Luke never did that. Nor did his father or his grandfather. And if his great-grandfather did, so what? They are good people."

Annie cut in with some venom, "God forgive me but the poisonous ould wagon used any excuse to keep Sal unmarried and tied to her side."

"So has your mother at last come around?" I asked, most shocked at the words Annie used in speaking of the woman who had given birth to her.

"Not at all. But she's going bewildered and can't lay down the law any more," Annie said, adding piously, if somewhat inappropriately, given her previous remarks, "God love her."

"I suppose you are a good catch with the farm." I said to Sal.

The women exchanged glances and laughed some more.

"When mam dies, the farm will go to our cousin, Brian, who lives in the County Monaghan," Annie said. "Daughters do not inherit, Martha. Luckily Brian is a good soul who is happy to see Sal settled and has agreed to provide the dowry and the two cows from the farm."

I sighed. How unfair ever is a woman's lot. My one consolation is that all over the world now there are brave women, agitating for change. I can only hope and pray it will happen in my lifetime, if not for the sake of my daughters, then at least for any granddaughters I may have.

"So where have Peter and... and the other gentleman gone?"

"Mikey Dan a gentleman! That'll be the day," Sal chuckled as if I had made a fine joke.

"They have gone to walk Luke's land, to make sure it is acceptable," Annie explained.

"Which of course it is," Sal added.

"After that, there will be some more discussion, probably more greasing of palms, and then, well, wedding bells can sound."

The two sisters got a hold of each other and danced around and around the kitchen, kicking up their heels. I could not stop myself smiling at the sight and was almost inclined to join in. Nevertheless, it all still seemed to me a primitive way of carrying on, until suddenly I called to mind our dear Queen and her many children. Were their marriages, too, not arranged? Was land not walked, metaphorically speaking at least? And were bloodlines not as equally important?

Soon Kitty returned with the children. They had been out in the woods picking nettles and gorse, with care I hoped, given the prickly nature of the plants. It seemed they were well used to the task for no one had got stung or badly scratched, excepting little Pegeen, and she made no great fuss, bless her. They had collected two basketfuls, and I asked what they would be doing with what they had.

"We can boil up a lovely soup with the young nettles," said Annie, "while the gorse blossoms make a fine syrup."

This was all of great interest to me and the remainder of the afternoon was pleasantly spent preparing these delicacies.

The next morning, Kitty and I set off for the barracks where Lily was being held until her case came up in before the magistrates. Our professed aim was to bring clean linen and something to eat for the girl, but we were hoping to meet with her as well. Peter had somehow found out that that Sergeant Hackett would be away for several hours down the country, Ballycanew way, investigating the theft of a horse, and this, we hoped, would make our underlying intention easier to realise. Indeed, the fresh-faced young constable left in charge received us most courteously. He was quite prepared to take the bundle from us, after apologetically explaining that he would have to search it. Since we had foreseen this, we had not placed anything inside, in the form of notes or similar that could cause problems for Lily. However, I needed to talk to the girl as a matter of urgency, and at first it seemed the constable was not inclined to permit us in to see her, presumably following strict instruction from his Sergeant.

My friend proved adept at playing on the lad's better nature, however. Added to which he must have been impressed by the sweet and gentle nature of his charge, so that when Kitty told him that we simply wished to try and lift the girl's spirits and pray with her – showing him the rosary that she had brought for the purpose – he relented and led us to the room in which Lily was being held. After all, he probably thought, what danger could two old biddies present?

Used to the official buildings that housed police stations in London, I had been amazed to find that this barracks consisted simply of a couple of knocked together, comprising a little front office, behind which the Sergeant and his constables lived. One of the back bedrooms served as a make-shift cell, and this was where Lily was presently languishing.

She lay on a hard bunk covered with a straw mattress, the only other furniture being a small table and a rickety looking chair. The floor was bare boards, the windows were barred, and a bucket stood beside the bed. No dignity here for the poor prisoner. As for Lily herself, her pretty face was puffed from weeping, though she tried to smile when she saw us.

Evidently the young constable intended to remain in the room during our stay, which did not chime with our intentions at all, positioning himself by the door, looking awkward but determined. I gave Kitty a little nod: we had devised a plan to deal with this eventuality. After banalities regarding Lily's health, to which she replied, with a glance at the constable, that she was well and was being treated kindly enough, she made the shocking disclosure that we were the first visitors she'd had, no member of her own family, not her father nor any of her brothers having yet made an appearance. As far as they were concerned, it seemed the poor girl was to be abandoned to her fate. Kitty then proposed the prayers, Lily being much surprised at this, knowing full well that I was not of her faith. However, we three knelt together, while the constable looked on, more and more uncomfortable.

Suddenly, Kitty collapsed as in a faint. I rushed to support her, while Lily hastened to bring her a cup of water from the jug on the table. When she tried to give it, Kitty started choking and fell back again, rolling her eyes.

"Oh, God," Lily cried. "Whatever is the matter? Oh, dear God."

"She is quite overcome," I said. "She was weak already but the journey here has taxed her strength terribly. She needs air." I made as if to lift her but showed that it was beyond my strength. "Will you remove her to the yard, constable, for I cannot?"

He showed panic then: a young man not used to dealing with respectable ladies of a certain age. I knew that he wished me to accompany him, as he supported Kitty out of the room, but I did not budge, stating firmly that we would continue our quiet prayers in the hope that Mrs. Melrose would soon be herself again. He did not insist, thank goodness, in his hurry to remove the poor moaning woman, and left us be.

Immediately I reassured Lily, who was quite distraught, that Kitty was perfectly well, her turn being a ruse to leave the two of us alone. We were striving, I explained, to prove her innocence, as we both truly believed in it, but that I needed her to tell me in as much detail as possible exactly what had transpired that night and who was present in the house, as far as she knew. Luckily the girl showed spirit and did not waste time in silly questions or laments.

What she described was this: Following the sudden break-up of the wedding party, after the row with the Straw Boys, Francis was in a foul temper, shouting oaths, stamping and tearing at his hair. His sister Briege seemingly was the one person able to pacify him, and after a while he calmed down. Or rather, Lily said, his rage abated but turned into an equally terrifying frenzy of high-spirits, demanding that the remaining stalwarts come back with them to the Kinsella farm, to continue the celebrations.

"He was laughing like a madman," she said. 'The men joined in. They were all for it, cursing the straw boys and vowing revenge… Mrs. Hudson, I was very much afraid." She paused at the memory, then continued. "We rushed back along the road, Francie dragging me tight by the arm, in case I might even then run away. I still have the bruises." She rolled up her sleeve. Indeed, dark purple marks marred her white skin.

"They continued the party, Mrs. Hudson," she went on, "with heavy drinking and feasting, swearing curses on their enemies, singing rough songs. You cannot imagine how horrible it was… Oh, how I wished you could have succeeded in getting me away before the marriage…"

"Who exactly was there? Can you give me their names?"

As she did, I duly marked them down in a notebook I had brought for the purpose. Mossie, of course, and her own father and brothers I knew. Jack Keane and Mikey Dan were among them, too. The other names meant nothing to me.

"To your knowledge, did any of these men hold a grudge against Francie?"

She shook her head.

"I do not think so. They all seemed on the best of terms. But maybe it could be so. He angered many people, you know."

"I can well imagine it."

She explained again how at last Francie had been persuaded to let her go to bed. Briege had then brought her the warm drink of herbs, telling her it would soothe her, and, indeed, she had very soon slept and knew nothing more until the morning.

"You didn't hear any shouting or quarrels?"

"Raised voices, yes, but only the way men shout when they have drink taken. Nothing that sounded like a quarrel. Not while I was awake. Though you know, I did bury myself under the blanket… Although…"

"Yes?"

"Well, now I remember I had the strangest dream. I was climbing up and up and up, a mountain I think it was, but every time I thought I had reached the top, there was more to climb and I was afraid because they were coming after me."

"Who was?"

"That I cannot say, Mrs. Hudson. Perhaps it was Francie and his friends, but truly I cannot say. In my dream I heard their steps getting near, so I hid myself under a rock, and they passed me by."

"You escaped then?"

"No, because then they started calling my name. They were coming back. And then just as they reached me, I woke up. And that's when I found... Francie..."

We heard the step of the constable approaching and quickly knelt as before.

"Your friend is recovered," he said, regarding us with some suspicion, which I hope our attitude of pious prayer dispelled. "You must go now."

"Goodbye, Lily," I said rising and embracing her. "God bless you, my child. Try to keep your spirits up."

"I will, Mrs. Hudson," she said, and looked direct into my eyes. Truly she seemed calmer than before and even managed a little smile. 'I am so glad you came... to pray with me."

"Thank you for letting us see her," I told the constable as we left the cell. "Prayer is a great solace, is it not?" God forgive me for the deception.

I explained all to Kitty on the way back. We tried to reassure each other that we were making progress, although there was little enough to show. We wondered too about the dream, considering that, in her deep sleep, Lily might have heard something happening in the room. To be sure, I myself have sometimes noticed a connection between my dreams and the wakened world. For instance, I recall once dreaming of a scene from my childhood in which a blacksmith from my home village was hammering a horseshoe, very loudly, only then to wake to the sound of Mr. H pounding on the door of my bedroom during one of his strange turns, demanding a midnight cup of coffee. I now related this to Kitty, to which confidence she nodded knowingly. My friend has never hidden her conviction that Mr. H presumed too much on my good nature. Perhaps, we now mused, in this present case, what Lily heard in her sleep was Francie calling to her in his final moments.

What then if she had woken up and seen his assailant? Not a happy thought.

When we got back to the farm, Peter was sitting at table, eating a plate of stew. Annie offered some to us but we both preferred, after the agitation of the morning, to confine ourselves to dry biscuits and tea.

"So how is Lily?" Annie asked.

"I think our visit encouraged her somewhat," Kitty said. "You know, not one of her family has been to see her."

Annie shook her head. "What a bunch of blackguards," she said, then looked at her husband, who seemed preoccupied.

"Tell them, Peter, what you said to me," she urged.

He swallowed a mouthful of stew and took a breath. He put down his fork.

"Now I'm not saying, ladies, that you are in the right regarding Lily's innocence..."

He paused.

"Tell them," Annie said again.

"How and ever, I was set a-wondering to myself who else might have a sufficient grudge against Francie."

"Among the hundreds," Annie added. "I'd say there'd be a shorter list of people who did not feel bitter towards the same feller."

"Hold your whisht, woman," Peter said, though not unkindly. He turned back to us. "Now, Kitty, you know how I have long been active in the Land League."

She nodded.

"You must realise, Martha, that we have been agitating for this many a year against the wrongs inflicted on the native Irish over centuries." His voice rose with emotion. "It is high time for those who toil on the land to own it, and not pay exorbitant rents to landlords who often do not even live in this country." He shook his head of pepper and salt curls. "Of course, there has been much

135

opposition from that parasitic class, aided by the forces of oppression, the Castle in Dublin, the judiciary…"

"The English," said Annie, glancing at me. "Not to say anything against you personally, Martha. I have seen how sympathetic you are, and know from Kitty that you refused to stay with the Timminses, when they asked you."

"The Timminses!" cried Peter. "That Colonel! He is has proved a dangerous enemy to our movement. He accuses us of being Fenians and sees plots against Crown rule everywhere."

"Did he think Francie was plotting something, then? Are you suggesting the Colonel might have had him killed over it?" I was astonished at the notion, though with an admixture of wicked pleasure.

Peter burst out laughing. "By God, that would be a fine thing. Not at all, Martha. No, just to explain further. You see, while I and most like me believe in peaceful methods to achieve our ends as promoted by Mr. Parnell and his ilk, there are admittedly those who would take a more violent path."

"Francie?" asked Kitty.

"Quite the opposite," Peter answered. "Although I suspect he might have played both sides for his own twisted pleasure. To be sure he would have had us believe he was in sympathy with our cause. But for some time we have been suspecting Francie of acting as an informant to the Colonel or his officers. There have been raids on members of our movement which could only have resulted from inside knowledge."

"Brutal raids," Annie added. "Women and children have not been spared."

"I understand," I replied. "So you think that someone might have taken revenge on Francie for these activities?"

"I am not saying it is so," Peter replied. "But it could be."

I drew out the list of names of those present at the Kinsella house the night of the murder and showed it to Peter.

"Are any of these people familiar to you as victims, then?" I asked.

He looked it over and shook his head.

"Not that I can tell."

Annie took the paper from him and regarded it thoughtfully.

"Dinny Doyle....Wasn't his brother raided a while back? Dinny might not be too happy with Francie, if he thought he betrayed Martin."

Peter considered the matter. "That's true enough, but I can't see Martin Doyle, or Dinny either for that matter, killing him over it. Certainly not in that way, in the bedroom. They would be more like to lurk down some boreen in ambush, to give him a good thrashing."

"But what if the drink had gone to their heads?" Annie asked. "If they'd had a skinful of poitín, Peter, they wouldn't be thinking straight. A false word could act like a match to inflame them."

Peter nodded, but reluctantly, and resumed eating his stew, which I thought must have got quite cold in the meantime.

So here, I thought to myself, was another line to follow and consider. If Francie indeed acted as a spy for the Colonel, he would have made many enemies, and ruthless ones at that. Then there was the question of the knife: according to Briege, it was not one from the house, which meant the crime must have been premeditated. Unless of course local men were in the habit of carrying knives around with them. Peter did not seem to think so, or at least not the sort of knife we had seen near the body. I sighed, quite out of my depth in among all the intricacies of Irish politicking, floundering about with no clear idea how to proceed. It still seemed that the only way to prove Lily's innocence was to unmask the guilty, but this was turning out to be the most difficult case in which I had yet involved myself.

Chapter Ten

There is in Ireland a strange and to my mind decidedly barbaric practice surrounding the death of a person. The night before the funeral, mourners visit the house of the deceased, ostensibly to pay their respects, but in fact, as I was soon to discover, to get drunk and often quite disorderly over the body of the departed, laid out for all to see in its coffin.

I knew nothing of this custom until Peter and Annie started discussing it, after news spread among us that Francie's body had been released by the coroner for burial. Our hosts were preparing to attend the wake, as they called it, though not, they assured us, to stay long, just to pay their respects. Clearly they did not expect me to accompany them, so when I expressed the wish to do so, they were most taken aback. It would not be appropriate, Peter said, under the circumstances, meaning, I suppose, because of the hostility of the Kinsella family towards myself. However, I argued that the death of any of God's creatures, especially in such a terrible way, was to be respectfully commemorated, and that, while Mossie and Briege were as convinced of Lily's guilt as I of her innocence, my sympathies towards them for their loss were sincere and heartfelt. After this most Christian speech of mine, Peter grudgingly agreed to my joining them.

My true motives, of course, were not quite so pious or transparent. I was longing to see the inside of the Kinsella dwelling again, and also closely to observe those who came to mourn.

Thus it was that, the day falling away to an angry sunset, purple clouds bulging over a sky the colour of sulphur, (and leaving Veronica in charge of the little ones), we piled into the rattle trap –

which I was getting quite used to by then – to bump once again over the dusty lanes to the Kinsella farm. There we found crowds present already, milling around the ramshackle yard – the vicious black dog by the sound of its angry barks banished to the same outhouse where Lily had been confined. As each newcomer entered the house, he or she commiserated with Mossie and Briege, who were seated by the door. I noticed how everyone seemed to be muttering the same phrase – "I am sorry for your trouble." Kitty did likewise, so I followed suit, and, though rewarded by surprised glares, it seemed to me that the bereaved were too numb with grief to be truly incensed at my presence.

Following a line of people, we shuffled into the bedroom, where an open coffin was set on two wooden chairs, candles lit at its head and foot. An old woman sat in the corner wailing loudly, and I wondered in a whisper to Kitty, if she were a member of the family, so upset she seemed.

"She may be for all I know," Kitty said, "but more like she is being paid to keen," explaining this as yet another funerary custom.

It was an eerie sound, more primitive than Christian. As I listened, I could make out some of the words, "Aye, aye, aye, no more, no more, your place is empty, evermore, aye, aye, aye..." I shivered and not just because the window was open, letting in the evening chill.

We moved with the others towards the coffin, an unadorned box of raw wood in which Francie lay, dressed in white and lying on white sheets, looking very different from the bloodied corpse I had seen only a few days before. He was clean and shaved, his golden hair carefully brushed, a wooden crucifix around his neck, his hands folded on his breast and a set of rosary beads made of jet entwining his fingers. A woman in front of me muttered, "Sure, doesn't he look like one of the saints in heaven, God love him," and then she bowed her head in silent prayer.

139

What she said was true. As I gazed upon that face, it was hard to credit that such beauty could cloak such viciousness. I stood for a moment contemplating the boy, and thinking that, whatever he was like, he was too young to have had his life so unkindly snatched from him. Just then a sudden gust of wind from the open window set the curtain billowing and the candles flames flickering. Francie's features seemed to quiver, a sardonic smile twisting those full lips, pale eyelids bulging, fingers clutching. I fell back, gasping in horror, almost expecting those eyes to burst open, that mouth to utter vile abominations, those hands to reach up and grab me. Kitty, who must have witnessed the same effect, blessed herself several times as if to ward off the evil.

Then, as swiftly as it came, the breeze died down and all was as before, that waxen face immobile, the hands piously clasped and still. My rational mind told me that it was a trick of the light, yet I found myself shaking with a supernatural dread that was most alien to me.

It was with great relief, therefore, we passed out of the bedroom and proceeded back to the kitchen, where a different mood altogether held sway. People were chatting and even laughing together. The air was thick with the odour of burning tobacco, worse than anything Mr. H might have used, and I noticed that most of the men, and even some of the women, were smoking from clay pipes which they picked up from the table and stuffed with black leaf left there for their use. With no care for hygiene, various foodstuffs were heaped close by on the same table – potato cakes, buns and biscuits, soda bread, sausages, a ham from which slices were even then being gouged with a knife that looked to me very like the one used to skewer poor Francie. Beside this feast stood a big pot of tea, bottles of porter and the inevitable poitín. A line from Mr. Shakespeare's Danish play came unbidden to my mind: something about the funeral baked meats furnishing the marriage table. Here, cruelly, the action was reversed.

Despite the convivial atmosphere, I could well imagine how all might soon turn rowdy from the way folk were pouring drink into themselves. Even the priest, Father Joe, as everyone called him, looking more apoplectic than ever, had a great mug of porter in his hand, and was already loudly slurring his words. Pointing him out to Kitty, I asked how anyone could revere such a person, but she explained that it was not the individual man but his role as representative of God that inspired reverence. Well, I thought to myself, that's as may be, but it doesn't change the fact that this particular representative is hardly worthy. Indeed, I strongly suspected that Kitty secretly agreed with me, but loyalty to her faith made her rise to the priest's defence.

At my request, Annie started discreetly identifying to me several of the other individuals present. I recognised Lily's brothers, of course. They had not bothered to visit their sister in prison, but now deemed it fitting to attend the wake despite Lily's presumed involvement in the crime. The big one, Ollie, was looking even more vacant and witless than usual, while the other two, Tighe and Seb, as dwarfish and repulsive as their father, were ogling from under low brows various young girls, grinning and nudging each other, and occasionally calling things out that made the girls blush or reply sharply.

A disgraceful way to carry on, as I remarked to Annie, who however surprised me by replying that wakes were a grand place for couples to meet each other, and that many a match had been made under such circumstances. Again, I felt myself on the wrong foot in this society.

She then pointed out Dinny Doyle, along with his brother Martin, the same who had been evicted possibly on the word of the deceased. Neither of the brothers looked at all guilt-ridden, but neither did they look heartbroken at the death of their supposed friend, eating and drinking with relish.

"And there's Jack Keane," Annie said, indicating a particularly disreputable individual, a dusty-looking older man with a deep scar on his cheek, as if someone had carved it with a blade, and perhaps they had.

"Jack is a shanachie, a great one for the storytelling. You could while the night away listening to him." She smiled. "He's good too for pishogues."

"Pishogues?" I asked. "Whatever are they?"

"Charms against the evil ones," Kitty put in. Her expression told me not to say anything more.

"Charms for cures, too. Jack is thick with Briege," Annie continued. "They say 'twas he taught her the secret ways."

At that moment, this person of so many dubious talents was accosted by an almost equally unsavoury looking individual, whom I recognised as the matchmaker, Mikey Dan. Noticing perhaps that we were looking his way, he raised his hand in greeting to Annie, and she acknowledged him back. Between them, they had speedily effected the terms of the match between Annie's sister Sal and her sweetheart, Luke, so everyone was happy.

"Excepting mammy, of course," Annie said. "She still thinks Luke not good enough. But no one ever would be. Anyway, it's all but done and dusted now, and nothing the ould biddy can do about it." Said with a degree of satisfaction. "You probably think me undutiful, Martha," Annie went on, perhaps noticing my expression. "You haven't met my mother, nor seen how she contrived over the years to keep Sal with her, an old maid."

"Mary Leary never was a very nice person," Kitty added. "Though I feel sorry for her now she is bedridden and losing her wits."

"She'll be fine," Annie said. "Better than ever with Sal and Luke to wait upon her. I expect Sal the fool will be round every day to keep an eye on her."

Kitty and Annie then moved off to talk to friends, while I stayed where I was to study the people around me. There were plenty of rough-looking individuals present who looked as if they well knew how to wield a knife, including William Cullen, himself. He had joined up with Mikey Dan and Jack Keane, the three seeming as thick as thieves, as the saying goes, looking about themselves in a surreptitious manner. I diverted myself with fancying that they were rightly thieves and about to make off with the family silver, although in this bare hovel they were surely unlikely to find any such thing.

In case you might think the whole room was full of low-life individuals, however, I should say that the majority were simply honest-looking neighbours of the deceased who, like Peter and Annie, considered it their bounden duty to pay their respects to the family. If they let their hair down somewhat at this wake, well, I conceded that they had little enough otherwise to distract them from the hard daily grind.

I am sure Mr. H would have noticed all manner of significant details amid this motley throng but I am afraid nothing struck me in particular. If the Irish way of doing things was unlike anything I had experienced before, that was all that was odd about it. I sighed in continuing frustration.

Suddenly I became aware of someone standing at my side, a little too close, and turned to find there Florrie Sweetnam. My surprise must have shown on my face, for he started to laugh.

"You did not expect to find me here, Mrs. Hudson," he said.

"No, indeed," I replied. "But then, I have not been in this country long enough fully to understand its customs."

"I am merely being neighbourly, you know,"

Neighbourly or nosy, I thought. I noticed all the same that he was not dressed as flamboyantly as usual, in a black jacket with a grey waistcoat. I remarked on this.

"Oh, if I turned up in my usual style, I expect I would get knocked about," he replied jovially enough. "Although I brought Thomas with me as protection against all these Romans." He chuckled some more and indicated his handsome servant, standing at a distance with a group of younger people.

"Funerals, you know, are the great Irish diversion," he continued. "Tomorrow, the church will be packed even though most of those present will only have had a fleeting acquaintance with Francie."

"I was quite surprised that he has so many friends here tonight." I laid ironic emphasis on the word "friends".

"Oh well, as to that… You know as well as I do that most people are here for quite other reasons. Including yourself, I rather think."

I had to admit to that one.

"All the same," I continued, "it seems to me to be more like an unseemly party than a dignified expression of sympathy. All this drinking and smoking…"

"It is not very English, I agree," Florrie replied. "However, for the Irish, it is a way of exorcising their grief. Actually, the Roman church is, as I understand it, quite against these wakes."

"Really!" I replied, looking across at Father Joe, now slumped comatose in a chair. "One would not guess it."

"Well, that is to say, the church bishops, the hierarchy, you know, are opposed, at least to the drinking. But there is not much they can do on the ground, try as they might. As for the smoking, that is very much part of the magic of the ritual."

"To choke the devils like it is choking me, I suppose."

"To choke the faeries, more like… You know, I like to collect folk beliefs where I find them, Mrs. Hudson. Someday, I might even put them in a book." He smiled lazily. The second book he had aspirations to write, after his family history. I would believe it when I saw it, I thought, but nodded politely.

Now he lowered his voice. "You were there, Mrs. Hudson. Is it a fact that Francie was dead before the priest came?"

"Certainly," I replied. "He had been dead some hours, as I think I told you before. That is why I am so sure of Lily's innocence."

"Hmm," he said.

"What is it?"

"Well, you know, the belief here is that the faeries take possession of the soul of one unshriven before death."

The faeries again. I just shook my head.

"Although, as I understand it," Florrie continued. "Father Joe is saying that there was a tiny flicker of life left, so he was able to anoint him."

"No, that's not true," I replied. "I remember quite clearly him saying that he could not do so, for the man was quite dead."

"Well, he has changed his tune now, for the family's sake, I suppose."

That was bad news, indeed. I was hoping the priest would repeat before the magistrates, that Francie was long passed by the time he arrived.

"No one believes him, of course," Florrie said cheerfully, adding. "No, Francie is well away with the faeries. I trust they are giving him a hard time."

I must have looked down-hearted, for my companion said that he expected the priest would tell the truth in court if required. "For he has to swear on the Bible, you know."

That was something at least.

"Going back to the heavy smoking here," Florrie said. "I recently came across a tale to justify the practice at wakes, which might amuse you." He paused. "The day her son was crucified the Blessed Virgin Mary was so upset that she picked up a pipe and tobacco for comfort, and took the first few draws herself."

I stared at him for a moment, then laughed. "You are joking, of course."

"Not a bit of it. There are all sorts of strange beliefs and practices on these occasions. Why, there are some fellows outside playing cards. I wouldn't be at all surprised if they come in shortly to play a hand with Francie."

Now I knew he was making fun of me.

Kitty rejoining us then, I asked her about it.

"Oh yes," she replied, to my astonishment. "I have heard it happens, although I agree that in the circumstances here it would be most inappropriate."

"In any circumstances, surely?"

She merely shrugged. I feared she was fast losing the veneer of civilisation she had gained over near enough thirty years in London, and was reverting to native ways.

Florrie laughed merrily and remarked, "You see, my dear Mrs. Hudson, I would never lie to you." He gave me a significant wink.

Thank goodness for Kitty, who now cut in to ask if I was ready to leave.

"Surely not so soon?" exclaimed our companion. "The fun has hardly started, you know, ladies. Wait at least until the piper arrives. And there's Jack Keane might entertain us with one of his endless tales."

That did not sound like a particularly enticing prospect, however, and, being fatigued enough with the evening, I agreed to go home with Kitty. Thereupon, expressing further regrets at our departure, Florrie excused himself to go and chat to a stout woman, overdressed in grubby purple silk, who had just entered.

"Moira," he cried out. "Moira Shaughnessy. As lovely as always."

"Ever the gallant," Kitty commented.

146

I nodded wryly and looked at the clock on the mantel to find what was the time. However, the hands pointed to the sixth hour, which was certainly not correct, and I soon observed that the hands on the clock were not moving. When I remarked on this to Kitty, however, she explained that the clock had been stopped on purpose to show the very time that Francie was supposed to have passed on, that is to say, at six in the morning, the moment when Lily had been discovered standing over him.

"Though, of course, as we know," Kitty said, "he died much earlier."

She also pointed out to me how the wall mirror had been covered over with a cloth.

"So as not to trap the spirit of the dead inside it," she told me, adding, "For the same reason the window in the bedroom was left open, you know, to ensure that the soul of the departed is not trapped in the house, and to enable it to fly away."

More superstition. At least, the rational side of me thought so. However, the memory of standing by the coffin and the tricky effect of the flickering candlelight still made me shudder, part of me almost believing that Francie's bad spirit was indeed trapped in the house.

"What are you thinking, Martha?" Kitty asked.

"Not very much, to be sure," I replied, shaking off the notion. "I was hoping to get some clue from the people here, but I confess, I am no wiser than I was before."

"Poor Lily," said Kitty. "It looks bad for her."

I am afraid I had to agree, for the talk we had overheard going around the room was all against the girl, and all for revenge, as if it were the innocent victim who lay cold in the other room, his young widow the wicked murderous one.

As if to underline this, two old women beside us were expressing that very sentiment.

"A noose is what she deserves," one was saying.

147

"A noose is too good for her, Eileen," quoth her companion, drawing her shawl about herself. "In the old days, the same hussy would have been burnt for a witch, and well would she merit it."

The two crones nodded in agreement. I guessed, all the same, that the pair might be seen at mass most days, and consider themselves the very best of Christians.

"By the bye, Maggie, how's your rheumatics, these days?" the first woman went on, à propos it seemed of nothing. "Did poor Briege's potion work at all?"

"It's a wonder, Eileen. Sure I don't know myself. The pains have all but gone."

"I must ask her about my bad chest. She has the gift, for sure."

"Ah, that she has, God bless her."

And with such more harmless chat, the two wandered off.

Maggie, I thought. Hadn't I heard that name before? It came to me then, the Timmins' terrible cook and mother to the Treasure. I looked after the woman but could see no likeness and Kitty, when I asked, could not say.

"Anyway," she said, "isn't Maggie a very common name in these parts," which was nothing but the truth.

"What is this gift they say Briege has?" I asked then. "I have heard something of it already. How she has remedies better than the doctors."

Annie had just rejoined us, and it was she who replied. "Briege, is it?" she said. "Isn't she great one for to know the herbs for the cures, better now even than Jack Keane himself. There are times you wouldn't want to go to a man for help. Sure to God, I was in terrible pain, Martha, after Pegeen was born, but Briege made up a bottle for me that had me well in no time at all." Annie looked across at the subject of our conversation, standing with Father Joe, or rather, seeming to hold him up, so drunk he was. The daughter of the house looked all spent, her face yellower than ever, with shadows like purple bruises under her eyes. Still, she was strong enough to bear the great weight of the priest.

"You can see the poor soul betimes in the woods and fields," Annie was telling us, "gathering berries and roots. Even up on Knocnacoill, and not many would dare to go there."

"Veronica told me of it," I said.

"Some even say," Annie lowered her voice, "that Briegeen was once taken by the faeries, for hasn't she the one leg shorter than the other. They let her go because she entered a pact with them, but no one knows what it is." She could see how doubtful I was from my face. "That's what they say," she continued. "Not that I believe it myself. Not necessarily... But come, let me show you her laboratory."

I was not at all sure of the propriety of wandering freely about the place, but since Annie seemed to think it was in order, we followed her into a poky enough room at the rear of the cottage, where a fire was burning in a small range. I should not have called the place a laboratory. To my mind, that definition was more in line with Mr. H's collection of test tubes, crucibles, boiling flasks, burners and so on. This place would more appropriately have been described as a devil's kitchen. Drying herbs and twigs hung like skeletal hands from the rafters, while jars containing seeds and berries and other queerer contents stood on the shelf below them. Even now, a big iron pot hanging from a hook over the fire, was bubbling with a noxious smelling liquid. Again I recalled Mr. Shakespeare, but this time it was the witches in his *Macbeth* with their foul cauldron.

"Double, double, toil and trouble..." I intoned. Annie looked at me sideways and Kitty giggled.

"Yes," she said, "it is rather like that, Martha."

We explained the reference to Annie, who, however, was none the wiser, the Bard of Avon seemingly not part of her education.

149

Looking around, I could not help but wonder how little Lily could ever have fitted into this strange household. It was so much Briege's place. Could Lily, as a married woman, ever have taken precedence over her unmarried sister-in-law?

At that moment, the same woman burst into the kitchen, not one bit happy to see us there.

"I was told you were in here. What are you about?" She was glaring at me in particular. "Spying, is it, missus? You'll get no satisfaction here, so." She gave a bitter laugh.

"Not at all," Annie replied in placatory tones, explaining how we were interested in her herbal remedies. Despite this, Briege continued to regard us with hostile suspicion, and I think would have thrown us out without further ceremony had Kitty not then intervened. She asked if Briege would be able to provide a cure for the back pain to which she was a constant martyr – this was the honest truth, as I knew well, since she had consulted with Dr. Watson on the matter. The young woman, in softer tones, started asking questions as a medical man or apothecary might, requesting Kitty to describe the symptoms in more specific detail. She even pressed gently on Kitty's back to find the source of the hurt.

"I can make up a rub for you," she said finally. "It may not cure but it should ease. Give me two days to prepare it. Tomorrow is Francie's funeral, as you know, and I will not have time before that."

Kitty expressed gratitude, but insisted that Briege should not put herself out.

"It will provide a good distraction," the young woman replied.

We quitted her then, again expressing our sympathy at the passing of her brother. This even earned a weary smile from her as she stirred the cauldron with a ladle. I wondered what was brewing there. It was surely no soup.

150

Back in the kitchen, the piper had at last arrived and was regaling the company with merry jigs, where solemn laments might, to my mind, be more in order. People were actually up dancing and I even espied Florrie Sweetnam in the midst of all, hopping about with the woman in the purple silk dress. He waved across at me, as if to say "What larks!"

However, Annie, I was relieved to learn, expressed herself as anxious as ourselves to leave, though Peter, when consulted, said he would like to stay on a while, if Annie could drive the bone-shaker back.

"He works so very hard," she told us, as if in apology. "You know well, Kitty, he is not one who goes for a jar as a general rule, but he does like the bit of company, and I am glad to see him out enjoying himself, even if it is at a wake."

We nodded in understanding, although I noticed Kitty pursing her lips in disapproval. Her late husband, Edward Melrose, was constantly boasting the fact that he never touched alcoholic beverages, Henry quipping privately to me that he himself didn't touch them either. Just swallowed them down, as he toasted me with a glass of claret. Not, I hasten to add, that dear Henry drank to excess, but, whether either of the men indulged or not, mattered little in the end. They were both carried off far too soon.

Leaving Annie to say her farewells to Mossie, who in any case was well into his cups at that stage, we went outside to find, as Florrie had mentioned, four men playing cards on a broken plough, a bottle of poitín on the ground beside them. I recognised William Cullen, Mikey Dan and Jack Keane, along with another equally unsavoury looking fellow. Would they really go in to the bedroom later, and deal a hand to Francie? Surely it was too macabre to imagine.

Annie came out then with mourners of her acquaintance, likewise heading home, and leaving behind the wilder elements, among whom I trusted Peter was not to be numbered. I pitied Briege having to stay in their midst all night and then clean up after them. The next morning, indeed, Peter informed us that an ugly row had broken out between the Kinsellas and the Cullens, not as you might expect, over the death of Francie, but over the loss of the field. Mossie, it seems, had vehemently insisted that, under the circumstances, the agreement was null and void, while William Cullen and his sons argued that the deal was done, dusted and over. The field was now legally theirs. I am glad we were not there to see the unseemly ensuing fisticuffs, which left both sides bloodied, Dinnie Doyle and other friends of Francie taking the side of the Kinsellas.

"Yet another case for the Resident Magistrate," Peter remarked.

Chapter Eleven

The morning of the funeral the weather broke at last. The balmy days of early summer gave way to angry skies of lowering clouds that held themselves back until we mourners set off in procession to the chapel, thereafter bursting over us as if to replace the tears that few were shedding at Francie's demise. I was glad of my stout black umbrella with the dog's head handle that had once belonged to dear Henry. It was big enough to cover both Kitty and myself, although it could not protect the hems of our skirts against the mud of the road. Having already spent a good hour brushing them clean from the last walk, I feared we should again be put to a great degree of trouble to get rid of it.

The old woman who had sat keening beside the coffin the night before had now been joined by several others, including Briege herself, and the lamentations they made along the way sounded raucous and primitive. It sent a chill over me, as if this gloomy train were journeying back through centuries to darker times, when old gods ruled this place. Really now, Martha, I thought, and shook my head to dispel such fancies.

The coffin itself was being conveyed without any pomp on the back of a cart, but, when we reached the church, it was lifted down by four black-suited pallbearers, to be carried inside. One of them I recognised as Mossie Kinsella, now sporting an ugly cut on his face and a blackening eye, the result it must be of the brawl of the night before. The men shouldered the coffin up the aisle and placed it on a trestle in front of the altar.

As Florrie had intimated, the church was as packed as it had been for the wedding, the locals coming to pay their respects or, more likely, to gawk. We managed to find seats for ourselves near the rear, squashed in among dripping coats and skirts. The service once more was in the Latin tongue that no one except the Pope in Rome and his bishops and priests speak anymore. It undoubtedly has a certain resonance, however, even coming from the less than wholesome mouth of Father Joe.

Once again, I sat down and stood up and knelt and sat again, along with the others, and bowed my head at appropriate moments, even though again I had little idea as to what was going on. At last it came to the moment when Father Joe was to say a few words (in the English tongue at least) about the deceased.

He stood up in front of the altar where only a few days previously Francie had lolled, awaiting the arrival of his bride. It already seemed an age away. Now the priest spread his arms wide and addressed us thus:

"Francis Kinsella," he began, "Yes indeed, Francie, as we all knew him, was a jewel, might I say, among the young men of our community. He shone like a comet in the sky, shooting across the firmament far, far too briefly..."

Father Joe carried on in this vein for quite a while, the congregation shuffling, peeking at each other with ironic or amazed expression on their faces, and in some cases, I am afraid, unable to suppress giggles. Surely no one could recognise in this effusive eulogy anything of the vile individual whose remains lay in the box. Of course, it is not the thing to speak ill of the dead, and yet to go so far in the opposite direction was most extraordinary.

Father Joe then moved on to the subject of revenge.

"*An eye for an eye,*" he intoned. "*A tooth for a tooth. Vengeance is mine, saith the Lord.* That's in the Holy Bible, don't you know. The cruel murderer of this pearl among men will rightly spend an eternity suffering the fires of hell, but," and here the priest smote fist against hand, "it is the responsibility of all good men speedily to bring this wicked, wicked woman to face her maker."

I had never heard the like from a man of God, and I hope I never shall again. I could only think that the man had been well bribed, maybe even with the strong liquor of which I am afraid his demeanour indicated he had only too recently partaken. I was strongly tempted to stand up and walk out, but refrained, not wishing to cause a scandal. I could only hope that the vast number of the congregation recognised this diatribe for the dung heap of falsehoods that it was.

Following the mass, we all trooped out into the graveyard surrounding the chapel. The rain had subsided into a mere drizzle, so we were at least spared another drenching. It was slippery underfoot, however, and the pallbearers staggered somewhat amid the grave stones – how truly frightful it would have been if they had dropped the coffin! – but at last they safely reached the pit into which Francie's remains were to be lowered. The wailing of the women continued until the priest managed to silence them, all except Briege who fell to her knees in the mud and stretched out her arms in the enormity of her grief. To me, but perhaps I am too English in my sense of propriety, it all seemed unnecessarily melodramatic. However heartbroken I was over the passing of my dear Henry, I should never ever have carried on like that.

At last the girl was prevailed on to stand, supported by a woman friend, and the priest went through the usual litany, or so I supposed, dust to dust, ashes to ashes, sprinkling a handful of soil into the pit. It was over.

This time our little party did not go back to the Kinsella house for the funeral meats. I could just imagine how unwelcome I would have been, and, as for the rest of our little group, I don't think any of them wished to see more drunken antics. Instead, we went home in a sombre mood and spent the rest of the day variously,

Peter seeing to the farm, Annie and Kitty to the house and the children, and I in my room, greatly in need of solitude and silence.

I removed my dress which was, as feared, in a parlous state from the muddy roads, and hung it up to dry. Then, having dressed myself in my robe for the time being, I lay down on my bed, though not to sleep, my mind buzzing as if my head were full of bees. Could it really be, I thought, that poor Lily was doomed? I knew her case was coming up before the magistrates, that is to say Colonel Timmins and his cronies, very soon. Despite what he had said to me earlier about leniency towards the girl, local pressure and their own prejudices might well cause them to recommend the maximum punishment. It was imperative to make progress towards discovering the real murderer, but, alas, I felt no nearer this goal. Kitty had brought me here to help her, and I was failing. Oh, how I wished I could consult erstwhile my lodger. I was sure he would have seen through the business long since.

Wednesday was overcast, with more threatening clouds, yet Annie was determined to go into Ferns for various 'messages,' and invited us to accompany her. Kitty stated her preference for staying at home, but, as I wished to send that telegram to Clara, I was pleased to go along. I also wanted to purchase, if possible, or at least order to be made, some serviceable garment, since my available wardrobe proved to be sadly lacking. Annie mentioned a seamstress who might do, though she said that I should have a better choice in Enniscorthy, suggesting a trip there later in the week. It was, of course, good of her, yet I shuddered at the thought of the long journey thither in the bone-shaker, and hoped that I could find satisfaction more locally.

Once arrived in Ferns, Annie and I agreed to go our separate ways for a couple of hours, to meet back in the square at the top of the town. I speedily managed my telegram, although the postmaster had some difficulty understanding my way of speaking, so I had to print it out for him on a sheet of paper. This recourse proved satisfactory.

"London, is it?" he said in his own country accent. "That's where your Queen Victoria lives."

"Well, yes," I replied. "Though I think she is more often at Windsor Castle, in Berkshire, you know."

The man had clearly never heard of the place, for he looked at me blankly, trying to process the information.

"Well it is for her, then, barking in her windy castle," he said at last, and spat on the floor, but otherwise showing himself not unfriendly. After all, it was not as if I were sending a personal message to Her Royal Highness. It had not escaped my notice, however, that our dear Queen is nowhere near as popular in Ireland as she is in England.

The telegram having been safely dispatched, the postmaster then directed me to the seamstress's premises, located as they were in a somewhat tumbledown house at the bottom of the hill. After some delay spent hammering on the door, I was welcomed effusively within by the seamstress herself, Mrs. O'Byrne, a slatternly enough woman of middle years with hair falling about her face and her dress somewhat undone. She apologised for that, explaining I had caught her at a bad time, glancing betimes towards the back of the shop, where behind an ill-drawn curtain there seemed to be a man in his shirt-sleeves smoking a pungent pipe. Nevertheless, she was pleased to demonstrate her wares, nodding and smiling and bobbing the while in deference to "your ladyship," as she kept calling me but, despite her courtesy, I very soon established that nothing here would do for me. The quality of the fabric alone was wanting, being rough and ready, and there was a profusion of the coarse red petticoats I had seen many of the country women wearing. As for the finish, I could have managed far better myself. Clara, indeed, could have managed better. I purchased a couple of the petticoats for the old woman, Mammo, and a shift for

Nell, thinking I could redo the seams myself back at the farm. As for my own dress, I left with a promise to think about it, which seemed the politer way, but I could tell that she was disappointed.

So now I found I had quite some time on my hands before I was due to meet up again with Annie. What to do? There is in Ferns an ancient castle of some historical note, since the town used to be a more important place than it is now. I regarded the picturesque ruins from a distance, but decided against exploring further, as the way to it led over a decidedly muddy field, and I dreaded ruining my only decent remaining dress. Instead, I made my way to the cathedral nearby. The solace and quiet there, I felt, would do my soul good, no matter that it was of the Roman Catholic denomination, for I was well used to visiting such by then. St. Aidan's called itself a cathedral, despite not being in great order, and needing much restoration. Nevertheless, it was possible to sit quietly and commune with Our Maker, which I did for a while, praying for Lily, barely disturbed by the elderly woman who was sweeping up and polishing the brass work. She acknowledged me with a nod, but otherwise left me be, and soon disappeared, presumably having finished her chores.

After a while, I became restive, and though I doubted there was much worth seeing in the place, took to walking the aisles to inspect the memorials and view the occasional window of stained glass. Coming upon a little guide book set upon a table, with a box for the ha'penny it cost, I took one up and paid the fee. Perusing it, I discovered the curious fact that remains of an older medieval cathedral, wantonly destroyed during the reign of Queen Elizabeth I, were incorporated into the fabric of the present building. I dutifully peered as directed at the pillars and the blind arcading, the episcopal effigy by the font, the lancets and viscae of the East Wall, but I am afraid none of it meant much to me. Of far more interest was the discovery that, after all, I was not alone in the place. A female figure sat huddled in a side chapel. I was inclined to pass on and leave her to her devotions, but I must have made a slight noise, because she turned her face to me. To my surprise I found that I knew her and knew her quite well.

"Augusta," I exclaimed. "Whatever is the matter?"

Mrs. Timmins' face was blotchy from weeping. In fact, as I approached, I could see that there was a fresh bruise on her cheek.

"Oh, Martha," she said, rising to her feet in some confusion, and attempting the hide the mark with her gloved hand. "How come you here?"

I explained my presence and then sat down beside her, so close that the sickly sweet smell on her breath suggested she had once more been sampling her husband's sherry. She was not, at first, inclined to confide the reason for her distress to me, but soon broke down. The Colonel had, she finally informed me in a shaking voice, got into one of his rages and had struck her.

"Goodness gracious, Augusta," I exclaimed, shocked. "This will not do. Does it happen often?"

"You know, Martha," she replied, "Mortimer is the best in the world, until he gets angry. It doesn't happen so very often, or at least he doesn't get angry with me so very often. And I probably do deserve to be punished, you know."

I took her hand. "No one deserves this," I said. "It is quite intolerable."

She bowed her head and the tears flowed again.

"But how come you to be in Ferns?" I asked. "And in a Catholic church at that?"

"As for that, I little thought I would meet an acquaintance in here, you know, as I might well in St. Mary's. Oh Martha," she continued. "I could not stay in the house, I was too fearful. I made an excuse and Barney brought me here. Barney is so good. Such a Treasure, you know. Whatever would I do without him?"

Yet the Treasure had proved unable to protect her from his master.

"But what will I do now" she continued, wringing her hands, "I am afraid to go back, in case Mortimer is still in a rage."

"Is there anywhere else you can go?"

She shook her head.

"What about your cousins in... Arklow is it?"

"No, no. I should be too ashamed to explain the matter to them. No, I must return home. And yet..."

She broke down again.

"What if I were to come with you?" I asked, impetuously. "The Colonel would surely not do anything to you then, I suppose."

"Oh, would you, Martha?" She grabbed my hand, as at the drowning man's straw. "That would be so very, very kind. And Barney could drive you home afterwards."

Having made the offer, I could hardly withdraw it. I confess I doubted the wisdom of the plan, given the Colonel's previous hostility towards me. In all decency, however, I could not abandon Augusta, especially not with the statue of the Virgin Mary gazing soulfully down at me from over the altar.

I hurried to our meeting-point to give Annie my packet of purchases and to inform her of the change of plans, without, of course, explaining the true reason.

"I suppose, Martha," said she with a smile, "that you prefer the comfort of a nice upholstered carriage to our old cart."

"Mrs. Timmins has promised me more honey," I said, improvising. "You know how much the children enjoyed the last pot."

It was not really a lie. When Augusta had presented me with the honey the last time, she had promised that I would be welcome to more in the future.

Nonetheless, it was admittedly a pleasure and relief to travel in relative comfort, especially since the threatened drizzle had started to fall.

On the way, to make lighter conversation, and in case the Treasure could overhear us, I explained fully my reason for visiting Ferns.

"I never expected to stay in Ireland so long," I said. "Yet given the predicament of poor Lily, I feel I must stay and see how it works out for her. But I must have a new dress. Unfortunately, I could find nothing here."

"Well, as to that," Augusta replied with more animation, "I wonder if I have something that would do for you."

I regarded her tiny person, comparing it to my considerably fuller shape, and expressed a doubt that anything of hers would fit me.

"I was not always the way I am now," she said. "There may be something."

"In any case," I agreed, "it will be a great excuse to explain my surprise visit."

"Indeed."

The Colonel must have calmed down in the meantime, for he was all affability when we returned. I have observed before that people of a sanguineous disposition are likely to blow up quickly, but also blow down with equal speed, if it is possible to say such a thing. Perhaps, too, he was worried, given his wife's impetuous flight, that this time he had gone too far, and the smiles expressed a thankfulness at her return, even in my less than looked-for company.

Maybe I am being unfair to him. He accepted genially the excuse that we had prepared, and even pressed me to stay on for luncheon. I did not particularly wish to do so – partly because of the tensions that must surely remain between the Colonel and his wife, and partly because I had not relished the previous meal I had eaten with them – but I agreed with thanks. Perhaps in this mellower mood of the Colonel's I could work on him, gently of course, with regard to Lily.

161

While the Colonel went out to check, as he told us, on his bees, Augusta and I repaired upstairs to her dressing room.

"Oh, Martha," she whispered. "I am so glad you are here. Mortimer has quite forgotten my fault and is on his best behaviour."

"I am glad to hear it," I said, keeping my thoughts on the subject to myself.

Thereupon she opened her wardrobe to me. I was quite confounded. Augusta Timmins turned out to be the sort of person who never ever throws anything away. Furthermore, perhaps the idea of passing clothes on to someone who could make good use of them had never occurred to her until now. She pulled out dress upon dress of an ancient vintage and design, many of them displaying the frivolous frills and flounces she had worn on my previous visit. Among the heaps of dresses, there was even one with a crinoline skirt from decades back, though without its horsehair petticoat. I could even see holes in the fabric where moths had feasted and there was a musty smell over all. It was not promising.

"Oh dear," she fluttered. "I do not think that after all there is anything here for you, Martha. I am so sorry."

It was at that moment, my eye having been caught, I think, by some movement, that I happened to glance out of the window. This looked over the kitchen garden and beyond to the beehives, and I was most surprised to see there the Colonel in conversation with Briege Kinsella. I commented on the fact to Augusta.

"Oh yes," she said. "Briege often comes here to talk to the Colonel."

"Really?"

"I think…" Augusta added. "Well, I don't know for certain because he does not confide much in me… but I think she tells him things, you know."

"What things?" This was most interesting.

"Oh, I don't know, Martha. Things she hears when she goes from house to house with her potions, I suppose. He told me she has interesting insights, whatever that means." She smiled up at me. "I suppose it helps him understand the people better."

"And poor Francie?" I asked. "Did he used to come around as well?"

"Oh dear me no. The Colonel couldn't stand the sight of him. If he so much as poked his nose over the wall, which he did sometimes, you know, the Colonel sent Barney to chase him off with the dogs." She chuckled at a memory. "Mortimer said Francie ran so fast it would be good sport to set the hounds on him. Like at a hunt, you know."

"Goodness me."

"Well, of course, he was only joking."

This was most intriguing news. Was it possible, then, that Peter's suspicions were awry, and that the member of the Kinsella clan who was informing on the neighbours was not Francie at all but his sister, Briege? As Augusta remarked, she it was went travelling around the countryside with her herbal remedies, and would thus be privy to all the news and gossip. And who would ever suspect her, a pathetic lame girl? She would be near enough invisible.

I continued to regard the two through the glass, now seemingly engaged in some heated argument. The Colonel's colour was up, and Briege, I saw, was even shaking her fist at him. Most odd. How I wished I could hear what they were saying.

"I can't imagine that I ever wore this," Augusta said. I turned back to see her holding up a shapeless garment in dark blue muslin. "But it might do for you."

I do not think she intended to be rude, but believed herself helpful, beneficent even. I took the proffered robe in that spirit, agreeing that I might be able to do something with it.

Luncheon was progressing smoothly, if not deliciously, with innocuous banter, and Augusta quite back to her old self. It was all so friendly, indeed, that I was on the point of raising Lily's predicament, when Augusta remarked brightly over the watery stewed rabbit, "Martha spotted you chatting to Briege Kinsella in the garden earlier."

The Colonel lowered his knife and fork and looked at me with his hard blue eyes.

"Did you, indeed?" he said.

"Oh, out the dressing-room window," I replied in an offhand way, hoping Augusta would not say more about my questioning on the subject. "I just happened to notice."

"You just happened to notice," he echoed me. "You happen to notice a lot of things, don't you, Mrs. Hudson?"

"Oh, no more than anyone else, I am sure."

"No more than anyone else? I don't think that's quite true, is it? You make quite a habit of noticing things, is that not so?"

"Well, you know, having been landlady to someone whose career was based on close observation," I remarked as coolly as possible, for I did not at all care for the threatening tone of the Colonel's remarks, "I suppose some of it was bound to rub off on me... This rabbit is quite delicious, Augusta."

"Barney caught it," she replied, unaware, I think, that she was leading the conversation back on to safer territory. "He's a wonder when it comes to providing game for our table."

We continued the meal with Augusta burbling happily on, and the Colonel and I largely silent with our own thoughts. I was aware of his eyes fixed upon me from time to time, but endeavoured to appear carefree. Now would not be the time, I realised, to raise the subject of Lily, though time was running out for the girl.

As I prepared to leave, which I did directly after luncheon, the Timminses for once not attempting to detain me, I expressed my willingness to walk back to the farm, the rain having eased and the skies holding enough blue to make a sailor a pair of trousers, as the saying goes. However, they would have none of it, the Colonel even insisting on walking me out to the coach house, to find the ever biddable Barney. This despite the old wound in his leg, which caused him to rely on a cane. He was all affability again, or seemed to be.

"I did not wish to say anything in front of my wife," he told me, "but she is the reason Briege came to see me, at my request."

"Is that so?" I replied. "May I ask why?"

"You may ask, dear lady, and I may tell you, since you are such a good friend to my wife. On the understanding, of course, that it is in complete confidence."

"Yes, I am fond of Augusta and care about her welfare. I will not break your confidence."

The Colonel nodded. "I am grateful for it. Poor Augusta has so few friends, you know, and often becomes lonely, a prey to her nerves." He paused. "Let us take a little turn in the garden while I explain something to you." He got hold of my arm, rather forcing me to accede to his request.

We walked again towards the pretty summer house, although now it appeared to me a lot less like an idyllic place to sit, and more like a gilded cage. We paused on the bridge and watched the little stream swirling under it. I wondered if an ugly troll might be found, living down there, although I did not share this particular fancy with my companion.

"It was because of Augusta's nerves, don't you know," the Colonel was saying, "that I asked Briege Kinsella to call round in the hope she could make up a soothing remedy for my wife. I am glad to say that she has agreed to do so. It is very good of her, so soon after losing her brother in such a terrible way."

"I have heard," I said carefully, "that she is very skilled at the herbal cures. I understand she is much sought after for it in the neighbourhood."

"Yes, indeed. In the past she made up a concoction for me against the gout which proved more effective than anything Dr.

Ross could give me. It even helped with the pain from my war wound, don't you know."

"I am glad to hear it," I said. "I hope for Augusta's sake that Briege manages a cure for her, too."

"I pray for it," he continued. "You see, Mrs. Hudson, my wife is in the habit, most regrettably, of taking comfort where she should not... You may or may not have noticed – and being such a very observant person," (again!) "I am sure you have – that dear Augusta is a little too partial to her glass of spirituous liquors. It has even, I am sorry to say, become something of a problem. I try to moderate her, don't you know, but she has become sly about it and, I am afraid, partakes in secret."

I said nothing and kept my expression neutral.

"The drink affects her balance, you know, and she is inclined to bump into things. You must have seen the bruise on her cheek today." He waited for my nod. "In this present case, I believe – for I was not there at the time, you know – she staggered against the parlour door." He smiled, but only with his mouth. His eyes stayed watchful. "She is quite likely to concoct some extreme story to cover what really happened to her... You understand me, I hope."

"Yes," I replied, "I understand you, Colonel. "I hope that Augusta will have no more accidents. That bruise on her face looks painful."

There was a pause.

"It would be most unfortunate if it were to happen again," I said.

"You know, Mrs. Hudson," the Colonel remarked, after another pause. "Augusta is not the most truthful of persons. I am sorry to say this, but as you are such a very good friend to her, you must realise this."

I realise, I thought, that the untruthful one is you, Colonel Mortimer Timmins, who is lying through your teeth.

166

"Well," I replied, "may Briege's remedy calm Augusta's nerves. And I trust you will do your very best, Colonel, to make sure that Augusta does not bump into anything in the future, whether affected or not... Now I think I must go home."

"Of course."

We retraced our steps in a somewhat uneasy silence. I supposed the Colonel was not at all sure if I had believed his explanation against that of his wife's.

Arriving at the coach house, he summoned Barney, who was polishing the paintwork. The ever amenable Treasure immediately went off to fetch the horse, and, while he did so, I decided, come what may, to broach the subject foremost on my mind.

"Mrs. Melrose and I are still most concerned about Lily, Colonel."

"Ah yes, the Cullen girl. I will have to consult my schedule but I think she comes before the bench early next week."

"It would be well for her if she could be given bail at least. She is hardly a danger to society."

"As to that," he replied, with a familiarly stubborn set to his expression, "it will depend on the evidence presented to the court. Murder is a serious matter, Mrs. Hudson, and those responsible cannot expect pity, however young and pretty they are."

"You have judged her already, without the evidence. Or only on the evidence of your friend, Briege."

I should not have spoken so rashly. The Colonel's face darkened with anger.

"The evidence will be weighed impartially, madam, and it will be decided then if there is a case against her. If there is, she will be taken to the Bridewell to await her trial. If not, she will be set free... Here is your carriage. Good day to you."

Barney whipped the horse and we departed, I fearing I had just made things worse for poor Lily.

167

Back at the farm, I showed Kitty and Annie the dress that Augusta had pressed upon me. They both laughed heartily.

"Was that the best she had?" Kitty asked.

I explained about the crinolines, the ribbons and frills, the flounces and the moths. It was good to talk of frivolous things. It was good to laugh.

"And the honey?" Annie asked suddenly. I had to confess that I had forgotten all about it.

Chapter Twelve

The next morning, as Annie, Kitty and I were sitting at breakfast, there was a hammering at the door heralding the most unexpected arrival of Florrie Sweetnam. He seemed flustered and his toilet was not as immaculate as usual.

"There you are," he said. "I thought you must know nothing about it."

"What is it?" I asked.

"Lily is up before the magistrates this morning. I heard it from Thomas. His brother is a constable."

"Good heavens," I said rising up. "The Colonel quite misled me yesterday. He said the case would be presented next week."

"What is to be done?" asked Kitty, rising as well.

"I can take you to Enniscorthy forthwith, if you would like to go," Florrie replied.

"But I wished Peter to be present," I said. "He saw with me that Francie had been dead for some hours and could give evidence to that effect."

"Peter is out in the fields," Annie said. "There's a sick calf. I doubt he could leave it at such short notice."

"I understand, of course," I replied. "But what a dreadful pity. Will anyone speak up for the girl, I wonder?"

"You and I can at least be there for her," said Kitty.

She had tried to visit Lily in the barracks on two further occasions, but each time Sergeant Hackett had turned her away. At least she had been able to leave some clean linen, some fresh milk and some of Annie's drop scones.

"Although I shouldn't be surprised if the Sergeant ate those himself," she had said grimly.

Now, we busied ourselves in throwing on our coats and gathering up other necessities, soon piling into Florrie's barouche.

What a contrast it was travelling to Enniscorthy in this well-sprung vehicle, with the previous drive thence, when Kitty and I had first arrived. We had little suspicions then of what lay ahead of us. I could have done without the present comfort, if only none of it had happened.

The vista of poor farms with their wretched inhabitants had not changed. Indeed, I seemed to recognise the same barefoot children, the same gaunt mothers, the same bowed elders: the shocking so soon become the familiar. The ten miles of the journey seemed endless and, cursing the duplicity of the Colonel in my mind, I feared the case would be over and done with before ever we arrived. Kitty I think felt the same, gripping my hand tightly in hers. Even Florrie caught the mood and abstained from his usual banter.

On arriving at the courthouse where the petty sessions were being held, we hurried in to find that indeed the case was well underway. Both the Cullen family and the two Kinsellas cast dark scowls at us: At least, I thought, the Cullens were there at last for Lily. She, held apart, the young constable we had met before beside her, looked pale and frail, as if about to faint, but gave a wan nod at the sight of us. If the Colonel, sitting in state on a dais with the two other magistrates, had spotted us, as surely he must have, he gave no sign of it.

During the ensuing presentation of evidence, I became ever more frustrated and angry. As I suspected, no one questioned the time of death, and it was all I could do to prevent myself leaping to my feet and shouting out what I knew to be true. Of course, as a woman and an outsider, I should have been laughed out of court, and would only have made things worse for the girl, but the injustice of it made my blood boil.

"Remember, this is only the preliminary hearing," Florrie whispered to me, sensing my wrath. "There will be time, Mrs. Hudson. There will be time."

"Will there?" I replied. "I pray to God you are right."

The magistrates deliberated among themselves for a few short moments, nodding gravely to each other. Colonel Timmins then banged his gavel on the table, to silence the hubbub in the courtroom, glaring around the room but again ignoring my eye so studiously I knew he must have seen me. He summed up the evidence, how Lily was discovered with the knife in her hand and the corpse at her feet, and then concluded with the devastating words, "We therefore judge that a strong case had been made against the aforesaid Lily Cullen, and so rule that she be taken hence to the Bridewell in Wexford town, to await her trial for the wilful murder of Francis Kinsella."

Lily cried out that she was innocent, while the Kinsellas and many others present shouted vile curses upon her. Even members of her own family turned their backs, William Cullen shaking his head and the brothers lowering theirs. I was at least gratified to see the young constable's gentle handing of Lily, raising her up to conduct her out the back door before the mob could react. Otherwise there was assuredly a real and grave danger that they would set upon her.

The Colonel must have recognised this, for he banged his gavel again.

"None of this," he roared. "Lily Cullen is to receive a fair trial, and justice will be done in due course." At last he looked across at me, full in the eye. Was it triumph? Was it defiance? Was it a challenge? At any rate, it was no very friendly expression that I found there.

171

Kitty was in floods of tears, but I refused to succumb in front of this man and stared back with what I hope conveyed my contempt for him and his obdurate ways.

"How distant is Wexford town?" I asked Florrie, while we waited for the crowds to leave the courtroom.

"From here, I suppose, twice as far again as we have travelled today."

"Far enough, then."

"Don't be too downcast, Mrs. Hudson," Florrie said. "Today's ruling was only to be expected, given the circumstances. With a good barrister, I am sure that when the case comes to trial, Lily will fare better. Being away from this place can only be an advantage, you know. Away from local influences."

"That is true," I replied. "But where can we find a good lawyer for the girl."

"Ah, as to that..." Florrie patted his nose, "it just so happens that I am acquainted with a capital fellow whom I am sure will fit the bill... I take it," he added a little more timidly, "that his fee will be covered by her friends, since I imagine her own family will not be able or indeed willing to do so."

"Of course," said Kitty, raising a tear-stained face. "Whatever it takes, I will pay it."

"Then let us call upon Malone forthwith," Florrie said. "His chambers are nearby."

Before we could leave the courtroom, however, I was most surprised to see Briege Kinsella heading our way, fighting against the flow of the crowd. Was it to crow over us? I prepared myself to face her down. But it was to Kitty that she addressed herself.

"I have that ointment made up for you, Kathleen," said she. "I can call over with it later, if it suits you."

She spoke in flat tones. I suppose for her the preceding was a hollow victory, after all. However vicious Francie may have been, the girl warranted pity, having lost someone so close to her.

"That would be most kind," Kitty replied, trying to control her emotions. "Thank you."

"Justice has been done this day, Kathleen O'Kelly, whatever you think about it," Briege said then, and turned to go.

We watched her silently, and then, without any other exchange with those present, set off on a short walk through the town to find Florrie's lawyer. Unfortunately, however, the gentleman in question had just recently gone out to luncheon, as we were informed by the spotty youth who opened to our knock. He could not say where his employer had could be found, but affirmed that he expected him back by two of the clock.

"In that case," said Florrie, "we might follow his example and find a place to eat, ladies. I have dined before quite satisfactorily at the Portsmouth Arms Inn, a most respectable establishment which has the advantage of private rooms."

Kitty and I acquiesced. I could see indeed that my poor friend was very much in need of a restorative, and a bowl of hot soup or the like would serve the purpose very well.

"Colonel Timmins is a spiteful man," I said later, over some excellent lamb chops: trust Florrie to know a good menu. "I am sure he influenced the other two magistrates."

"I thought he was your friend," said Kitty. "You seemed to get on so well before."

I remained silent. I was not about to divulge poor Augusta's secret.

"Clearly friendship does not count for very much with him," Florrie said. "But what fun it will be, ladies, when he has to judge between the counter-claims of the Cullens and the Kinsellas regarding that disputed field. You could see the two families looking daggers at each other, more because of the field than the murder, I reckon." He chuckled and rubbed his hands together. "Oh yes, indeed, I shall make a point of attending that particular contre-temps."

I am afraid that neither Kitty nor myself was inclined to see the funny side of anything at that moment, and especially not a mention of daggers, so the rest of the meal passed in a gloomy silence.

There was still time in hand after our meal before we were due to go back to the lawyer's chambers, and while Florrie expressed a wish to visit a bookshop – "For I have quite run out of sensational reading matter, you know" – Kitty and I went off in search of a dressmaker's. In fact, we had noted such an establishment on our way to the inn, and now repaired thither to try and find new outfits for the two of us, Kitty being as much in need as myself. I shall not dwell on the outcome, except to say that it was most satisfactory. Kitty picked out a neat linen suit in pale grey, while I found a serviceable gown in puce silk. This was not a colour I should normally have chosen but, even if I say so myself, it became me surprisingly well, and the price, I was delighted to see, was far less than I should have paid in London to my usual dressmaker. I also managed to pick up more sturdy garments for Mammo and Nell, regretting my previous inferior purchases from the slatternly Mrs. O'Byrne. Florrie, when we met up with him again, was likewise pleased with his acquisitions, a package of "delightfully scandalous reads in those tell-tale yellow covers, don't you know."

Happily, by the time we reached the lawyer's chambers, Brian Malone was returned, a tall, thin, serious young man, with pale skin and the blackest hair I had seen since arriving in Ireland, where most people appear either sandy haired or red. Later, when I remarked on this to Florrie, he replied that there was probably Spanish blood in the lawyer's ancestry, and, answering my surprised query, explained how sailors, shipwrecked here from the Armada of Elizabethan times, had never gone home but had intermarried with local women.

"You can find quite a number of people who look like that in the West of the country," he said. "They are probably of Iberian ancestry, although some historians even claim such characteristics go back to the Phoenicians, don't you know, who traded here in the Middle Ages."

However curious that was, and whatever Mr. Malone's origins – Florrie as usual showing himself to be a font of irrelevant information – the young man impressed me. He listened attentively as we explained the business, evincing especial interest in the evidence I provided regarding the appearance of the corpse compared to the alleged time of death. He did not even appear shocked that I, a woman, was in a position to provide this information, and thus duly rose in my estimation.

"You claim," he said, making a note, "that from the condition of the body, the murder must have happened much earlier in the night than when Lily raised the alarm."

"Yes," I replied, "and Mrs. Melrose's brother, Peter O'Kelly, who viewed the body with me, will verify that fact." Or I hoped to heaven that he would. "The parish priest also commented that Francis had died a considerable time before he arrived on the scene, although..." I paused.

Mr. Malone raised his eyebrows. "Although?"

"He may not be reliable," Florrie said. "Father Joe Molloy is a drunkard, and moreover changed his tune after, and said that Francie was still alive when he came to anoint him."

"That was to comfort the family, wasn't it?" asked Kitty. "They would hate to think that Francie died unshriven."

"Perhaps so."

"Well, he can at least be approached," said the lawyer, taking down the name and parish of the priest. "I know you are convinced of Lily's innocence," he continued, "but I have to ask. Is there any chance that she stabbed Francis in self-defence? The courts look quite kindly upon women who have been attacked, you know, even by their husbands."

"She denies any involvement," I replied, "and claims to have been in a deep sleep all night, having been forced to drink strong spirits earlier. In any case, Francie was stabbed in the back. Surely, if she were defending herself, he would have been killed by a knife to the chest."

Mr. Malone nodded and made another note.

"Unless she did it in her sleep," Florrie remarked. "I read a novel once where that happened. The murderer, you know, had no memory of committing the fatal act."

We all looked at him with expressions, which, I am pleased to say, for once quite silenced him

After further discussion, Mr. Malone expressed himself happy to represent Lily as her defence council. I was delighted, for he came across as a man of sound principle who would do his best for the poor girl. His fee, additionally, was moderate enough, although I suppose I was appraising it, as with the price of my new dress, against the staggering amounts that London lawyers habitually charge.

"I will endeavour to get bail for her as well," he said. "The Bridewell is no place for a young girl, and assuming you can put up the bail money, I know a judge that may agree to sign temporary release papers."

People knowing people. It seemed this was the way things were done in Ireland.

"That would be truly wonderful," said Kitty. "No expense spared for my dearest girl."

I had to say it. "If she gets bail, that would, of course, be very good news. But where would she then go, Kitty? Certainly not to her in-laws and hardly even to her own family. And I do not think Peter and Annie would be happy to accommodate her either."

Kitty looked thoughtful. "I suppose we could take rooms in here in Enniscorthy, Martha, or even in Wexford town."

The expenses involved in that, I thought, would be considerable, on top of the lawyer's fees and bail. I knew Kitty to be comfortably off, but she was not what one would call rich. I, of course, could help out from my savings, but they were not substantial, either.

After a pause, in which we reflected on the matter, Florrie suddenly burst out with an offer to have the girl stay with him.

"Oh, no," said Kitty. "It is most generous of you, Mr. Sweetnam, but I could not think of it."

"Nonsense, dear lady. It is the perfect solution, you know. As Mrs. Hudson can tell you, I have plenty of space. And with my housekeeper in residence too – Mrs. O'Meara, who is a perfect model of respectability – Lily will be quite safe from scandal."

This was some kindness, indeed.

"An even better thought," he added, ever more enthused. "Why don't you two ladies come to stay, too, to be with her, you know, for company? I should be more than delighted, you know. I should be honoured."

He really was a phenomenon.

"Of course," Mr. Malone put in, bringing us back down to earth, "it will all depend on whether I can get bail for her. It is by no means certain, you understand."

"But you think there is a chance?" Kitty asked.

"Oh yes, indeed. Judge O'Boyle is a humane man... Can I tell him then that you would take responsibility for the girl?" He looked from Florrie to Kitty, who both nodded.

We left his chambers with assurances from him that he would be in touch very soon, and so it was in a much happier frame of mind that we left for home. Kitty indeed was ecstatic.

"He will get her bail," she exclaimed. "He will get her off. Oh, thank you so much, Mr. Sweetnam, for everything. I cannot express my gratitude enough."

Florrie and I exchanged glances, the two of us perhaps rather less sanguine than my friend for a favourable outcome.

As promised, Briege turned up at the O'Kelly farm later that afternoon with a pot of ointment she claimed would help Kitty's sore back.

"What is in it?" I asked.

"Nothing to be concerned about," the girl replied tartly. "It's not poison, you know."

"No," I said soothingly. "I am sure it is not. I am simply interested."

"Well now, there's feverfew and the sap from a silver birch and bilberries and nettles, if that means anything to you."

Kitty smelt it.

"And poitín, I think," she said.

"Just a tiny drop. Rub it on to your back where it pains you several times in the day. It will tingle but that's good. It shows that it's working. And come back for more if you need it, Kathleen. You know where I am."

"Thank you," said Kitty. She reached into her reticule for a coin which she pressed on the girl. Briege took it gravely, and left without another word.

We of course had not mentioned to her anything about our hopes for Lily. I could just imagine how that particular piece of news would have been received.

Chapter Thirteen

Brian Malone was as good as his word. Indeed, Kitty, Annie and I were most astonished when, just two days later, the man himself arrived at the farm to give us the most excellent news. Lily had been released on bail under the recognisance of Mr. Florence Sweetnam of Castle Florence, Ferns, in the County of Wexford and Mrs. Kathleen O'Kelly of Baker Street, London. At that very moment, as he told us, and after all her ordeals, Lily was enjoying the tender care of Mrs. O'Meara, he himself having driven her down that morning, then coming over to us after a necessary visit to the barracks to inform Sergeant Hackett of the developments.

"He was none too pleased, I am afraid."

"I can imagine," I said.

"Nevertheless, the Sergeant has to abide by the ruling of the judge. At least he seems to be a man who goes by the book. I foresee no trouble from him."

"But from others?" asked Annie. "There is strong feeling here, you know, on the part of the Kinsella family and their friends, and they are rough types, likely to take the law into their own hands."

"I assume the Sergeant is aware of that possibility and will be on his guard," Mr. Malone replied. "Florence Sweetnam understands full well what he has taken on and has a staff of stalwart men. I trust Lily will be safe."

Annie blessed herself. "Please God," she said. I silently echoed the sentiment.

"And how is Lily in herself?" Kitty asked.

"She is, as you can understand, very shaken by her experiences. She was hardly eating before I visited her and had become very weak."

"Oh dear God!" exclaimed Kitty.

"Indeed. I think she had fallen into despair and hardly wished to continue to live." He paused, while we received this news with horror. "However, ladies, I trust I was able to give her hope. Having spoken with her at length, like you I am convinced she is incapable of committing this terrible crime. It is thus a most welcome development to have managed to arrange bail, and get her out of the Bridewell."

Kitty clapped her hands from sheer joy and hugged me.

"We will feed her up," she said. "We will restore the bloom to her cheeks."

"Was it hard for you to persuade the judge?" Annie asked. "It is most unusual for bail to be granted in a murder case, is it not?"

"It is," the lawyer agreed, "but, apart from the evidence I was able to present to him, which clearly indicated an over-hasty judgment of guilt, and mentioning, too, the poor state of the girl's health, it could not hurt our case that Judge O'Boyle is an enthusiastic follower of the chronicles of Dr. Watson regarding the exploits of the late lamented Mr. Sherlock Holmes. When I told him of your involvement, Mrs. Hudson, he even expressed a strong interest in meeting up with you on some occasion to discuss the great man."

"Goodness," I exclaimed.

"Although," he went on, "it would of course not be proper until the conclusion of the present case, which, I am afraid, given the timetable of the courts, may be some time in the distant future."

The distant future! I heard his words with a sinking heart. Was I never to escape from this ill-fated country and return home?

It was considered advisable then that, while Mr. Malone travelled back to Enniscorthy, Kitty and I should pack our bags in all haste and repair to Castle Florence, to be with Lily and provide support. Despite the kindness of Florrie and Mrs. O'Meara, they were strangers to the vulnerable girl.

"Mr. Sweetnam is to send his carriage over to fetch you in an hour," the lawyer told us. "I trust that is agreeable."

We said that it was and bade our farewells to the young man, along with our eternally grateful thanks.

Peter, meanwhile, having seen a strange carriage departing, soon arrived to find out what was the matter. He was most astonished to hear that Lily had been released.

"So soon, and so simply," said Peter, with grudging respect and even a degree of disapproval. "I never thought you good women would pull it off. It just goes to show how different rules apply to people of privilege and the dissident religion."

"Nonsense, Peter," Kitty replied. "It was all about the righting of an injustice. As you must tell by their names, Mr. Malone and Judge O'Boyle, are doubtless good Catholics like ourselves."

I could see that Peter was not convinced, but Annie was delighted at the outcome.

"I hated to think of that sweet girl in that terrible prison," she said. "Who knows what horrors go on there?"

Despite their protests of regret at our departure, Annie and Peter must have been glad to see the back of us after the two weeks and more we had imposed upon them. Dear Henry was fond often of quoting the maxim, "visitors are like fish: they start to stink after three days," and there is much truth in it. At last, our forbearing hosts would get their house back again, although it has to be said that the boys had got so used to sleeping in the barn, they seemed quite sorry at the prospect of a return to civilised ways. Veronica, Pegeen and Sairie, for their part, wept bitterly to see us go, even though we assured them that we would visit as often as we could.

181

It was Florrie's boy, Thomas, who arrived to fetch us and help us with our bags. Young Veronica was evidently much taken with this fine fellow, hastily wiping away her tears, smiling a lot and fussing around to call attention to herself, while Kitty, I was impressed to find, had no difficulty penetrating his thick accent. Thus it was, waving back at that most hospitable of families, we set off for Castle Florence. I had not told Kitty much about the place, since it rather diverted me to think how amazed she would be at the sight of it.

As indeed she was.

"This is the old Devine house!" she exclaimed as we turned into the drive. "I should never have known it."

"Mr. Sweetnam has been busy with improvements," I remarked. Although perhaps "improvements" was not quite the right word. Transformation into "something rich and strange," more like.

As we drove up, we were delighted to see Lily already waiting for us outside the door, sitting perched beside a great stone urn on the edge of its plinth, Mrs O'Meara beside her, and the huge wolfhound, Bran, at her feet. Kitty jumped down from the barouche and rushed across to hug the girl. Many were the tears exchanged before words could be uttered. The dog, excited too, could hardly be restrained by Mrs. O'Meara, barking frenziedly and trying to leap up.

When at last girl and godmother were separated, it was possible to see how, in such a short time, poor Lily had changed. She was horribly thin, emaciated even, her pale skin almost translucent, and her lovely auburn hair looking dull and straggly. Moreover, she needed a good hot bath after her ordeal, for she was not quite clean. I assumed she must have wished to wait until our arrival before indulging in that particular luxury.

However, she had perked up somewhat at the sight of us, and was quite bright-eyed while recounting how kind everyone had been to her, how reassuring Mr. Malone, how welcoming Mrs. O'Meara... and Mr. Sweetnam too, of course, how very nice the dog. And she leaned down and scratched Bran behind his ears, smiling the while and telling him what a good boy he was, the beast's great tail thumping off the ground in delight. Of her ordeal before this happy day she said not a word, and we did not ask. There would be time for that.

Now Florrie came out to welcome us. He was an astonishing sight, a round ball in a flame-coloured jacket and black waistcoat, a purple cravat at his neck, a white rose in his buttonhole. It must have been in our honour, but I could tell that Lily was quite overwhelmed by this extraordinary apparition, and clung to Kitty, who looked almost equally taken aback. On her previous encounters with Florrie, he had dressed down – for him that is.

"Come in, come in, come in, Thomas will bring your bags," he insisted, rubbing his hands.

Kitty was even more bemused than I had been at the interior of Castle Florence. After her brother's farm house, this was a whole other world, something she (and I) had perhaps only encountered in occasional visits to stately homes owned by lords and ladies. She stared about herself, lost for words, at the crimson panelling, the parquet floor, the naked cherubs nestling in the plasterwork of the vaulted ceiling. Although when she finally managed to speak, she exclaimed in all sincerity, "It is utterly delightful, Mr. Sweetnam. Like a palace. Martha never told me."

"I wanted to surprise you," I replied, and Florrie chuckled approvingly.

But however astonished Kitty and I might be, it was surely nothing to how Lily was feeling, coming as she did from the ramshackle farms of the Cullens and latterly the Kinsellas, with their dirt floors and windows of broken glass, not to mention the privations of the Bridewell. Later, indeed, she told Kitty and me that she feared she had been carried away to faeryland, with Florrie the

King of the Leprechauns. Only for Mrs. O'Meara she might have run off straightway. Luckily, Florrie never learnt till a long time after what she had thought on arriving at his beloved Castle, and by then he was able to laugh it off.

Just now he was all set to bring us into his dazzling parlour, where a small spread was to be laid on. Mrs. O'Meara, however, displaying her womanly wisdom, suggested that we might be more comfortable for now in her kitchen. Florrie agreed, though clearly disappointed. He did so love to show off his house.

We duly repaired below stairs. Florrie had not taken me there on my first visit, perhaps because it reflected his housekeeper's homely and practical nature rather than his own flamboyant one. The room was spacious, and well-appointed, with a large cast iron range on which a tureen was bubbling, smelling deliciously of a meaty stew. A fresh-faced young scullery-maid, introduced as Betty, was stirring the mix, which I hoped we would be tasting later in the day. Highly polished copper saucepans of all sizes hung from the walls, while a Welsh dresser was set with china plates embellished with an emblem I recognised as that of the Sweetnams, the same that featured in the stained glass of the parlour windows. A large and well-scrubbed wooden table stood in the centre of the room, plain and serviceable wooden chairs set around it. Dishes of biscuits and rosy apples had been placed upon the table, along with side plates and cups and saucers all ready for our tea. Kitty and I approved wholeheartedly, and soon, over that restorative beverage and oaten flapjacks pleasingly enhanced with raisins, the mood relaxed somewhat, although Lily still clung to Kitty, and hardly managed more than a couple of bites of her biscuit and a sip or two of the tea.

After this light repast, we were shown to our rooms, and once more amazement was the order of the day. Mrs. O'Meara, revealing again her natural sensitivity, had placed Lily in with Kitty in one of the less fancy chambers on the topmost floor. It was neat and clean and contained two beds, perhaps being usually reserved for upper servants or secretaries, rather than honoured guests.

"I cannot imagine why they are to be squashed into one room," Florrie complained, "when we have an overabundance of lovely bedchambers. But for some reason Mrs. O'Meara insisted."

"I thought you two might like to stay together," she explained, "although I can have other rooms made up if you prefer it."

"Not at all," replied Kitty. "This will do very well indeed." The expression of gratitude on Lily's face confirmed her words.

I was perhaps not quite so lucky, although I am sure Florrie would have judged me to be the more privileged, being placed in the room complete with four-poster bed and the full suit of armour. I anticipated this latter would quite disturb my rest, reminiscent as it was of the ghost of Hamlet's father, as so memorably seen by Henry and myself on the stage of the Lyceum Theatre, with the great Irving as the Prince. I knew I should never be able to bring myself to pull the heavy velvet drapes round the bed to obscure the thing from view, for I should then only imagine all sorts happening behind them, unseen by me. I am not fanciful in general, but in addition, I could not but recall the terrible events in such a room, so recently related by Dr. Watson in "The Adventure of the Speckled Band." Luckily there was no bell cord here for a poisonous swamp adder to slither down, and, as I consoled myself, why indeed should it do so, even if there were? I am no young heiress. In the end I pulled myself together, and threw my shawl over the suit of armour. Poor Florrie. How taken aback he would have been. I am sure he considered that he had given me the very best of the rooms. It had a fine prospect, all the same, over the gardens designed by his second wife, and I looked forward to exploring them later.

In the meantime, I unpacked, placing smaller items of clothing in the chest of drawers and hanging the meagre rest of my belongings in the gigantic mahogany wardrobe. My goodness, I thought, that particular piece of furniture alone was almost big enough to house one of those poor families I had seen on the road – Mammo and Nell for instance.

I then went in search of Kitty. She had indeed arranged for Lily to have a bath, laughing merrily at the way the girl had reacted to the roll-top "bateau," as Mrs. O'Meara had been pleased to call it, no doubt echoing Florrie. Apparently the girl had never had a bath before. She had always washed herself from a basin of water, and had been quite terrified at first to climb into the tub, thinking she would drown. However, she had soon accustomed herself to the delights of the experience, especially since it was enhanced with a bar of Pears soap, and was soon, so Kitty told me, making lather and blowing bubbles.

The Lily who emerged a little later from the bathroom, pink from the hot water, was already starting to look more like her old self. She was robed in a huge white towel, her wet hair hanging loose about her, to be lovingly brushed by Kitty. I stayed chatting with them for a few moments and then left them to their mutual confidences, deciding this would be an appropriate moment to take a turn in the famous garden.

It was no surprise to find Florrie lurking downstairs, waiting for one or other of us to appear. When hearing of my plans, he insisted on accompanying me on the tour, even though, to be honest, I should have preferred some quiet time by myself.

"I think I have already informed you," said he, as we walked out, "that it was my dear Blanche who performed such a wonderful job of transformation here, inspired by Gertrude Jekyll, of whom I believe, though I still can scarcely credit it, you say you have never heard."

"I confess my ignorance," I replied. "The only Jekyll I know is the Doctor in Mr. Stephenson's thrilling novel."

"Then you will be diverted to learn that Stephenson was friendly with Gertrude's brother, and so borrowed their family name for his character."

"Ah," I replied. "Then there is an actual connection."

"Indeed.'

I have to say I liked the garden considerably more than the house. In fact, the contrast in styles was quite striking. Castle Florence, it seemed to me, should properly have had a formal garden, all fancy fountains and marble statuary and paved walkways between low box hedges, very neat and tidy, and quite unlike this daisy-spotted lawn, these gravel paths winding between a profusion of flower beds, albeit with blooms carefully chosen in complementary colours as on an artist's palette. I suspected that dear Blanche had created a world for herself here, away from the artifice of the house, somewhere in which to take refuge. If I were to live here permanently, I too should have spent as much time as the Irish weather would permit outside in this enchanting garden, or, when it rained, in the Orangery, looking out at it.

I did not, of course, express these thoughts to Florrie, though I lavishly and most sincerely voiced my delight at all that surrounded us. We were at that moment following one of the paths leading to a charming woodland glade, and here Florrie suggested we pause awhile on a stone bench under the shade of an aged oak tree. It was most restful, after the stresses and strains of recent times, to sit peacefully listening to birdsong, the light wind soughing among the leaves above us and the babbling of a little stream beside us. I was reminded of Tennyson's inestimable lines;

> Myriads of rivulets hurrying thro' the lawn,
> The moan of doves in immemorial elms,
> And murmuring of innumerable bees.

Florrie was most gratified when I quoted them, and insisted I write them down for him when we returned to the house.

"Perhaps I will have them carved upon a stone and set right here," he said. "It will always remind me of you, dear Mrs. Hudson."

I hoped he was not about to become gallant again.

"It is most good of you to do all this for Lily," I said. "Especially since it will not render you popular either with the Colonel or with the Kinsellas. I hope they will not make trouble for you."

"Mrs. Hudson," he replied, brushing a catkin from his jacket, "I care very little for the opinion of others, good or bad. As for trouble, I do not think you need to worry about that. Lily will prove to be a delightful addition to the household, I am sure. At least, when she stops being afraid of me."

"I doubt she has ever seen anyone like you in her whole life."

I trusted I could say this without causing offence, and indeed Florrie began to chuckle.

"Of course," he went on, "her being here has brought you to me as well. Mrs. Hudson... Martha..." and his tone, I was dismayed to hear, became warm with passion. "I stated just now that I care little for the opinion of others. But there is one exception. You must know that, even in the short while of our acquaintance, I have developed feelings for you. Nay, strong feelings...No, don't speak..." For I was certainly about to. He reached into his pocket and took out a large linen handkerchief which he laid on the ground at my feet, and, to my extreme embarrassment, proceeded to place one knee upon it. He even took my hand.

"I do not expect an answer now," he said, "but I must tell you, dear lady, that it would be the greatest honour for me if you and I could spend our twilight years together. In short, if you would deign to become the fourth Mrs. Florence Sweetnam."

Oh dear, I am afraid I burst out laughing, it was all too preposterous. What unlikely lovers we were. The elderly little man kneeling in front of me in his absurd clothes, and myself a stout matron well into my middle years. I could not but see the funny side of it.

"I am not joking, Mrs. Hudson," Florrie said in offended tones, hauling himself up with some difficulty. "I mean what I say. I wish you to consent to be my wife."

"Mr. Sweetnam, Florrie," I replied after a pause to gather myself. "I apologise for laughing. I am sure you spoke in all sincerity, but I can give you my answer right now. And it is no. I am most honoured that you would make me this offer, but my life is in England, in London. I could never settle here. It is all so very different from what I am used to."

"My apologies, also," he said, lowering his head. "I see that I have been too forward. I have sprung it upon you. But please say that you will give my proposal some thought before you dismiss it utterly. Please, Martha."

"You are a good man and a very good friend," I replied. "I should like us to continue our friendship, but there will never be more than that. You see, I am devoted to the memory of my late husband, Henry. I could never consider replacing him."

Florrie shook his head vigorously.

"It would not be a question of replacing anyone, Martha. Each one of my late wives remains here in my heart." He was still gripping my hand and now pressed it to his breast. "Mary Elizabeth, Blanche and Emma Jane. I shall never ever forget those darling, darling ladies. But it is my strong contention, you know, that love is broad and can be shared among many. Or, if you cannot love, dear lady, then consider companionship. It is assuredly something we all crave, to find someone to walk with through the rocky pathways of life, especially as it reaches towards its inevitable end. I feel I have now found that person in you."

I gently withdrew my hand. The poor man was desperately lonely. I could have told him that he had fixed on me simply because

189

I was here and a novelty, and for no other reason, but I could not bring myself to do so.

"I will think about it," I assured him at last. The kindest I could be.

He smiled then, his wide pink face lighting up, and we retraced our steps through the flower garden, that could have been mine, Florrie pausing only to pluck a crimson peony, which he presented to me with a flourish.

Unfortunately, the petals fell off as soon as I reached my bedroom.

Later, we all sat down to a good dinner of the delicious stew that had been bubbling on the kitchen range earlier, along with fluffy boiled potatoes, and a lemon tart to follow, that balanced the sweet perfectly with the sharp. I was most impressed.

This time it was served not in the comfortable kitchen but on a highly polished mahogany table in the formal dining room, a long and imposing hall of a place. The table stood at a right-angle to two arched windows resembling those in a church, looking out on to the back lawn of the house. An elaborate crystal chandelier hung over us, dripping beads of light as we ate. The walls were painted pearl grey and sported, on one long side, another fancy white marble fireplace, surmounted by a large elaborately gold-framed mirror.

"Venetian glass," Florrie said, pointing at the mirror. Then at the fireplace. "Carrera marble, Napoleon III style, don't you know."

Facing this on the opposite wall hung a couple of still-life paintings, lavish with fruit, vegetables, hourglasses, dead game and skulls. They looked far too antique, never mind too competent, to be by Florrie, and indeed he identified them as the work of a seventeenth-century Dutch master with a complicated name. If he expected us to recognise it, he was disappointed, for both Kitty and

I confessed our ignorance, while feeling we must admire the, to my mind, somewhat gruesome subject matter.

"They are vanitas pictures, don't you know," Florrie said, pausing significantly for a reaction.

"What is that?" duly asked Kitty.

"Memento mori, my dear Mrs. Melrose, reminders that we must die." He chuckled, casting at the same time swift glances at me, as if, like Satan in the wilderness, he was tempting me with the offer, "All this can be yours" (I hope I am not blaspheming by the analogy, for I should never wish to set myself beside the Christ). Given Lily's presence, moreover, and the threat of the noose that hung over her, I found his words most insensitive, and caught the girl glancing up anxiously thereafter at the morbid images.

However proud he was of it all, it was not a cosy place to be. And if Kitty and I felt somewhat intimidated by the room itself and its appurtenances, by the elaborate place settings, crystal glasses, silver cutlery and all those porcelain plates embellished with the Sweetnam emblem, how much more must little Lily, crouching over her plate as if she would be happy to disappear altogether. She once again hardly ate a thing. I suppose even this relatively plain fare seemed rich to her, especially after prison rations of gruel and hard tack, and she took only a potato mashed up with a little gravy from the stew. Kitty cajoled her to eat more but she protested in low tones that she was not hungry.

The rest of us, however, tucked in with relish for it really was very good. I am ashamed to report that I could not help comparing it favourably with the meals that Annie had served us, even though she did her best with limited time and means. Mrs. O'Meara on the other hand had little to do but think up dishes to delight her master, presumably with no expense spared. Thus, I was surprised at the simplicity of the stew, though grateful for it as well. I should have thought Florrie's tastes in food would be somewhat more exotic. In fact, as I discovered later from Mrs. O'Meara, her master actually preferred bland nursery food above all others.

Soon after dinner, for we were all fatigued, Kitty and Lily took themselves to bed. For my part, I wandered into Florrie's library, to try for some suitable reading matter, and was gratified to find, beside shelves filled with those notorious yellow-covered novels favoured by our host, some more to my own taste, including a very comprehensive set of the works of Mr. Anthony Trollope. The author must have spent time in Ireland, from the titles and subject matter of some of the works, and indeed Florrie later informed me that Mr. Trollope had worked for the postal service all around the country. I picked out, for fun, an early novel titled *The Kellys and the O'Kellys*, in honour of Kitty's family, and withdrew with it into my bedroom. In all honesty, I should have preferred to stay in the library, but feared I might shortly be joined there by Florrie with his hang-dog eyes. Luckily, I was soon gripped by the book and quite forgot about the sinister suit of armour lurking in the corner of the bedroom, not to mention deadly snakes slithering down bell pulls.

Chapter Fourteen

The next day, being Sunday, Florrie and I prepared once again to go to church. Thomas drove us there, in the company of Mrs. O'Meara, whom he was then to take on to the Roman Catholic Church of the Annunciation, the location of Francie's doomed marriage and funeral. We had all agreed that it would not be a good idea for Lily to show her face there, so Kitty was to stay home with her.

Mrs. O'Meara was clearly thrilled with the chance of a ride. She usually walked, as she informed me, the few miles to chapel, along with the other servants. On this occasion, Florrie, I suspect, wished me to see him in the role of Lord Bountiful, generous with his servants, and so, with him and me inside the barouche, and his housekeeper up beside Thomas, we set off in style.

"I have been thinking," Florrie told me, "of building a chapel here, modelled after Mr. Walpole's construction at Strawberry Hill in Twickenham. A chapel in the woods." His eyes grew dreamy at the thought. "It would make life so much easier, you know. I could employ a resident priest. Maybe a hermit. What do you think of that, Mrs. Hudson?"

That you have more money than sense, is what I thought. However, I merely replied that it was an original idea, but that I had not heard of the particular chapel he mentioned.

"Oh, goodness me, you should certainly try and visit Strawberry Hill, you know. The place has been an inspiration to me."

"You visited England, then? Twickenham, you say?"

"Oh certainly, dear lady, in my misspent youth, you know." He winked. "Yes, indeed, I passed some of the happiest years of my life in your London metropolis. I am not quite the country bumpkin you think me."

I of course protested with a laugh. "Goodness, Mr. Sweetnam, I never thought you that."

"My father wished for me to study law, but I am afraid I disappointed him sorely. I was only ever interested in art, and London is full of art and artists, as you well know."

I nodded, though not entirely without sympathy for his father.

"Not to mention all the other delights," he continued, with a knowing smile.

I was not inclined to enquire about the nature of those, but hoped he meant the theatre, the opera, and other cultural activities.

"Sadly, you know," he confessed, "when my father discovered I had been skipping my classes, he cut off my allowance and summonsed me back to Ireland forthwith."

"Your father was in the legal profession, too," I asked.

"Him? Goodness, no, he was in trade." Florrie spat out the words as if it were something shameful. "Manufacturing this and that, you know. He hoped for better things from me, as he saw it, but when that plan failed, I was forced into the business… Until he died, of course, and then I sold up. Dear mamma," he beamed, "was quite all right with that. She could see that sort of life was not for me… And then, alas, she too went to a better place."

At least the source of Florrie's wealth was now explained as an inheritance and I could not help musing that, since his father's most convenient passing, Florrie had probably never worked another day in his life.

Arriving in due course at St. Michael's, we alighted and bade farewell to Mrs. O'Meara and Thomas for the time being.

As we entered the church, there was some stirring among the congregation, as well as glances and mutterings in our direction. The news of Lily's release must already have reached these good people, and I wondered how that could be. Florrie said it was probably thanks, or no thanks, to Sergeant Hackett, who would have hastened to impart the news to the Kinsellas and Cullens, as well as to Colonel Timmins. I could see the back of that gentleman's head in the front pew, stiff and upright, while Augusta peeped round at us with a frightened face.

"Fun and games," whispered Florrie. "What a lark!"

Which was not exactly how I should have described it.

It was a relief that Mr. Webber's sermon made no mention of Lily, though he did gallop through a discourse on God's mercy, a pleasant change from his earlier bellicose pronouncements. It seemed his words made no impression on the Colonel, however. At the conclusion of the ceremony, he hurried out of the church with a face like thunder, while Augusta delayed, creeping over to us with the news, in case we had not noticed, that Mortimer was very, very cross.

"He feels you have stabbed him in the back," she said to me in hushed tones. Not a very happy choice of words under the circumstances.

"I hope he will not take it out on you," I whispered back.

To this she just made a little face. At least her bruise had faded, and there were no others to be seen.

Once outside the church, I found there was no escaping the Resident Magistrate's wrath. He came right up to Florrie and myself, almost spitting in my face.

"Mrs. Hudson, I trust you realise that you have quite undermined my authority with your meddling."

He spoke loudly, and people were turning to look. Even the vicar raised his head in some surprise.

"If you had exercised your authority properly in the first place, Colonel," I replied, "there would be no reason to meddle now. Excuse me." I turned towards Florrie's barouche.

"Don't you dare walk away from me, madam," the Colonel shouted. "I haven't finished with you yet."

"Well, I have quite finished with you." I spoke as coolly as I could. Really, it was all most unseemly. I hoped I did not look as shaken as I felt.

"You will never be welcome at my house again," he yelled after us. "Never. As for you, Sweetnam, you've guzzled your last glass of my Amontillado."

"Oh dear," said Florrie, as we clambered aboard the barouche, "that is punishment indeed. Although," and he grinned, "he only ever gave me a thimbleful anyway. Now, Mrs. O'Meara,' he said to the housekeeper as Thomas drove us off, "how did you get on?"

It was only then I noticed that the housekeeper, too, looked distressed. Surely not on our behalf.

"Oh Mr. Sweetnam, sir, it was horrible, so it was."

"Why, my dear. What is the matter?"

To our dismay, the woman burst into tears, and it was Thomas who answered. I found I was at last getting used to his strong local accent and managed to understand him completely, without having to turn to Florrie for a translation.

"Them Kinsellas and their lot waited outside the church, crowding up against us." Thomas told us. "Quite threatening they was. Now I can handle it, Mr. Sweetnam, sir, but to do that to an old woman like Mrs. O'Meara, well, it wasn't right."

"No, indeed."

"Worse, the ould priest took their part, didn't he, Mrs. O'Meara."

"He did so," she sobbed. "Father Joe preached from the pulpit that people should be ashamed of themselves to let a Catholic girl into a black Protestant house where they would try and turn her away from the true church. He was looking at me the whole time he said it, so he was. God would judge, he said. God would punish.

And he shook his fist and pounded the pulpit. It was horrible, Mr. Sweetnam, horrible."

"I am indeed very sorry to hear that," Florrie replied. "You had best not go back there again."

"Oh, I couldn't miss mass, sir."

"I see. No, of course not." He smiled. "Then perhaps next week Thomas can take you to another church. Even, perhaps," he added rather grandly, "to the cathedral in Enniscorthy. How about that?"

"Oh no, sir. I wouldn't want to put you to the trouble."

"Not at all. It is I who have brought trouble down upon your blameless head."

"I'd be very grateful to go to any other church than that one... But you won't, will you sir?"

"What, Mrs. O'Meara?"

"You won't try and turn the girl, will you?"

Florrie laughed and patted her hand. "Not at all. Not at all."

The next few days passed quietly and, for Kitty, Lily and myself, mostly in the Orangery or in the garden. Lily particularly seemed to find solace in the idyllic setting, though she must have known full well that this period of calm would not last, and that, sooner or later, she would be summonsed to trial. Nevertheless, she had been greatly heartened by her conferences with Malone, the lawyer.

"He believes me, you know," she told us, almost surprised at the fact.

From time to time, I tried to solicit from her more memories of that terrible night, but she really could remember very little.

"I felt quite dizzy and fearful when I left the men. They were all laughing and roaring. Men with drink taken, you know, always talk more loudly."

The poor girl had much experience of men with drink taken, I suppose.

197

"I could hardly walk straight, which had them laugh the more, and say things to Francie that made me ashamed. Luckily Briege was there to support me and brought me a cup of herbal tea she said would help me sleep. And it did, because no sooner had I lain my head down that I was gone. The next thing it was morning and… and…"

She started to shake, and Kitty put her arms around her to soothe her.

"What was in this drink that Briege brought?" I asked.

"I don't know. It was quite bitter."

Not camomile, then, which is sweet. So had Briege deliberately drugged the girl? That would account for Lily not waking up, even when Francie was being attacked right beside her. Yet that, in turn, might well suggest Briege had knowledge of the planned attack, or even that she had attacked him herself. On the other hand, maybe the drink was simply a draught of valerian or even henbane, kindly meant and kindly given. It was after all surely too far-fetched to imagine the sister wanting her brother dead. Even less if he were in fact her own son. What possible reason could there be? Surely if she were jealous of the new bride, then the obvious person to get rid of was the girl herself. Oh, how I prayed that some of the deductive powers of my erstwhile tenant would descend upon me, to clear my head and show me the way to truth.

As I have recorded previously, Lily had provided me with the names of the men present in the farmhouse that night, and a right bunch of blackguards they were, as Annie had described them. I still considered it most probable that, after the women had departed, a row had broken out among them, or that a long-held and bitter grudge had at last overtaken one or other of them under the influence of the drink. Murders under those circumstances, as Peter had informed me, were frequent in Ireland, and classed somewhat quaintly as "melancholy accidents." Apparently such crimes were regarded more leniently as a result, the which I am quite sure never would happen in England where murder is murder full stop.

How to find out if a "melancholy accident" were the explanation in this case seemed, nevertheless, an impossible task for me, who could hardly go around and interview the suspects. The Colonel and Sergeant would certainly not tolerate my further meddling, even if any of the men were prepared to talk to me, which was of course most doubtful.

It was so frustrating. Mr. H and Dr. Watson could have infiltrated local society so much better than I. Hardly could I don a disguise, as a peasant woman or similar, to hunt around in search of clues. No one would have been taken in for an instant.

Trying to look on the bright side, however, I hoped that maybe it would all prove unnecessary. Maybe the legal arguments of Mr. Malone would be sufficient to throw doubt on a conviction. Yet in my heart of hearts I felt that, unless another perpetrator were unmasked, Lily would stand little chance of acquittal.

Meanwhile, for much needed distraction, I liked to visit Mrs. O'Meara in her kitchen to learn some local recipes I could bring back with me when I finally returned to Baker Street. I particularly required details of her delicious fruity and moist barmbrack, which I was surprised to learn contained cold tea. As a favourite of Florrie's, it featured most days on the table, and was particularly tasty smothered in creamy locally made butter.

I hoped, all the same, that Mrs. O'Meara was not under the impression that I wished to learn these recipes because I was intending one day to usurp her place in the household. Some remarks she made about me being a favourite with the master, accompanied by a knowing look, suggested just that, but I tried as best I could to dispel those suspicions, insisting that I could hardly wait to go home to London and was only staying on for Lily's sake. In reply to which, Mrs. O'Meara merely shook her head, an annoying little smile playing over her lips.

Another fine dish she had served up, which I had never heard of in England, was boxty, a flavoursome pancake made with mashed and grated raw potato, mixed with flour, salt and pepper, and fried in butter. As she showed me how to prepare it, Mrs. O'Meara turned to the scullery maid, and said, "Tell Mrs. Hudson the rhyme, Betty."

The girl immediately piped up, "Boxty on the griddle, boxty on the pan, if you can't bake boxty, sure you'll never get a man."

"Well," I replied firmly, "I certainly don't want a man, but I shall be happy to make boxty back at home in my own kitchen."

Mrs. O'Meara merely smiled and nodded.

Chapter Fifteen

On the third day the unspeakable happened. It was late in the afternoon and growing cool in the garden. Kitty and I wished to go to prepare ourselves for dinner, but Lily expressed the desire to remain out for a little longer.

"It is so beautiful here," she said, wonderingly. Nature for her previously must have often seemed an enemy to be fought and overcome, a cruel and demanding mistress, loath to give up the fruits of her stony soil under hard frosts and deluging rains, sometimes even a parching sun. Now, all was still and peaceful under God's heaven. It helped of course that this summer evening was balmy with the fragrance of roses and jasmine and honeysuckle.

"Please let me stay here a while," she said. "I love to see the darkness come over all, like a soft blanket, so it is."

Seeing no harm in that, we left her be.

Dinner time came and Kitty informed me, with some surprise, that Lily had not yet returned to their bed chamber. Perhaps, she surmised, the girl had gone straight into the dining room, but when we entered it, we found there only Florrie already seated at the long table, his napkin round his neck in anticipation of culinary delights to come. He, as he told us, had seen nothing of the girl. Perhaps, we wondered, had she peeped into the room and, observing that only the master was present, had in her timidity hidden herself until we arrived. We waited a little while longer, but there was still no sign of her. It was then we started to get really anxious, rising from the table, leaving the soup, and going out into the gathering dusk to look for her. We called her name but were answered only with silence.

Florrie then summoned Thomas and some of the men to do a wider search, spreading out along the road in both directions, in case she had decided on a walk and got lost.

"Where ever could she have got to?" Kitty was distraught, as was I.

"We will find her," Florrie assured us, but I could tell that he was worried, too.

After what seemed like an eternity, Thomas came rushing back with terrible news. An old man, seated outside his cottage smoking a pipe, told him that a group of men had gone by, dragging a girl with them. When he called to ask what they were about, they had answered only with curses.

"Who were they?" Florrie asked. "Did he recognise them?"

Thomas looked grim. "Mossie Kinsella was one of them."

Florrie then instructed him to make haste and go for Sergeant Hackett.

"Tell him to hurry to the Kinsella farm. There's mischief afoot and no mistake."

Kitty blamed herself. I assured her that no one could have foreseen such an outcome, although privately I too felt guilty that we had relaxed our guard. Had Mrs. O'Meara not told us of the threats Mossie and others had made at church, and had not the priest, Father Joe, virtually encouraged them to take matters into their own hands?

"I do not think we should wait on Sergeant Hackett," I said to Florrie. "He may not be at the barracks, or he may not take the matter seriously, and time is of the essence here."

"Do you think we should go there alone?" Florrie said, somewhat fearfully. As I had observed on a previous occasion, he was no hero.

"You should stay here with Kitty," I said. "I will go to Kinsellas with a couple of your men, perhaps Con and Liam."

The two I mentioned were sturdy lads, good to have on your side in a fight, if it came to it.

"You should not go either, Martha," said Kitty.

"For Lily's sake, I think I must."

I fetched Henry's umbrella, while the two lads prepared the barouche.

"Are you expecting rain?" Florrie asked. "Or are you planning to hit someone over the head?"

"If it comes to it," I said.

I have never hit anyone in my life, with or without an umbrella, but there is, as the saying goes, always a first time, and the umbrella, I felt gave me a small measure of protection.

"Hey ho," said Florrie, admiringly. "You are quite the Amazon, Mrs. Hudson." He waved us on our way, while Kitty looked on anxiously.

Con proved a worthy driver, and we fairly sped along the few miles to the Kinsella's farm. When we arrived, the first unusual thing that struck me as we drove into the yard was the pitiful whining of the dog, the same mutt that usually greeted newcomers with fearsome barks. We could see it tied up, but, at the sight of us, it slunk back into the shadows.

I marched up to the farmhouse, the two lads behind me, and, hearing a commotion within, threw open the door.

Now that it is all over, I can recollect, as Mr. Wordsworth said in another context, emotion in tranquillity, but for a long time after I would tremble at the memory of that terrible hour.

The scene that presented itself to us was as barbaric as something from the Dark Ages, some medieval version of hell fire, the air, heavy with the stench of burning peat, catching in the throat and stinging the eyes. The kitchen, lit only by a flickering oil lamp and the embers of a fire, was crowded with the shadowy figures of men, like the souls of the damned. With their backs to us, they formed a wall around something I could not yet see, and their voices emitted deep-throated growls that sounded hardly human – wolves surrounding their prey. Then one of the men moved and, to my horror, in the midst of this unholy circle, I discerned two women: Briege Kinsella, hopping like some demented sorceress, was brandishing a flaming stick of wood in the face of poor Lily. She in turn was struggling vainly against the two big men who were restraining her, two men whom I recognised from the wedding, their eyes wild, their faces reddened with drink.

"Tell me, witch, tell me," Briege was yelling, waving the stick ever closer to Lily's face.

"I don't know," Lily was crying back. "Men, I beg you all, have pity on me. I swear to God, I am innocent. I did nothing that night, I swear it, Briege."

"Don't speak of God, you witch." And the flames near caught on Lily's long hair.

"Stop!" I cried out, speaking in as commanding a way as I was able. "What is this horror?"

It was only then that people became aware of my presence.

"You, woman!" roared Mossie. "Get away out of here. This is no place for the likes of ye." He looked beyond, at the two men with me. "And Con Bourke and Liam Bolger. Off with ye. This is family business here."

"Oh, Mrs. Hudson, save me," cried Lily. "They are all gone fierce mad. They are going to kill me for sure." She screamed out then. The men holding her must have crushed her arms.

"No, they will not, Lily," I said in a firm voice. "Don't be afraid. We have come to fetch you home."

Briege came up close to me then, still grasping the flaming pole.

"You know nothing about it," she said in a threatening whisper. "Any of it."

"If you harm this girl, you will be severely punished by law," I said.

"What care I for your laws," screeched Briege, with a cackling laugh that chilled the soul. "We are beyond your Sassenach laws here, lady."

The men muttered agreement and crowded round me. I could smell their sweat, their dirt, their rage. How glad I was to know that Con and Liam were behind me.

"Leave the girl alone," I repeated, trying to keep my voice steady.

"This girl, you say." Briege threw back her head in ghastly merriment. "This is no girl, lady. This is a faery changeling."

"What!"

"No," Lily cried. "No. It's not true."

I was aghast. More magic and superstition, this time not confined to quaint little tales for children, but manifesting as something deadly serious. I tried to step forward, but someone grabbed my arm and pulled me back.

"Look at this thing," Briege whirled around, addressing the men. "Is this Lily Cullen?"

There was a murmuring.

"Oh, to be sure it looks like her, but not like. This worn drawn thing is not the pretty girl my brother married. Look at her." She paused triumphantly. "No, this thing stole into my brother's bedroom the night of the wedding, and took the place of his innocent bride."

Did they really believe this? I could not credit it. Yet there was something in the atmosphere, something primitive and oppressive. The faces around me, bucolic, roughened by hard work, hard lives and drink, came from places far, far from my experience of the world.

"No, Briege," Lily protested, her voice breaking. "It's not true. I'm no faery witch… Look at me, men. I'm Lily, your neighbour. You've known me all my life. Daughter to William Cullen and Nora Hayes, God rest her soul. … Briege, I beg you, I am your sister!"

Her pleas enraged the woman even more.

"Lies, lies! The faeries took her and left this creature in her place," Briege screeched. "It killed my brother. My Francie. Didn't da and I find it with the knife in its hand?"

"I'll never forget the sight. Not to my dying day," Mossie cried out. "Our poor Francie all blooded and dead. My son's innocent blood spilled all over her, the witch."

He fell to his knees, hands on head, his face distorted by grief, sobbing loudly.

"Think, men. Would little Lily Cullen have been capable of that?" Briege asked

More mumbling and shaking of heads.

"The magistrates found it guilty, didn't they? We all saw how they sent it off to the Bridewell," Briege lowered her voice. "But it worked its faery magic and got set free."

"Not true," Lily insisted again. "I found him cold and dead. Cold and dead." But no one was listening to her.

"Did you see your one at church yesterday?" Mossie continued, getting to his feet. "No, you did not, because she couldn't take communion. It would burn her faery tongue."

"Yes," the men said, nodding. "Yes, yes, yes."

"I'll burn its faery tongue to get the truth out of it." Briege approached Lily once more, the flaming stick raised up.

She was quite, quite mad. They all were. I pulled myself free and turned to Con and Liam.

"Help me get Lily away," I said.

"Don't you set a foot closer, boys," Mossie ordered. "This is our business, so it is. You don't need to get mixed up in it."

"Go your ways, lads, and be quick about," said another man. It was Jack Keane, the strange looking creature with the scarred face who had been at cards with Mossie at the funeral. The man who taught Briege all she knew about remedies and charms.

"Go home, Liam, son," urged yet another.

"Da?"

"Get away, son. You was never here," the man said.

"If you leave," I told the boys. "You will be responsible if anything bad happens tonight."

But they were already shuffling towards the door.

"Take the ould witch with you," Briege cried out.

"Yes." Mossie said. "Take her. Or something bad might happen to her, too."

I stepped in front of Lily.

"I am not leaving without the girl," I said. "Really, men, you cannot believe she is a faery. Not in this day and age. There are no faeries. Lily is flesh and blood like you and me."

"Ha!" Now Briege waved her flaming stick so close to my face that I could feel its heat. "Like you is it? So maybe you're a faery too. Are you? Are you a faery, lady?"

"Don't be ridiculous. Of course I'm not."

"Of course I'm not," Briege parodied my words, my accent. "Ha! That's what you witches want us to think. That's your trickery. Your shape-shifting."

"Get out while you can," Mossie hissed at me. "I won't be telling you again, missus."

"No," I said. "This is barbarism. Con, Liam…"

"Sorry, missus, sorry," Con said. "Sorry, Lily." He looked terrified, remorseful. Liam's head was down. He could not look me in the eye.

The door opened and shut behind them. They were gone.

So now it was me against the rest, and I confess it was all I could do to stop myself running out after the lads. Yet I could not bring myself to abandon the girl.

The next thing I knew, I was again grabbed by rough hands. They tried to drag me to the door and throw me out, but I was having none of it, fighting back as best I could. Henry's sturdy umbrella was put to good use, I am pleased to say, inflicting a few bloody noses and crowns, including on the men holding Lily. Vile curses were flung at me, and while words, as they say, can never harm you, what could I, a woman no longer young, achieve in the end against a roomful of strong men? They swiftly overcame me and forced me down by the girl, to be held as fast as she.

"Oh, Mrs. Hudson," she said. "What will become of us at all?"

I could not answer for I did not know.

Now I could see Mossie talking urgently in low tones to Briege, pointing at me. Maddened with drink and the wild atmosphere of the proceedings, he was still, I suppose, hazily aware that it was one thing to abduct and torture one of their own, but that I, as a middle-class English woman, presented a problem. No talk of faeries or witches would be any defence if I suffered at their hands. His daughter, however, shook her head vehemently.

"They are both in this," she muttered. "I see it clearly. Two witches in league. Remember, da, how she came so quick after the murder to look after her faery kin. She's as guilty as the other. They both must be made to confess. And fire is the key."

Terrifying words, indeed. I felt Lily tremble against me. Could this really be happening? Surely God could not permit it. I sent up a silent prayer.

Briege then ordered the men, to carry Lily to the fireplace. The girl started screaming in terror. Was she to be flung upon the fire? Even though the flames were not high, the embers glowed bright, and she would be badly burned.

However, they just held her there, for now well above danger.

"Confess," Briege said. "Tell what you have done with Francie?"

Poor Lily sobbed and burbled again that she was innocent, that she had nothing to do with his death. Briege stirred the fire under her with her stick and sparks flew up. I gasped, but thank God none caught. Yet the vision of Lily held over that fire about to be roasted has etched itself deep on to my memory, where it haunts me to this very day.

Meanwhile, Briege had crouched down and was staring intently into the embers as if reading something there. A waiting hush descended on the room, the men seemingly deferring to the higher wisdom of this strange little woman, somehow transformed into a dark priestess or sibyl. As for me, despite the heat, I suddenly felt shivery. If I were of a superstitious frame of mind, like the rest of those poor benighted folk, I too might have thought there was a supernatural presence in the room.

"No." Briege spoke finally, a new queer ecstatic quality to her voice. "I see. I see it is nothing but the truth it tells. Put it back. The fire has forced out the truth."

The men holding Lily restored her to the bench beside me. She was near fainting with shock. I tried to give her a reassuring smile, though it was far from reassured I felt myself to be.

Briege started to laugh then, the same chilling sound as before.

"It did not kill Francie, do you see, for one good reason. It did not kill Francie," she repeated, "because he is not dead."

I felt the men holding me recoil in confusion at these words.

"We saw him in his coffin," one muttered. "We saw him buried. Six foot under."

"He is not dead!" she cried in exultant tones. "It is more faery trickery. Don't you understand? The faeries wanted my beautiful Francie for themselves, so they left another changeling in his place. To fool us. Oh, how nearly we were fooled."

There were stirrings. Wasn't this beyond the credulity even of these most credulous beings? Yet I too suddenly remembered my unnerving experience looking into Francie's coffin. The way he had seemed to look up at me, to sneer, about to clutch. A faery changeling, he? I shook my head. Absurd! A mere trick of the flickering candlelight. Surely that's all it was.

Now Briege seemed in a trance.

"I know what we must do," she intoned. "I read it in the embers, men." She stirred them again with the stick and more sparks flew up. "Yes, yes. We must go to the rath of Knocnacoill at midnight. Lily and Francie will appear there together on a grey horse. We must take black handled knives to cut them loose from their fetters and free them from the enchantment. We must get them back."

The men stared at her. Mouths open, eyes wide.

Then "Yes," I heard whispered all around me. "Yes, yes, yes."

It was as if they too had entered her hallucination.

"And this one?" asked Mossie. "What do we do with her?"

Briege turned slowly and looked Lily full in the face. She smiled.

"This faery must be sent back to faeryland," she said. "And fire will speed it on its way."

She picked up the oil lamp with the intention, I guessed, of throwing it over the girl. Lily screamed.

"Stop," I cried. "It was you, Briege Kinsella, and none other, who killed your brother Francie from jealousy, and now you plan to murder the one he preferred over you."

I do not know to this day what prompted me to say such a thing. Until that moment, I had hardly thought it possible. Maybe, as Kitty said later, the faeries inspired me. Whatever about it, Briege

210

gave a great scream and fell in a faint on the floor. The oil lamp spilled and flames flared up, engulfing the woman. In the rush to save her and extinguish the fire, both Lily and I were let go. I grabbed the girl by the hand and dragged her away through the thick smoke. The moment I opened the door, the inrushing wind fired up the flames even more, but we managed to stumble into the yard, then out of the yard and into the shadows. I could hear shouts and someone behind us, and tumbled the two of us into a ditch where we could not easily be seen. I held my hand to the girl's mouth, for she was unable to stop gasping from terror.

Now the road was filled with men. We could hear them arguing as to where we might have gone. In the end some went one way and some the other, while a few lingered at the gate. None thought to search the ditches, thank God, but we were not safe. We could not move, and I feared that at any instant we would be discovered. All we could do was to stay as still as possible, the damp and cold seeping up around us.

And then Mossie came out with a lamp and the dog. He must have given it something of Lily's to smell for it snuffled around, a terrifying sound. We could hear it coming closer and closer, panting with excitement. A hell hound set to tear us to pieces. The girl started trembling uncontrollably against me and moaning. All was lost.

"What in heaven's name is going on here, lads?"

An authoritative voice. The voice of Sergeant Hackett. I had never thought to be pleased to hear him but now his words were like the proverbial music to my ears. Then another voice I liked even better. Florrie Sweetnam calling my name.

Muddied and dishevelled, I rose up from the ditch with Lily in my arms. What a sight we must have been. Dear Florrie stood amazed, Thomas at his side.

"By God, they was here all the time," Mossie said, lunging at us, the dog barking in a frenzy, its mouth foaming. "You near killed my daughter, you cursed witch."

"Briege would have killed Lily," I replied, my voice shaking, shielding the girl with my body. "I did nothing but speak my mind."

"You said my daughter murdered Francie! That was a damned lie."

I think he would have let his rabid dog loose upon us, even in front of witnesses, had the Sergeant not intervened.

"Now, now," he said in a firm voice. "Control yourself, Mossie, and get that dog of yours away. We'll get to the bottom of the matter in due course, I promise you that." He looked at Lily, her pale face trembling. "This girl should be taken home."

"She should be taken to the barracks," said Mossie. "She should be locked up."

Somehow I felt that he at least did not believe Lily to be a changeling, for surely no locks could confine a faery. Or maybe out in the fresh air the spell had broken.

"Lily should come back with me," said Florrie. "Where she can be looked after properly. As the judge ruled, don't you know. It's these men should be arrested, Sergeant, for abducting the girl and planning worse. For threatening poor Mrs. Hudson here."

"That's all as maybe," the policeman replied in appeasing tones. "As I said, Mr. Sweetnam, sir, we'll get to the bottom of the matter in due course. Now then, Mossie, you must understand that Lily has been released on bail into the care of Mr. Sweetnam here, and it is not for me to overrule that judgment however misguided you or I might feel it to be."

He was not our friend and, I think, never would be, but, thank goodness, he at least felt himself duty bound to uphold the law of the land.

Mossie made no further appeals, but withdrew back to the house, muttering that he must see to his daughter. The men with him crept away into the night, whether ashamed or not at what they had tried to do, I could not tell.

Florrie helped the still trembling Lily and myself, who was no less shaken, into his barouche. Then with Thomas driving, safe at last we travelled back without delay to Castle Florence. On the way, Florrie explained how Con and Liam had arrived in a frightful state, guilty at having abandoned Lily and me to the mob. After they explained all to him, he set off at once. The arrival of Sergeant Hackett at the same time was a happy coincidence, Thomas having previously managed to convince the policeman of the gravity of the situation.

All the way, I hugged Lily to me. How slight she was. I remembered my own daughters at that same young age and thanked God that we, at least, lived in a civilised country where such practices as these have long been forgotten.

Chapter Sixteen

It was later the next day and Lily was resting in her room, with Kitty sitting by her bed, reading to her. Because of the heavy rain, I could not walk in the garden but was sitting in the Orangery, unable to concentrate on my Trollope, staring out at the dreary afternoon and reliving the events of the previous night. Would we be safe now, or should Castle Florence, metaphorically, pull up its drawbridge and prepare for further attacks?

I was also regretting my new puce silk dress, utterly ruined by its immersion in the ditch, although I suppose it would have been worse had I been wearing my good black bombazine. Oh, how I wished more than ever to be back in Baker Street in my own cosy little place. My head was pounding horribly, and I idly wondered what concoction Briege might supply to ease it. Certainly, Kitty had benefitted from her ointment. Whatever else the woman was up to, she knew her herbs.

As if my thoughts had conjured up the Kinsellas, I was astonished and not a little frightened to see Mossie enter the Orangery with Florrie, Thomas, acting the bodyguard, behind them. The man's demeanour, however, was totally changed from that of the night before. Cap in hand, head bowed, he seemed lost for words. I stared at him and then at Florrie, who shrugged his shoulders.

"He begged to see you," he said.

"Well, what is it, Mossie?"

"I brought back your fine umbrella, your ladyship." He tried out a bow. "You left it behind you. You'll be needing it in this weather, so you will."

Was that it? He did not need to see me face to face to return it.

"Thank you," I said, and waited. Clearly there was more. He coughed.

"And a basket of new-laid eggs from our fine hens."

A scrawny lot as I remembered them.

"I hope you'll enjoy the hen's eggs, your ladyship."

"Thank you," I said again, still at a loss.

There was more then, and it came in a sudden rush.

"I am most heartily sorry, your ladyship, for the troubles of yester eve…" He banged his chest as if to verify the whereabouts of his heart. "I trust your ladyship is quite recovered by now." Still staring at the floor. "May I be so bold as to say you're looking well, so you are."

"I reckon Sergeant Hackett put you up to that, didn't he, you scoundrel?" said Florrie. "To try to stop Mrs. Hudson from bringing charges against you and yours."

"No, no, Mr. Sweetnam, sir. No, the Sergeant isn't in it at all. Not at all, so help me God. 'Tis myself, Maurice Kinsella, that is heartily sorry, and that's God's honest truth." He shuffled a bit. "Wasn't it bad poitín got to us all last yester eve. Sent us crazy, so it did."

"And Briege," I asked. "Was she maddened with the poitín too?"

"Ah well, Briege, you know…"

"She's just mad," commented Florrie.

"It's for Briege I'm here now," Mossie went on, ignoring the remark. "Well, and to give you back your umbrella and the hen's eggs and tell you how heartily sorry I am, your ladyship… I pray to heaven above you believe me."

"Yes, yes. All right." I almost preferred the old Mossie to this snivelling wretch.

"See, Briege," he said at last. "Well, she's very bad."

215

A moral judgement or a description of her physical state?

"She's been asking for you, so she has."

"For me?"

"She wishes to tell you something."

"I hardly think," I replied, "that I wish to hear anything from her. Do you really believe after what happened last night, Mossie, that I ever again intend setting foot in your house? You must think I'm as mad as you are."

He was miserable. He was broken, hanging his head.

"That was… that was… There was bad drink, like I said, missus, your ladyship. No real harm meant."

I could not believe my ears.

"No harm! You were threatening our very lives, man. Your daughter was about to throw burning oil over Lily."

"Well, now, I won't admit to that. No, you took us up wrong there, your ladyship, and I'm heartily sorry if you was afraid… Still and all, you must understand our strong feelings against Lily, after her killing Francie and all..."

I started to object, but now he was in full flow.

"Any road," he said, "you've nothing to fear from us now, I promise you. We'll be as meek as new born lambs, from here on in, so we will. We will let justice take its course, like the Sergeant said… She's awful bad with the burns, missus. Please…" He looked up at me at last, his eyes watery and pleading, and I could not but feel pity for the man, brutish and uncouth though he was.

"I don't know," I said.

"Please… Mr. Sweetnam here can come along wi' ye."

Florrie as my knight in shining armour. The thought made me smile.

"Well, maybe Thomas," I said relenting. I knew I should feel safer with that young man by my side, even if I remained dubious about the wisdom of the enterprise.

I could tell that Florrie did not wish me to go, and that Thomas was less than enthusiastic as well, particularly given the inclemency of weather. Nevertheless, curiosity, that wayward friend, persuaded me finally to agree to return with Mossie.

I was mightily glad of Henry's umbrella, somewhat buckled though it was from its use as a cudgel the night before. Even travelling the short distance from the door of Castle Florence to the barouche would have drenched me without it, for the rain was veritably bucketing down. Indeed, the vehicle itself, though no doubt stylish, was not really suited to intemperate Irish weather, and the rain drove in upon us so hard that I soon regretted my decision. By the time we reached the farm, poor Thomas must have been soaked to the very skin. The same for Mossie, although I am afraid I did not feel any great sympathy for him. Myself in the back under the hood was less afflicted, but still very damp.

The farmhouse presented a more dismal aspect than ever, and the inevitable barking of the dog as we arrived made me shudder, recalling the creature's menacing demeanour of the night before, quite ready and happy to tear out throats out. It was with much relief, then, that I could see the dog was once again safely tied up.

The kitchen looked to be in ruins following the fire. The wooden table was singed black on one side with a leg so charred it would need replacing, while all that remained of a chair was its broken back. All was wet from the buckets of water that must have been thrown to quench the flames, and a sour stench hung over all. Thomas peered around himself in disbelief, while Mossie showed me into the bedroom, the same where I had last seen Francie laid out in his coffin. Now Briege was huddled in the bed, more yellow-looking than ever, her face twisted in pain. I could see no marks of the burns, however, which had, I supposed, to be on her lower limbs.

"Has she seen the doctor?" I asked Mossie.

"She won't. She has her own remedies."

217

"Still, I think…" I began.

"Never mind what you think." Her voice sounded cracked and hoarse, and hardly friendly. "Come over here. And you," she ordered the men. "Go away."

I supposed it was safe enough now, and I nodded to Thomas, who left with Mossie.

"I'll stay near," he promised.

I sat on the edge of the bed, for want of anywhere else.

"What is it, Briege?" I asked, kindly enough I hope.

"You made a dreadful accusation against me last eve, missus."

"It's not true, then?"

"How can you think it? That I would kill my own brother…"

"It would not be the first time such a thing has happened." What about Cain and Abel? "I am still sure that Lily is innocent. And if not her, then who?"

At the mention of the name, Briege laid her head back. "I curse the day Francie laid eyes on that young one. But there was never any gainsaying him. When he wanted something he must have it. And he wanted her." She paused. "I told him in that case to surprise her in the fields or woods some day and take her there by force. But no, he had to have the same little girleeen for wife."

How shocking to hear her words, to talk of ravishment so lightly.

"I think 'twas because she was so pure." She sneered. "Oh, how much he wanted to bring that fine lady down. To hear her cry out under him."

Had she asked me here to listen to this kind of talk? I stood up.

"No." She grabbed my hand. "It's not that I want to tell you. Not that."

Her hand in mine was burning hot, and I feared she was become delirious.

"You said I was jealous," she said. "Yes, I was. He was mine. No one else should have him. But… I did not kill him. I swear it on the Bible."

Her eyes blazed at me, and I could not doubt her, even though it was little thought she had given to the holy book on the previous night.

"What do you mean, he was yours," I asked. "Your brother, surely."

She gestured to me to come near. I bent my head to hear her whispered words, expecting confirmation of the rumoured incest. But it was not that at all.

"My brother?" she muttered. "No, not my brother. Not my brother, but my son and my bedfellow."

I shot back as if hit. Never could I have imagined such a terrible confession.

"Oh, I know what he was," she went on. "How corrupt he was. But he was so beautiful, Mrs. Hudson. The moment he was born, I knew there would be no one else in the whole world for me."

I waited. I could not speak.

"We hid it from folk. When I started to swell, that is. The disgrace of it, do you see. My mother made as if the boy was hers. 'Twas proclaimed a miracle for she was thought, after me, to be barren." Some miracle, indeed! "After dada," she continued, "spread the word that mammy was with child, the two of us stayed home mostly near the confinement. 'Twas easily done."

Hardly, I thought. Did Briege really not know what people were saying about Francie's parentage?

She paused.

"You must have been very young," I said.

"I was twelve, going on thirteen."

Younger than Veronica. My God!

"And the father?" Even now I dreaded what I might hear, though she had disclaimed Francie as her brother.

"That's what I have to tell you now."

And she did. It was not what I expected. Not at all.

I returned to Castle Florence in a daze. My head was spinning as I tried to make sense of it all. The throbbing ache had stopped, though, swept away perhaps by the shock of the revelation.

Thomas made no effort to talk on the journey, and I was grateful for his reticence. Shaking his head from time to time and muttering under his breath, he may, as I suspected, have been in some agitation at what he had seen, though not heard, for that must remain a secret. I had sworn to Briege I would not divulge anything even to Kitty. Both she and Florrie, of course, enquired as to why the woman needed to see me so urgently. I simply replied that she wanted to apologise, face to face, although in fact I suddenly realised that she had done no such thing, and could not help but wonder if she still believed Lily to be an evil changeling who had spirited her Francie away.

My friends accepted my explanation somewhat doubtfully. It is not in my nature to lie, and I think they could tell that I was being less than open with them. Quite genuinely, however, I was able to plead exhaustion. I took to my room where I stayed for the rest of the day, Mrs. O'Meara bringing me some tea and toast, for it was all that I could face. Me, who usually has such a healthy appetite.

I lay on the bed, staring across at the suit of armour, which I had got quite used to by then, regarding it almost as a companion, a protector. Should I act, I asked it now, on what I had learnt? Surely the new information pointed to quite another suspect as the murderer, and threw other explanations out of the window. Yet could I prove my suspicions? It would surely be impossible.

Sleep must have overcome me at some point, for when I returned to consciousness, it was the middle of the night. Troubled dreams I could not quite grasp slithered away from me. In need of air, I crossed to the window and opened it. The rain had stopped, the skies had cleared, and a fingernail sliver of a crescent moon hung over the garden from which Lily had been so roughly snatched. Now all was peaceful. Sweetness rose from the night-scented stocks under my window, and I had a sudden urge to walk out and feel God's clean air upon my face. Assuredly there was nothing to fear out there this quiet night.

I crept down, hoping the dogs would be quiet and docile with me, and not raise the household with their barking. In fact, Bran, the huge wolfhound on guard duty, ran up to me and nuzzled my hand. Thank goodness he did not try this time to jump up, for he was quite capable of knocking me over, as he had nearly done to Lily on several occasions. Out of affection, for he seemed to love her as much as she him. What a shame he had not been able to protect her on that fateful night.

He followed me now around the paths, for company. The stars made a white canopy over us, so all was not obscure. Yet there were flickering shadows and everywhere strange rustlings almost akin to whispering. It was not so hard at that moment to believe in the presence of faery folk, and I wondered fancifully if I should have even been terribly surprised if a leprechaun had come out of the bushes to accost me. Perhaps I was already turning native.

I shook my head to dispel such foolish notions, and then gasped out because there was indeed something unusual there, something white, flitting through the wood. Common sense told me to turn on my heels and rush back to the safety of my room, but once again curiosity overcame me and, protected, I hoped, by Bran, I entered that darkness.

Now I could see nothing at all, and was about to retrace my steps when I heard weeping ahead of me, a very human sound. I proceeded towards it with all caution, and soon could make out a paler patch of ground where the starlight penetrated the trees. It was the same glade again where Florrie had got down on one knee in front of me, so long ago, it seemed, although it was only the other day. Now I spied sitting on the very same bench the hunched figure of a girl, Lily. How she had not heard us up to now was most strange, for Bran and I had rather crunched through the undergrowth.

The dog raced forward to greet his friend. Lily, not recognising us in the dark, started up in terror, and would have fled, I am sure, had I not called her name.

"Oh, Mrs. Hudson," she said, "it's you." And threw herself into my arms.

Bran jumped on both of us, wanting to share the moment. Lily stroked his head and gently pushed him down.

"For goodness sake, girl," I said. "Whatever are you doing out here at this time of night? Especially after what happened before."

I sat her down beside me, and held her tight, the dog at our feet, sensing the mood and looking up at us.

"I thought to run away," she said at last. "I cannot bear it. I cannot go back to that awful place, and there is nowhere else for me to go. I thought maybe after all I could find the faeries and they would take me in and be kinder to me."

"Lily, Lily," I replied, stroking her hair. "There are no faeries. That's just stories."

She stiffened slightly, and I realised I had to reassure her differently.

"Are we not kind to you?" I asked. "Kitty and Mr. Sweetnam and I?"

"Oh yes, more that I could have imagined possible. But even you cannot stop them taking me back there." She burst into more bitter sobbing.

Perhaps I can now, I thought, after what had been disclosed to me. I did not say anything of this to the girl; however, for, to be sure, it might all come to nothing.

At least, thanks be to God, Lily gave up thoughts of finding the faeries that night, returning with me in docile enough manner to the house, the faithful dog plodding behind. She had become chilled in her light shift, and I took her straight down to the kitchen, where I was pleased to see the remains of a fire glowing in the range. I heated some milk and gave it to her, hoping it would soon soothe her into sleep.

She drank it up obediently. I thought again of the other draught she had been given on the wedding night, wondering how much, after all, I could believe of Briege's account.

Soon Lily started to yawn, and I brought her upstairs. Before she entered her bedroom, she begged me not to tell her godmother about her nocturnal roamings.

"For Auntie Kitty will worry so very much."

I agreed, though reluctantly. However, as I told myself privately, it would not break my promise to charge Kitty with keeping an eye on the girl at all times, in case, as my excuse would be, Mossie or others decided again to take matters into their own hands.

Giving me a last hug, Lily crept back into her bedroom, as did I to mine, but it was many, many hours before I was able to sleep again.

Chapter Seventeen

I wish I could say that I rose from my bed invigorated and with a definite plan of action, but instead I felt dull and listless. I washed in cold water, hoping to shake off this most unwelcome miasma, but merely ended up shivering. Let us hope, I thought, that I am not coming down with a summer chill. I am a healthy woman, and yet recent experiences were surely enough to affect even the most robust.

Descending for breakfast, I half feared Lily might have run off again. That was part of the reason, I am sure, that I could not sleep, straining my ears all night to hear soft footfalls on the stairs. It was a relief then to find her at table and eating her porridge – Mrs. O'Meara had been almost offended when I described the dish, the first morning, as stirabout. That, apparently was for peasants, and nothing like the rich mixture she prepared with cream and raisins. Whatever about that, Lily was tucking in, and even gave me a small conspiratorial smile.

After a clear night, the day had started bright, although clouds were already gathering and it looked as if it might again rain later. It was proving difficult enough, restricted to the house and grounds, to plan how to fill our days, without our usual domestic chores. That time in Enniscorthy, as well as our dresses (my ill-fated puce silk), both Kitty and I had picked up wool, knitting needles and crochet hooks, and, when not doing anything else, we were able to pass the time pleasantly enough in peaceful conversation, while making up little garments for our grandchildren. However, to spend many hours that way eventually becomes tiresome, and I envisaged with some dread, the stretch of days ahead of us until the July assizes, when Lily would be sent for trial. Unless I managed to clear her name before that, Effie, Henry and little Alistair would have a whole new wardrobe finished by the time I returned home.

To stretch our legs before the rain, we took a turn in the yard and looked in at the stables, where Thomas was brushing down Florrie's horses. Lily was entranced. Her father had an old nag, right enough, but these were beauties gleaming under the care of their groom. A beaming smile lit up her face as she caressed Dove's grey muzzle.

"Do you ride?" Thomas asked her.

She nodded, shyly.

"Mebbe I can get the master to let you and me take these two for a jaunt some time."

"Oh, can I? Can I?"

She looked at us, her eyes widened in delight, but I was alarmed, recalling suddenly how Briege had said something about faeries and horses. I wished I could remember exactly what it was, but the last thing needed just now was for Lily to be seen cantering around the countryside on a grey mare.

"Just for now," I said, pouring a bucket of cold water over Lily's hopes, "it would not be a good idea for you to leave the sanctity of Castle Florence. I am sure in any case it is against the terms of your bail."

I knew no such thing, but to invoke the law of the land seemed preferable to be seen laying down the law myself.

Kitty nodded in agreement. "Best you stay here safe with us, lovey."

The girl nodded, but she was clearly disappointed.

"Well now," Thomas said comfortingly, "ye are most welcome, Lily, to come and help out with the horses any time you like, and take a turn on Dove here in the paddock."

It was kind and perhaps something more, for I saw how the young man looked at the girl with admiration. Thomas, too, it seemed, did not believe her to be either a murderer or a faery.

At that moment, before Lily could respond, Florrie came out to join us.

"I have a letter for you, Mrs. Hudson," he said, "and Barney is waiting for you."

This was most puzzling. I could not imagine what was the matter. Had the Colonel not said most forcefully that I would never be welcome to visit them again?

I opened the letter. It was from Augusta, and read as follows:

Dear Martha, I wish to apologise in the strongest terms for the intemperate language with which my husband addressed you last Sunday. You know, I hope, that I do not share his animosity. In fact, I am appealing to you as my only true friend. The Colonel is away in Wexford town on estate business just now, and his return is not expected until Thursday. Dear Martha, I should like nothing better than for you to visit me this afternoon. If not today, then tomorrow for I am quite sick with loneliness. Additionally, there is something of an urgent nature which I have to tell you and which cannot be written. You may perhaps guess to what it relates.

I hope it will be today. Please come alone as I am not fit for company and do not wish to share my secret with anyone but you.

Yours in hope and expectation,
Augusta Timmins

I showed the missive to Kitty and Florrie.

"It is quite well written," he remarked, scanning it. "Lots of long words. I had not thought Augusta so literary."

"Oh, we women tend to develop a fine style from our novel reading," I replied with a smile.

"Intriguing too," Florrie added. "I wonder what this dark secret can be. Can you guess it?"

He looked searchingly at me, but I kept my face bland. If he did not know of the Colonel's propensity to violence against his wife, I was not about to reveal it.

"Well, I shall soon find out," I said.

"Will you go then?" Kitty asked. "I did not think you considered her such a great friend."

"Of course, I do not," I said. "You, Kitty, are my dearest friend, of course." I smiled and she smiled back. "Nonetheless," I continued, "I think that I will go and straight away. The message intrigues me." I did not tell them that there was another pressing reason why I was inclined to visit Augusta Timmins.

I collected a few necessities for the journey, including Henry's umbrella. I do not quite know why I took it: the Timminses' carriage being closed, I should not get wet even if it rained. Still, the umbrella had served me well so far, and holding on to its familiar dog's head handle made me feel dear Henry was close to me, like a guardian spirit.

I hurried out to the drive in front of the house. The carriage was all set to go, with Barney in his green uniform, expressionless as ever, already in the coachman's seat whip in hand, the sleek chestnut horse tossing its fine mane as if anxious to be off. Florrie helped me up into the carriage, and soon I was bouncing along behind the Treasure, wondering, with some dread indeed, whatever it could be that Augusta had to impart to me so very urgently.

The Timminses' mansion presented its usual somewhat forbidding foursquare aspect. I was a little surprised when Barney drove round the side rather than stop at the front door.

"They said to go to the summer house."

They? I supposed it had to be a turn of phrase.

"D'you know the way, ma'am?"

I told him I did, and thanked him. He nodded back solemnly.

The garden was as lovely as ever. Blue and copper-winged butterflies were dancing over the massed flower beds, and bees were burrowing into the jaws of the snapdragons. A laburnum tree had come into bloom since my last visit, its golden chains hanging down in rich profusion, while a few late bluebells clustered at its roots.

I started over the little bridge, but could not resist pausing for a moment to watch the glittering water tumbling beneath, pulling thin strands of weed with it. The sight called to mind Lily's long hair, though the thought of her drowned like Ophelia was not a happy one. I shivered, again, wondering if I had caught cold.

I approached the summer house and tapped on the door. It was shadowy inside, and through the glass I could only make out vague shapes, the table, two chairs, one of which, its back to me, was occupied. Augusta was already arrived. I opened the door and went in.

"Ah, here you are at last, Mrs. Hudson. Good day to you."

My heart gave a jolt. For it wasn't Augusta sitting there at all, but the Colonel, who swivelled round in his chair, sneering at me.

"Despite what I said before, you are most welcome, you know. Yes, indeed. Most welcome."

"I am come to see Augusta."

"I know that, but sadly my poor wife has taken to her bed. You will have to make do with me, I am afraid."

What had he done to her? Had he returned early, discovered her letter and punished her? Yet how could that be, when it was I who had the letter? My mind rushed in several directions at once, and it was all I could do to maintain a calm exterior.

"I hope she is not badly ill," I said.

"Not at all. A headache perhaps from too much…" He lifted the glass of amber liquid that stood on the table in front of him, and mimed drinking from it. "I think you know what I mean."

"I should like to see her all the same."

"Please sit down, Mrs. Hudson. I have something I must discuss with you."

"I don't think we have anything to say to each other." I turned to leave.

"Oh, I think we do. I think we have a great deal to say. Just sit down for a moment, if you please. Perhaps we can clear the air. Perhaps you would like a tot of this most excellent *uisce beatha*, as the locals call it."

"No, thank you."

He drank some himself, and sighed with satisfaction. "The water of life, you know."

His tone was genial, but there was a cold glint in those ice-blue eyes. Those eyes. Suddenly I realised that Briege had told me nothing but the truth. I think he must have recognised this too, for his smile broadened, revealing long discoloured teeth like the fangs of a wolf.

"Sit down," he said again, this time more firmly, and glanced beyond me.

I looked where he was looking, behind me, out the door. Barney, the Treasure, was idling near the bridge. Surely it was not possible that he would stop me if I tried to leave. Once again, however, my curiosity overcame my better judgment. I sat down.

"Good," he smiled. "Now…" He picked up a paper that was lying on the table. "Like you, Mrs. Hudson, I too received a letter

229

this morning. Not as well-written as yours I am afraid, for the author is barely literate."

I said nothing. So he knew more about my letter than he should. Was it indeed he, and not Augusta, who had written the note to me? Had I walked into a trap? Yet the calligraphy had looked like a woman's hand.

"Barely literate and barely clinging to life, I am sad to say," he went on. "For which you, madam, have some no small responsibility, I think."

It was Briege who had written to him, then. I waited.

"You have nothing to say. I am astonished. In my experience the fair sex usually has plenty to rabbit on about, whether or not it is to the point." He laughed. "Of course, usually it is not."

I still kept silence.

"Well, I shall have to read it out to you, then. That is, if I can grope my way through the frightful scrawl."

He held the paper a little way off, being, I supposed, long sighted.

"*To Colonel Timmins,*" he read. "Both titles horribly misspelt." He barked a guffaw. "But hardly unexpected. Well, to proceed. *Here I am near death but not...* What now? Ah *willing* (spelt w-i-l-n) Ha! Comical, is it not."

"Colonel," I said. "Please just read it without any asides. They are most tedious."

"Tedious, is it?" He raised those bristling eyebrows. "Well, as you wish."

The letter informed him that being near death, as she thought, Briege had confided everything to Mrs. Hudson under an oath of silence, because she did not wish to take her secret to the grave.

"An admirable sentiment," the Colonel said, tearing the letter up and scattering the pieces on the floor. "But stupid. If you

230

have had to take an oath of silence, madam, what point in telling you in the first place?"

"I should not have termed it an oath, Colonel," I replied. "For instance, I should not feel bound by it if another's life hung in the balance."

He clapped his hands. "Oh, casuistry, thy name is woman. Are you sure you are not a Roman Catholic, Mrs. Hudson?"

I was rapidly tiring of his game. I leant forward on the table.

"You know what Briege told me. That she was not the sister but the mother of Francie." Even, shockingly, more than that, but I would not say so to him.

The Colonel leant back and sighed.

"She also told me who the father was," I went on. "The villain who seduced a little girl of twelve."

"Seduced!" he sat up again. "Ha! She knew exactly what she was doing. She knew full well, the baggage. The way she looked at me. The way she flaunted herself."

"A child doesn't know, Colonel."

"She grew up with animals. An animal herself. Of course she knew."

How vile he was.

"Nevertheless," I said, "you took advantage of her powerlessness."

"And have paid for it ever since." He spat out the words. "The bitch."

"I do not think you have paid very much, from the way she lives."

"That is her choice. Anyway, it is the threat more than the money. The threat to tell that gives her power. I should have dealt with it long since."

His fingers curled into fists.

"But you have continued to… to see her. To have relations with her."

231

"Is that what she said?"

"Yes. Even now."

He hammered his fists on the table.

"You don't know anything about it. How could you, a woman like you? Smug, moralising, holier than thou, clutching your bible to your unappetising bosom… Men have certain needs women like you know nothing about…"

I was shocked. "They also have wives."

"Augusta, is it?" He threw back his head and laughed. Those teeth again.

"But then Briege told Francie," I said.

He drained his glass and poured another.

"The stupid…" The Colonel shook his head. "I cannot make it out. Why now? Was it spite drove her to tell him?"

"Who can say? Francie was getting married. The only person she loved, and he was leaving her. Maybe she thought it was time for him to know."

"He invited me to the wedding. Can you imagine that? The insolence of it. As if I would have anything to do with that cockroach." His colour had risen. "What proof is there he is my son at all? Perhaps she has been lying all these years. A slut like that. The local whore."

If she is, I thought, who made her that?

"You know he was your son," I said. "He had the same eyes."

The same pale blue eyes like splinters of ice.

He stared at me. If he could have ground me to dust with that glare, he would gladly have done so. I shivered but returned his gaze.

"You are some foolhardy woman," he said. "But you have spirit, I'll give you that. Much good it will do you now, though."

I tried to ignore the implications of that remark. I had something to find out, to confirm my suspicions. "So what exactly happened, after you got your invitation?"

He looked at me thoughtfully. "You might as well know all," he continued. "Of course, there was no question of attending the damnation wedding. Imagine, me sitting at the top table, newly reunited with my prodigal son. It was grotesque to think of it." That bark of a laugh again. "I sent Barney to Francie before the wedding to tell him that I would meet him that night. That I would visit under cover of darkness when all was quiet and come to some arrangement, so long as he kept his mouth shut in the meantime. I knew that would work. He was greedy, like all your wretched Irish peasants."

His ugly arrogance was boundless.

"Instead," I said, "you killed him."

More laughter.

"Not at all! Look at me. You think a feeble old man like myself could overpower a strong country lad like Francis Kinsella."

"Yes, if you surprised him. If he turned his back on you. Francie was, after all, stabbed in the back."

He shook his head. "No, no, no, Mrs. Hudson. You cannot lay that on me. I never had any intention of going to the Kinsella farm that night. Me? Colonel Mortimer Timmins, hero of the Crimea. Scuffling about in the darkness like some low-life cut-throat. Never."

His eyes drifted past me. He was looking out the window again, a little smile on his lips.

"Barney!" I exclaimed, the truth suddenly revealed. "Barney did it."

What had Augusta told me the very first time I met the Timminses? How the Treasure was utterly devoted. How he did everything for them.

The Colonel sat back. This time he sipped at his glass.

"Are you sure you don't want a taste?" he asked. "It is so very good."

I shook my head.

"Augusta would not have refused. But then, Mrs. Hudson, you and I know all about her little weakness."

"You would let Lily hang for something she didn't do. An innocent young girl."

"Oh dear lady, which of us is entirely innocent in this life? I am sure Lily's confessor could tell us certain things about that little miss that would make your respectable hair stand on end." The man really had a totally perverted view of human nature. "In any case, as I told you before, she would not have hanged. I am not such a monster as to allow that."

You had your own flesh and blood killed, I thought. It is difficult to imagine how more monstrous one could be.

"Sadly, Mrs. Hudson," he continued, "you now know too much. I suppose I cannot buy your silence?" He looked quizzically at me. I said nothing. "No, I thought not. You are an upstanding, not to say priggish, English lady, with a horribly overdeveloped sense of right and wrong, not like those other animals. It is a shame. A pity for you."

He stood up and crossed by me to the door. It seemed Barney had been waiting for the signal, because he started up towards us. I observed him to be carrying with care a large box that I soon recognised as a beehive.

"Ah, here they come, my little darlings," the Colonel said. "I think I have already explained to you, dear lady, how my bees have been bred to defend the hive against attackers. You should not have attacked the hive, Mrs. Hudson. You should not have threatened the King."

His face screwed up into a mask of rage, and I understood with horror his dastardly plan: to leave me in the summer house with a swarm of disorientated and angry killer bees! I was to be stung to death.

"You cannot do this, Colonel. For the love of God. It is inhuman. I beg you."

"Believe me, I am truly sorry, Mrs. Hudson," he replied. "It is not a very pleasant way to die, for sure. But you see, you have left me no choice. Better all the same, than if I were to set the hounds on you." He laughed. "That would be a sight. Foxy Hudson running through the fields, with my hounds in hot pursuit. Tally ho!" He clicked his fingers. "But sadly, as I told you before, it's not yet hunting season."

"You will surely be discovered." I was becoming frantic. Was this to be my end?

"Not at all. It will be judged a horrible accident, for who could suspect anything else. Of me, who am a pillar of the community, a Resident Magistrate, Master of the Hounds, the last word in integrity and respectability? Of course, I will be truly remorseful." He put on a tearful voice. " 'I should never have let the dear lady wander in the garden by herself. I never dreamt she would go anywhere near the bee hives.' That is where your body will be found, Mrs. Hudson. 'I warned her about them many, many times, but curiosity, as you know, killed the cat'. Ha! The old cat. Yes." His eyes flashed malevolently. "Oh, it will be a performance to rank with Irving's. Yes, indeed. A shame you won't be there. You should see me when I am mortified, Mrs. Hudson. So utterly convincing, you know. Mortified Mortimer." He chuckled. He was mad and I was doomed.

I struck out at him then with Henry's umbrella, and he staggered and nearly fell. I managed to run past, but whatever chance I might have had against the Colonel, I had none at all against Barney. He came rushing up and knocked me back into the room, throwing the hive in after me. It overturned, sending the bees buzzing furiously. I heard the key turn in the lock. The two men were gone leaving me to my horrid fate.

It was at that moment that the blessed spirit of Mr. H visited me and I remembered what he had told me, apropos of his plans to spend his latter years keeping bees.

"They will not sting you, Mrs. Hudson," he had said, "unless they believe they are being attacked. If you ever find yourself caught in a swarm of bees, stay still as a statue and you will be safe."

It was all I could do to try what he had said. I stood, motionless, frozen indeed with terror, hardly daring to breath. Hundreds of bees were climbing all over me, exploring my clothes, my hands, my face, my hair, for my hat had fallen off. Little feet like tickles everywhere. My eyes were closed, and I prayed to God the Father to save me, or if I were to die here, to forgive my many sins and admit me to His Heavenly Kingdom, to reunite at last with my beloved husband.

That was surely the most likely fate, for I could not stay still like that forever. Even if I were not stung, the Colonel would soon return to seal my fate. I could hear the buzzing around my head and around the small confines of the summer house becoming ever more frenzied, the insects banging against the window in their vain efforts to escape. It continued like that for an age. Perhaps it was ten minutes, perhaps even less. When would the Colonel return to view his deadly handiwork? I heard the key turn in the lock. Was this it? Would this be the end?

"Martha," I heard whispered. "Martha, oh my God, are you all right?"

It was Augusta Timmins. I had never been more glad to hear her voice.

The open door drew the bees and they swarmed out, while I collapsed into the little woman's arms.

"He made me write that letter, you know, standing over me, rubbing his knuckles. Then he ordered me to stay in my room. Believe me, Martha, I had no idea he was going to do this to you. I thought he was just going to talk… just talk."

I was looking beyond her. The Colonel was returning. I was not yet saved for I knew Augusta could not stand against him for me. We watched him approach, Barney behind him.

"Whatever is he doing?" Augusta exclaimed, for the Colonel had suddenly launched himself into a grotesque dance, leaping, hopping, waving his arms wildly. The bees, freed, and in a swarm, were attacking him, and Barney was enraging them even more by trying to drive them off, shaking a stick at them. And what a stick it was! Henry's umbrella! Augusta and I watched in horror as the Colonel fell to the ground, shuddering.

"Mortimer should be wearing his gear," she said with concern. "He reacts very badly to bee stings, you know."

I almost laughed, so grotesque it was. After everything that had happened, she was still loyal, ready to run out to him. I pulled her in the opposite direction.

"This way, Augusta," I urged, making for the thicket behind the summer house, thinking to hide there. "You don't want to get stung yourself, do you?"

Now, however, servants were emerging from the big house, drawn by all the commotion. While they were distracted, I judged that it would be safe enough for me to make my way out by a circuitous route, avoiding the plume of bees. I did not wish to linger in a place that had proved so perilous to me, for whom among those here could I trust with my life? Not even Augusta, though she urged me to stay.

I hurried to the front of the house, and, shaken and trembling though I was, I started to walk away from the estate. In one direction the road led to back to Castle Florence, but that was far distant, and I decided the better choice would be to try to reach

Peter and Annie's farm. Even then, as I remembered, it was a good three miles, more, I feared, than my reduced strength would allow. My hope was to meet a Good Samaritan on the way, and it was then that I remembered the old woman, Mammo Kinsella, and her granddaughter, Nell. Their little cabin was not so very far from where I was, although, in my enfeebled condition, it took a deal longer than usual to reach it. At the same time, I was fearfully listening out for any sound of a pursuit, for the Colonel would surely not let me escape so easily, and would soon send Barney after me.

It was with great relief therefore that at last I discerned the tumbledown shack ahead, the old woman outside, chopping turnips as ever, a clay pipe in her mouth. She welcomed me with a lengthy address in her own language and I presumed from her smile that she was thanking me for the small services I had managed to render her. Her shawl looked to be the one I had sent over, and a red petticoat peeped out under her skirts. Nell came out then. I was pleased to see that she was cleaner than before, no longer in the rags she had been wearing when first I met her, but presentable in a blue cotton dress and white apron.

The girl looked at me with concern, being more sharp-sighted than her grandmother, for she perceived that I was on the verge of collapse. She brought me into the gloomy cabin and sat me down on a chair. Then she fetched some water. I gulped it down – seldom had any drink tasted so good – and then, overcome with a weakness, I started to weep.

This would not do. I took a deep breath to pull myself together, and started to explain some of the matter. The old woman had followed us in and stood looking on in amazement as the girl translated what I told her.

"Nell," I said, "there are bad people after me. If they come looking, I beg you in God's name, please don't tell them where I am."

"Not at all," she said. "We wouldn't do that after your great kindness to us… You can hide in the loft, missus."

She helped me up the rickety ladder, and put me among the sweet smelling hay, pulling down the ladder again after her. Just in time, as it happened, for we could hear a galloping on the road. Peering through the slats in the loft, I could see it was Barney on horseback.

By then, Mammo had gone back outside to resume chopping up the turnips. The Treasure started ordering her to tell if a lady had passed that way. His voice was high-pitched and discordant, like a squeaky bagpipe. Mammo muttered back in Irish, which seemed to enrage him.

"You stupid eejit, can't you speak proper! I'll give you Irish gabbling, so I will."

I feared he was about to strike her with his whip, but then Nell hurried out.

"A lady, is it? No one has been past here these few hours, excepting yourself, sir."

Sir, indeed.

"You won't mind if I look in the house, sure you won't," he sneered. His tone forbade a refusal.

"Not at all, sir," Nell replied, "but there's divil a thing you'll find there, never mind a lady."

He must have dismounted, for I soon heard him stomping about beneath me.

"What a filthy hovel!" he exclaimed. I heard him kick a few things over, opening a cupboard door as if he might find me crouching in there, and slamming it shut when he didn't.

I held my breath. If he found the ladder and came up, I would surely be discovered.

"Would your honour like a sup of milk?" Nell asked.

"I would not. I'd be afraid to be poisoned in this place."

"Poitín, then?"

"Damn you, no."

I wondered that she asked, but probably it was to distract him.

He rattled around a little longer.

"Have you an outhouse?" he asked Nell at last.

"Just a shed out back."

He must have gone to look, for I heard him cursing the while. Then he came back.

"Maybe she passed when you didn't see her," he said. "With you in here, like."

"No, sir, that cannot be. Mammo was out all the time. I asked her. There was no lady came past here. It's something you'd notice, sir."

His voice changed, taking on an oily, cajoling tone. "What about if I give you this nice silver coin? Will that help you remember, girleen?"

There was a pause. I imagined her considering the coin and held my breath.

"I'm sorry, sir," she said at last. "I'd like the coin, sure I would, but I can't remember what I didn't see."

His voice hardened again. "God damn your insolence."

Through a crack in the floor, I saw how he grabbed Nell by the hair, and started pulling her head back.

"You better not be lying to me, Nell Kinsella," he said, "or it'll be the worse for you and your ugly old grandmother too."

The girl whimpered piteously. "Why should I lie to you, sir? I don't know any lady, I swear it."

He struck her then, and, with another curse, he left, galloping back the way he had come.

Nell took up the ladder again and climbed up to me.

"He's gone," she said. "Bad cess to him."

"Thank you, Nell," I said. "You could have given me up."

"To him, is it? The dirty blackguard? I wouldn't give him so much as a fig, Mrs. Hudson, ma'am. Pulling out all our presses, he was. Tearing the covers off the bed. Oh yes, I know him all right. He's the one comes by every month to squeeze the last farthing of rent out of us."

They were tenants of the Colonel's, then. As if I didn't have reason to think badly of that individual already, I was now learning how he left these good people in wretched poverty, while importing his expensive sherry and keeping his hounds and his bees, his fine carriage and his fine house. Oh, Onward Christian Soldiers, Colonel Timmins. No Christian you.

Not Barney either. Who would have believed such a devil lurked behind that seemingly stolid front.

Nell was also wondering at Barney. "I don't know what happened to your man, though," she said. "His face and hands were all over red lumps, like he had fallen down flat into a bed of nettles."

So the bees had stung him too. I could not be sorry.

I made to start down the ladder again.

"No," Nell said. "Best you stay there, ma'am, in case your man comes back along the way. I can go for your friends. It's the O'Kellys, amn't I right?"

I nodded, nearly weeping again for the kindness of her, sank back into the sweet-smelling hay and stared through gaps in the thatch at the sky above. I was not heaven-bound yet. No, indeed I still had unfinished business here on earth.

Chapter Eighteen

Now that all is over and I am safely home in Baker Street, I can look back on those terrifying days with a degree of equanimity. It was not so at the time. Not at all. I am not a woman given to hysteria, but I confess I nearly broke down during the long hour waiting for Nell to return, tuned as I was there in the hayloft to every strange sound, every squeak, every footfall, expecting at any moment to hear Barney come back looking for me. To hear him enter the cabin and start climbing the ladder. To see his angry mottled face peering up over the hay loft floor.

In the end, it was Peter who arrived, and never was I more delighted to take a ride in the bone-shaker, first hugging Nell and Mammo tight for helping me escape. I promised that they would get their reward, though wondering at the same time how ever could I repay such a great debt.

"Don't you mind about that, ma'am," Nell said, hopping and dancing with glee. "I was just happy to thwart that nasty old steward"

Barney old, in her eyes, and he not much past thirty!

"All the same," her little eyes sparkled. "Our poor cow might like a friend."

I nodded. Surely that was easily provided.

We drove back in silence. Peter was sensitive enough to understand that I was too overcome to explain all right away, though I noticed how he glanced at me with concern from time to time. I was having difficulty holding all in, and if I had started telling it at that moment, I was not sure I could maintain any degree of composure. In fact, as it turned out, Nell had already blurted out a lurid tale to him, the which at the time he could scarcely credit. When he learnt what had actually transpired, however, the girl's version seemed tame by comparison.

"She said Timmins' man was chasing after you with murder in his eyes. Her actual words were "I knew your woman would be kilt for sure if ever he got his dirty paws on her.""

Back at the farm, I was fussed over by Annie and the little ones who were not at school, my special pet, Pegeen, in particular, delighted to see her Auntie Marta again, and wanted to climb on my lap and hear more stories. The tale I had to tell, however, was not suited to little ears, and the children were sent out to find hens' eggs by Annie. She told them she wanted to make drop scones as a special treat for us all, and they scurried off happily, each with a little basket.

Then I related my misadventures to the kindly couple. When I came to the revelation that Colonel Timmins was behind the murder of Francie, I could see they had difficulty believing me.

"I always knew that Timmins was rotten," said Peter, "but, Martha, this beats all. Are you sure?"

"It sounds very strange," Annie added. "Why ever should he do such a thing?"

I hesitated then. Why break my confidence and blacken Briege's name any further unless absolutely necessary?

"I am not sure," I replied. "There was bad blood between them, I suppose."

Peter thought about that, and then said, "So why turn on you, Martha, if you didn't know anything?"

It was a fair question. They both looked at me askance.

I had to admit then that there was something I had found out about the business which I did not feel I had the right to share, because it involved another person. Peter and Annie had to make do with that, and finally I convinced them enough to send Peter for Sergeant Hackett. Although how that particular individual would receive my accusations filled me with some dread, for the Sergeant had never shown himself inclined to credit me in any way. In addition, he would assuredly take the side of his patron, the Resident Magistrate. Nevertheless, it had to be done, and Peter duly set off for the barracks, while Annie plied me with restorative cups of tea. It was comforting to be in an ordinary domestic setting at last, watching her help the children make the scones, such a contrast to the nightmarish horrors I had so recently experienced.

Peter returned soon enough, not with Sergeant Hackett, however, but with the pleasant young constable I had met before, the which, I admit, was something of a relief.

"The Sergeant has been called out to a commotion at Colonel Timmins' place and has not yet returned," he informed us.

"A commotion, John?" asked Annie. She glanced at me.

"That's all I know. They said it was a very pressing matter."

"Maybe I can explain a little more," I said, and told something of my involvement there. The constable, like the others, was at first disbelieving, although far too deferential to say as much to an English lady. Once I had partly convinced him, he suggested I should accompany him to the Timminses, to tell what I knew to the Sergeant, something I was of course loath to do. I never wanted to set eyes on the place again. However, Peter, obliging as ever, said that he would take me there as my protector.

Back we went along a road become far too familiar to me, the constable cycling beside the cart, me wondering what further shocks were awaiting us. Passing again Mammo's cabin, I noticed that she was in her usual place outside, and, giving her a wave, saw how she followed our progress with wondering eyes. I wondered myself.

Indeed, the developments that soon presented themselves to us were so astonishing that they could hardly have been imagined.

It will make things clear, I hope, if I first recount what had happened after I made my escape from the estate, as recounted to me subsequently by Augusta.

The last I had seen of the Colonel was him being attacked by the swarm of bees with Barney trying to drive them off, but making things worse by brandishing Henry's umbrella (the which I recovered eventually, though in such a sorry state that it was become useless as a means of keeping off the rain. Nevertheless, I cherish it still. It served me well). It seemed the bees finally dispersed or died, but left the Colonel prostrate after his bad reaction to the stings. Barney carried him to the house, and placed him on the chaise longue in the parlour, whereupon, according to Augusta, who had bustled along behind, he instructed the Treasure to go after me, and under no circumstances let me get away.

"What," Sergeant Hackett had asked, taking notes that were after, as I understand it, used in court, "did you take that to mean, ma'am?"

"Well you know," Augusta had said, guilelessly or not, I cannot tell, "Mortimer had already tried to kill Mrs. Hudson once."

She was pleased to recount that the Sergeant had looked thunderstruck. (I wondered if perhaps indeed he thought Augusta drunk.) But then she led him to the summer house, to show him the overturned hive, and how the key to lock the door was on the outside.

"It gave me a terrible turn, you know, when I went in, to see Mrs. Hudson all over bees," Augusta had told him. "Then they flew off out the door and attacked poor Mortimer."

She actually said, "poor Mortimer," even though I can report that her husband did not die from the stings and, in fact, made a rapid enough recovery. Maybe, after all, his bees were not quite the assassins that he had boasted they were.

"Why ever should Colonel Timmins wish to kill Mrs. Hudson?" This had been the Sergeant's next question.

"Oh, because she had found out it was he who killed Francie… Well, not him, of course. Not directly. He sent Barney off to do it."

How dearly I should have liked to see the Sergeant's face, when she made that assertion. You might indeed wonder further, as did I, how Augusta Timmins discovered the truth of the matter? For a few seconds, I suspected that she had known all along, but that, thankfully, proved not to be the case. I should have felt the betrayal hard.

What exactly had happened was this, as I finally understood it from Augusta's rambling account. Barney, having returned from his fruitless search for me, came to get further instruction from the Colonel. That gentleman was still lying stretched on the chaise longue with Augusta in passive attendance, while a maid applied soothing honey to the stings. On hearing Barney affirm that I was nowhere to be found, and maddened by bee venom, it seems the Colonel leapt up in a rage and insisted Barney search me out and deal with me, or it would be all the worse for him. Ignoring the presence of the women – the Colonel never rated our sex worth much, after all – he threatened the Treasure, assuring him that it would be he who paid the ultimate price for the killing of Francie ("I was aghast at that particular revelation, Martha, as you might imagine," Augusta had averred, looking most gleeful, however). The Colonel further swore that he would deny all involvement, and his account would be assuredly believed, as an Englishman and a gentleman against that of a mere servant and Irish bogtrotter.

Thereupon, Barney, himself also suffering from many painful bee stings, showed himself not quite the faithful retainer the Timminses had imagined him to be. There was a line he would not cross, and taking all the blame for Francie's murder was that line.

A terrible row ensued, and in a frenzy Barney seized the Colonel by the throat and would have throttled him there and then, had two men servants not come on the scene, having heard the noise of the shouting and the screams of the women. They managed to drag the Treasure off and lock him in the cellar, where apparently he had proceeded to smash up all the precious bottles of imported Amontillado. The Colonel meanwhile had subsided on to the chaise longue again, quite overcome, and Augusta had taken it upon herself to order that Sergeant Hackett be sent for.

"I don't think Mortimer liked that I did that," she told me after, surely the understatement of the century. However, just as the worm that was Barney had finally turned, so too it seemed had Augusta, after so many years of marital oppression.

Peter, the constable and I arrived just as the Sergeant was interviewing the Colonel, the former merely raising an eyebrow at the sight of us, the latter presenting a sorry sight indeed, all over swelling bee stings. For his part, he regarded me with hatred, realising no doubt that I could well and truly cook his goose. Indeed, with so many witnesses against him, it would have been useless for the Colonel to deny all involvement in Francie's murder. However, his defence, which he must have been fabricating while waiting for the Sergeant to arrive, was the very same as that of King Henry II regarding the murder of St Thomas à Becket in Canterbury cathedral. Colonel Timmins now claimed that he had simply mused, in Barney's hearing, some equivalent to the royal wish "who will rid me of this turbulent priest?"

"Barney," he said, shaking his head sadly, (mortified Mortimer, I thought), "must have taken it for an instruction. Of course, I had no such intention. After all, Sergeant, why ever should I wish the lad dead? I simply did not like the way he kept hanging around the estate, and suspected his motives to be criminal ones, robbery or indeed worse. My information, indeed, was that he may have been part of a secret society bent on the violent destruction of British rule on this island. Until that could be proved, I meant for him to be warned off. I feared for my own life, my beloved Augusta's life. That's all. That's all. It has come as much as a shock to me as to anyone else, don't you know, that Barney killed poor Francie."

I was livid, hearing his lies.

Did he really believe, under the circumstances, that I would keep my promise to Briege and not reveal that the Colonel had in fact a very strong motive? No, I could not keep silent any more. How, indeed, could he explain away the murderous attack on me? The Sergeant listened, stony-faced, as I spoke, while the Colonel shot me further glances of hatred.

"It was a joke," he claimed, when I finished, "which I admit got a little out of hand, Sergeant, when Mrs. Hudson herself knocked over the hive and enraged the bees. I never locked her in. I never meant any real harm to her. I simply did not like her interfering and wanted to take her down a peg or two. Women, don't you know, born meddlers in what is none of their damned business. As for me fathering Francie, what a perfectly absurd claim." He barked a laugh. "No, no. Mrs. Hudson was easily taken in by wicked lies, because she wanted so much to clear Lily's name. As if I would have anything to do with such an ill-favoured slattern as Briege Kinsella."

Colonel Timmins emphasised the "I", setting himself thereby above the rest of us mere mortals. Sergeant Hackett narrowed his eyes a little at that – maybe after all there had been talk, or maybe he disliked the bald-faced arrogance of the man – but said nothing, just scribbled in his notebook.

Barney, for his part, when dragged up from the cellar and stinking of good sherry, maintained that he was ever obeying his master's clear orders, both with regard to Francie and with regard to me. He claimed that he did not know why the Colonel wanted the boy killed, and never asked, adding, chillingly, that the Colonel had told him not to hesitate but to kill anyone else who was witness to the deed, William, Briege or even Lily. However, the house had been quiet, William no doubt dead drunk, and no sign of Briege.

248

Barney had chased Francie into the bedroom, where the new bride was deep asleep, so he let her be. I believed him, as I am sure did many others, then and later in court. However, to leap ahead in the narrative, I am afraid that justice is sometimes blind, and not in a good way. Briege was not asked, or else refused, to testify, and Barney was hanged, while the Colonel was exonerated of all but poor judgment. As a result, he lost his position as Resident Magistrate and Master of the Hounds, and ceased to be part of the social scene, shunned rather by his peers and seldom even being seen at church any more.

Lily, of course, much to our delight, was cleared on the instant. Kitty informed the Cullens and Kinsellas that the girl would henceforth stay with her. None of them challenged that.

The dispute over the field continued under the aegis of the new Magistrate, who judged it had been fairly gifted to the Cullens, and that what happened thereafter was irrelevant. He did add that under the circumstances the Cullens might, out of compassion, like to return the field to the Kinsellas. However, they had no compassion and did not like. As I understand it, the bad feeling between the two families persists to this very day.

Working the field, indeed, uncovered more secrets. The skeletons of several babies were found, and Briege, who had not died of her burns, was called to account for them. She claimed they were all still born, and Dr. Ross, who examined the poor little bones, agreed that none were full term or anything like it. Giving birth to Francie at such a young age must have damaged the poor girl's insides beyond repair. For a while her spirit was broken, too, but eventually, I am told, she could be seen once more, gathering her herbs, and even ministering to local people when they fell ill. Though it was noted how she had turned more strange, muttering constantly to herself as if in conversation with someone or something unseen by others. Francie was a name never mentioned by her, although once or twice, as Veronica wrote to me in the

careful hand she was taught at school, Briege had been glimpsed
near midnight, heading to the rath of Knocnacoill, as if hoping that
the faeries might deliver him back to her again.

Chapter Nineteen

To return to my narrative, there was nothing more to keep me in Wexford after Lily's acquittal. I was indeed urged by the family to stay on for the wedding of Sal and Luke, which was yet a few weeks off – they weren't going to make the mistake "marry in May and rue the day". The middle of June had been fixed on for their nuptials. I should have liked to attend because they were good people, and it would be a joyous event, but I longed to go home. Kitty, for her part, decided to stay on, moving back with Lily to her brother's farm, even though Florrie most kindly said that they were both welcome to remain at Castle Florence for as long as they liked. He had become very fond of the young girl, and she of him, once she had got over her early fears.

Nonetheless, I had things to arrange before I left. In particular, to obtain a cow as gift for Mammo and Nell, to thank them for saving me from the Colonel's murderous intent. Peter proved happy to organise that for me, even bringing Nell along with him to the mart, so that she could choose the beast that she liked the best. From his own resources he added some healthy hens. Moreover, with Annie's help, I made up a basket of goodies for them, to ease their lot.

Nell was thrilled.

"I shall call the cow Daisy," she said. I was only glad she did not name it Martha in my honour. "And we can sell the eggs in the mart and make butter. Oh, Mammo, we'll be so rich. We can buy ourselves boots for the winter."

She clapped her hands and did a little dance. I confess the sight brought a tear to my eye – to be so happy with so little – and I gave her a great hug on bidding her farewell, as well as the price of boots for the pair of them.

In answer to the worries I expressed regarding the girl, Annie engaged to keep a watchful eye on the little family, and promised that if anything happened to Mammo, Nell would not be abandoned.

Another little duty had then to be performed. Mr. Malone, the lawyer to whom we owed so much, arranged for me to meet up one afternoon with Judge O'Boyle, the man who had granted bail to Lily, and who had professed such an interest in hearing about Mr. H from one who knew the detective well. The Judge turned out to be a small, round, rosy-faced man with a shiny bald head, reminding me of a nice ripe apple, a Cox's orange pippin, perhaps. We had a pleasant enough chat in Enniscorthy, in the same Portsmouth Arms Hotel which I had visited before with Kitty and Florrie. When I broached the Judge on the subject of Francie's murder, however, hoping he might take up Barney's case against the Colonel, he demurred. Although he was delighted to hear of Lily's release, he informed me firmly that he was not prepared to intrude on another judge's jurisdiction, and was sure that, in any case, justice would prevail. While sympathetic, I am afraid he was also of the conviction that my imagination had carried me away. He simply could not believe the Colonel guilty of the dark deeds of which I accused him.

"I am afraid, Mrs. Hudson, that you have been reading too many of the accounts of Dr. Watson, as well perhaps as more sensational works of fiction," he said, smiling and patting my hand. "I suspect that they have given you a lurid and distorted view of human nature, and must assure you that I have always found the Colonel a most reasonable man. He's a hero of Crimea you know. And he runs a fine pack of hounds."

"Yes, he told me about his hounds," I replied, shivering at the memory, though I could now see that it would be useless imparting more on the subject to the Judge.

Raging inwardly against the man's condescension and prejudice, I yet parted on friendly terms with Judge O'Boyle, who after all had served Lily well. I could do no more.

If justice on earth would not serve the case, however, then heavenly justice could. It was shortly after I was back in London that I learnt from Kitty of the Colonel's sudden death from a severe stroke. I instantly penned a letter to Augusta. However, I could not quite bring myself to commiserate with her on her loss but simply asked how she was faring. I also took the liberty of informing her of the poverty and plight of her tenants, Mammo and Nell Kinsella, and asked if she would be able to help them in some way.

She wrote back by return of post, expressing surprise and ignorance that any of her tenants were quite so indigent – I suppose the Colonel had always excluded her from the practical side of estate management – and agreed to get some of the her workmen to rethatch Mammo's cabin, and in general make improvements to ease their lot. Although I had doubts, she was as good as her word. I think it pleased her, after bending to her husband's will for so many years, to be in charge, and even to be making decisions that would have riled the Colonel.

You may be interested to learn, Martha, that I have a new cook, the letter went on, *having at last dismissed the abominable Maggie. Mortimer insisted we employ the woman for her son, Barney's sake, but I never liked either her or her cooking. Now I am getting quite plump on the delicious food I enjoy every day.*

I chuckled at that particular piece of news, although I could never imagine Augusta plump.

She added that she was managing well enough, with assistance from her Arklow cousins.

Mortimer did not like them, she wrote, *but they have proved good people and I am glad of them. Their daughter, Philomena, has moved in with me as my most delightful companion, and her brother Thaddeus (Thady) is become my new steward.*

Nonetheless, she added that she sorely missed Barney, *for no one can replace him, you know. He did everything for us. He was such a Treasure.*

She made no mention of missing the Colonel.

All that, however, is again getting ahead of my story.

The day I was due to leave Ireland, all packed and ready, Florrie requested that I take a walk with him in the garden. I think I knew what was coming.

It was another beautiful morning of early summer – whatever happened to the greyness and rain for which Ireland is supposedly famous? Leaves of all shades of greens and copper were uncurling in the sun; the creamy white blossoms on the horse chestnut trees stood like elegant candles; a bed of calla lilies trumpeted joy to the world; the pink petals of the flowering cherry were falling about us like confetti. All things in short to make one think of a wedding, if Florence Sweetnam Esquire ever needed prompts.

He himself was even more of an exotic than usual that morning, in his blue velvet jacket and burnt orange waistcoat. His little patent leather shoes had shiny buckles on them as if he were about to dance a polka. As we walked, he plucked two red rosebuds, one that he put in his buttonhole.

"I am heartbroken, dear Mrs. Hudson," he said presenting the other flower to me, "that you are leaving so soon. I trust that you will never forget us. Indeed, is it too much to hope that you will soon return?"

I murmured something, out of politeness, to the effect that it was not impossible. Someday, maybe.

"How thrilled I am to hear that, to be sure, to be sure. Oh, Mrs. Hudson, Martha, let me hope that you will." He paused. "You cannot have forgotten the offer that I made to you a while back. In this very garden."

Hey-ho, here we go, I thought.

"Let me assure you that my feelings have not changed since that day. I remain your most devoted and steadfast admirer, and cannot let you go away without repeating that it would be an honour if you would consent to become Mrs. Florence Sweetnam. Oh, please say yes. Please do."

"I am honoured in turn," I replied, "that you should be so kind as to think of me in such a way, Mr. Sweetnam. But I have not changed my mind. My life is not here and never can be."

"That is your final answer?"

"It is. But believe me when I tell you that I shall always think of you as a good friend, Mr. Sweetnam. The very best."

"A friend," he sighed, crest-fallen. "I must be satisfied. Alas." He sniffed at his flower.

We took another turn around the garden, during which time I was glad to see his customary high spirits soon restored. We ambled over to the paddock, where Lily was riding on Dove, with Thomas looking on, smiling.

"I think my stable boy has taken quite a shine to that young person," Florrie remarked. "Love is in the air, Mrs Hudson."

"Mm."

Lily could do worse, I thought. Indeed, she had done worse. Yet, in my opinion, she was still far too young to enter into a state of matrimony. Indeed, I assumed that when Kitty eventually returned to London, she would bring Lily with her. There she would be turned into a proper young lady, and forget all about handsome stable boys. That, at least, is what I thought would happen.

That afternoon, Florrie himself drove me to Enniscorthy for the train to Kingstown. I had previously said all my farewells, hugged lastly by Kitty and Lily with tears in all our eyes, though we expressed the hope that we would meet again soon enough.

Even Florrie, on the train platform, shed a few tears, and I was sorry for his sake that my eyes remained dry.

"Safe journey," he said with emotion, and stood waving a voluminous lacy handkerchief at me, turning a few curious heads, as the train started to chug out of the station.

Had I really broken his heart? It seemed unlikely and, as it turned out, if I had, then it was very soon mended, for, not long afterwards, maybe some three weeks following my return to London, I received the following extraordinary missive from Kitty.

Dear Martha, she wrote, *I hope that you are well recovered after your ordeal. All is good here and we are looking forward to the forthcoming nuptials of Sal and Luke.*

However, I have news that will no doubt astonish you. Florrie Sweetnam has asked me to become his wife and I have agreed! Imagine! Me the mistress of that beautiful house... Our tastes clearly differ there, I thought. *Oh, Martha, I have found it so delightful to be home in Ireland. I never knew how much I missed it until I returned, despite the several unpleasantnesses that accompanied our trip.* Unpleasantnesses, indeed, I thought: something of a euphemism there surely. I read on. *London, you know, was never home to me after dear Edward passed on, especially with our two boys away in far off Canada and unlikely ever to return. Florrie is a good man, and at this stage of my life I do not expect a grand passion, although he constantly expresses his strong and steadfast feelings for me.* I was glad, reading this, that I had never informed Kitty of his similar protestations to me. *He has even, you know, consented to convert to Catholicism. Indeed, he says that he has always been attracted to the Roman ceremonies, and plans to build a little chapel on the Castle grounds.*

I am afraid that, at this point, I put down the letter and burst out laughing, so heartily that Clara entered to see what was the matter. When I explained that Kitty Melrose was getting married in Ireland, Clara nodded and withdrew. I could tell from her expression that she did not quite see the joke.

The letter further informed me that Lily was doing very well. That she was learning, under Kitty's tutelage, all manner of skills which would serve her well in future life, and that she and Veronica were now inseparable friends.

Moreover, she continued, *Lily and Thomas seem to have an understanding, though I have insisted that nothing come of it until Lily is at least eighteen. He is a sound young fellow, all the same, and appears truly to be very fond of her.*

I suppose, when I thought about it, I could not regret that particular outcome. Lily, a wild flower transplanted to London, might very well have withered in a place so unlike everything she had known before. Indeed, her innocence and beauty might have made her a prey to men far less scrupulous than Thomas.

There was more in the letter about Peter and Annie and their brood, including a picture that Pegeen had drawn for me, perhaps of a cow, perhaps of a dog, perhaps of a hen. Whatever it was, I cherished it, placing it in my journal. The further details of their life, however, would hardly be of great interest to my readers, dealing as they did with mundane matters.

I sat back, letter in hand, considering the news. Fickle Florrie, I thought, without rancour, for I was never vain enough to believe his declarations of undying love. Like myself, however, and even more so, Kitty is "a woman of property," an attribute I rather cynically believed more warming to Florrie's heart than any physical or spiritual qualities we might possess. I could be quite wrong, of course, in judging him mercenary, for hadn't he explained his wealth as inherited from the despised father in trade. No, I had no good reason to suspect anything untoward regarding Florrie, who clearly had an affectionate nature, despite the unusually rapid turnover of wives. Yet the fact remained that he was a gentleman of expensive tastes and little obvious income. I confess, I sincerely hoped Kitty's dowry would be sufficient to see the two of them into comfortable old age, the new chapel on the grounds notwithstanding.

I penned a reply forthwith, to congratulate my friend on her impending change of state, but added, somewhat facetiously, that I hoped she would think twice before permitting Florrie to paint her portrait. I am not superstitious, not really, but I would hate to think of her ill-drawn image hanging beside those of the previous dear departed ones. Just in case.

As to accepting the invitation, when it came, to attend the wedding, I made my excuses and sent my sincere regrets, explaining that since Mr. H had miraculously returned from the dead, my duties to him now kept me in London. I sent on gifts of an amethyst brooch for Kitty and, for Florrie, a cravat pin in the form of a horse-shoe, embellished with a ruby and two emeralds, too showy for my taste, but I thought he might like it. Indeed, he did, sending back an effusive thank-you note, which, however, made no mention of his previously professed feelings for me, addressing me simply as 'dear friend'.

I was a little regretful not to be present for Kitty's happy day, and to have the opportunity of meeting up with good people. My excuse was feeble enough, indeed. Mr. H's presence would not have prevented me spending a week away in Ireland, for Clara could have managed perfectly well. It was not even the prospect of the long and wearisome journey that put me off. No, it was the nightmares that came to me – Francie stabbed, Francie in his coffin, Lily roasting over the fire, Briege in flames, Lily and myself shivering in the ditch while Mossie came looking for us with his slavering dog, myself beset with angry bees, myself chased through the fields of county Wexford by the Colonel's baying hounds. It was such terrifying images convinced me that even wild horses, as the saying goes, would never ever be able to drag me over St George's Channel again.

A Note on Sources

I have endeavoured in this novel to be as accurate as possible with regard to the early 1890s in Ireland, its local history and traditions, and so, if there are errors, I beg my readers' indulgence and forgiveness. In particular I researched matchmaking, wedding and funeral customs, including the wake. Folklore plays a big part in the book, and for that I consulted many sources including the National Folk Archive. All the tales relating to fairies and the banshee are drawn from these sources. In particular I have to mention the excellent work of scholarship that is Angela Bourke's *The Burning of Bridget Cleary: A True Story*. In this, the author investigates in detail a notorious case in rural Tipperary in 1895 when one Michael Cleary, believing his wife had been exchanged for a fairy, and in the company of others, burnt "the changeling" to death. The power of belief and superstition around fairies, fairy forts, charms and cures remained a powerful presence in rural Ireland alongside conventional Christianity even well into the twentieth century, and some say even to the present day.

Also By Susan Knight

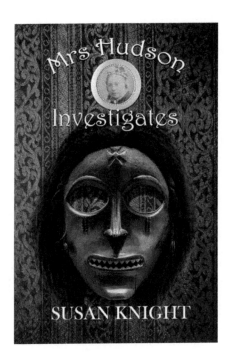

A distraught young woman arrives at Baker Street urgently requesting the assistance of Mr Sherlock Holmes. But the great man and his assistant Dr Watson are away. What to do? She confides in Holmes's landlady, Mrs Hudson, who over the years has developed certain powers of deduction from observing her tenant at work. The young woman, responding to this, begs her for help. Reluctantly, Mrs Hudson agrees... Thus begins a series of adventures, recounted engagingly by Mrs Hudson herself. Adventures and investigations which take her across the country, from the Midlands to Sydenham, from Eastbourne to Edinburgh. Her warmth and down-to-earth practicality are brought to bear on a range of strange and startling crimes that occasionally lead even Mrs Hudson herself into mortal danger.

Also from MX Publishing

MX Publishing is the world's largest specialist Sherlock Holmes publisher, with over a hundred titles and fifty authors creating the latest in Sherlock Holmes fiction and non-fiction.

From traditional short stories and novels to travel guides and quiz books, MX Publishing cater for all Holmes fans.

The collection includes leading titles such as *Benedict Cumberbatch In Transition* and *The Norwood Author* which won the 2011 Howlett Award (Sherlock Holmes Book of the Year).

MX Publishing also has one of the largest communities of Holmes fans on Facebook with regular contributions from dozens of authors.

www.mxpublishing.com

Lightning Source UK Ltd.
Milton Keynes UK
UKHW021044171220
375366UK00006B/202